Terry Jones was born in 1942 in Wales. He read English at Oxford University and retains a passion for medieval history and literature: his study of Chaucer's Knight received wide critical acclaim when it was published some years ago. Terry Jones became well known to the general public as a member of the Monty Python team. He co-directed *Monty Python and the Holy Grail* and directed Monty Python's *Life of Brian*, *The Meaning of Life* (which won the Grand Jury prize at Cannes in 1983), *Eric the Viking*, *Personal Services* and *The Wind in the Willows* (which won the Best Film in the International Children's Film Festival in Chicago, 1998).

Terry Jones is married and lives in London.

N

ENGLISH CHANNEL
(La Manche)

A T L A N T I C   O C E A N

BRITTANY

No

FRANCE
1360

SPAIN

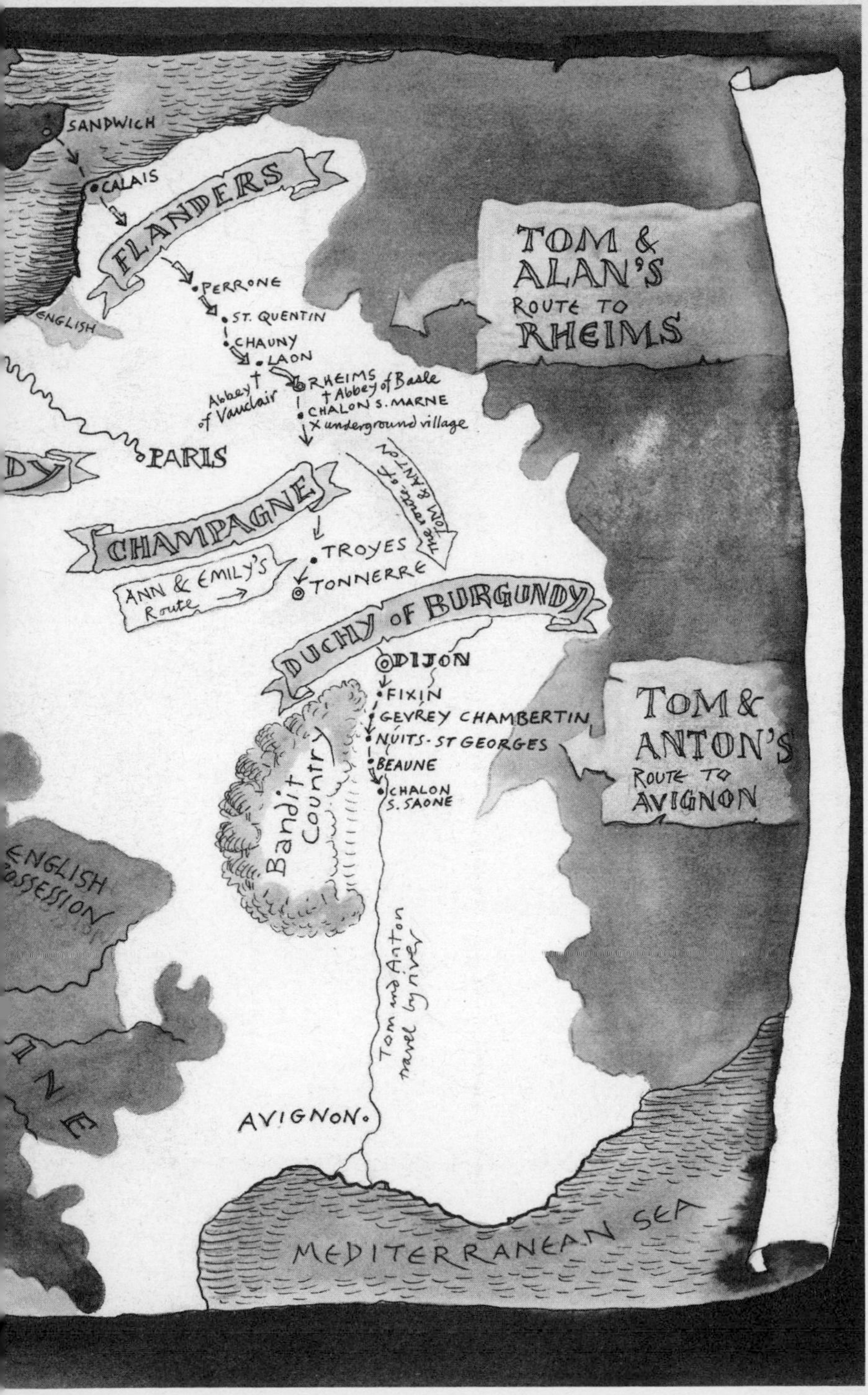
SANDWICH
CALAIS
FLANDERS
PERRONE
ST. QUENTIN
CHAUNY
LAON
Abbey of Vauclair
RHEIMS
Abbey of Basle
CHALON S. MARNE
X underground village
PARIS
ENGLISH
TOM & ALAN'S ROUTE TO RHEIMS
CHAMPAGNE
the route of TOM & ANTON
TROYES
TONNERRE
ANN & EMILY'S Route
DUCHY of BURGUNDY
DIJON
FIXIN
GEVREY CHAMBERTIN
NUITS-ST GEORGES
BEAUNE
CHALON S. SAONE
TOM & ANTON'S ROUTE TO AVIGNON
Bandit Country
ENGLISH POSSESSION
Tom and Anton travel by river
AVIGNON
MEDITERRANEAN SEA

TERRY JONES

THE LADY AND THE SQUIRE

Illustrated by

MICHAEL FOREMAN

PUFFIN BOOKS

PUFFIN BOOKS

Published by the Penguin Group
Penguin Books Ltd, 80 Strand, London WC2R 0RL, England
Penguin Putnam Inc., 375 Hudson Street, New York, New York 10014, USA
Penguin Books Australia Ltd, 250 Camberwell Road, Camberwell, Victoria 3124, Australia
Penguin Books Canada Ltd, 10 Alcorn Avenue, Toronto, Ontario, Canada M4V 3B2
Penguin Books India (P) Ltd, 11 Community Centre, Panchsheel Park, New Delhi – 110 017, India
Penguin Books (NZ) Ltd, Cnr Rosedale and Airborne Roads, Albany, Auckland, New Zealand
Penguin Books (South Africa) (Pty) Ltd, 24 Sturdee Avenue, Rosebank 2196, South Africa

Penguin Books Ltd, Registered Offices: 80 Strand, London WC2R 0RL, England

www.penguin.com

First published by Pavilion Books Ltd. 2000
Published in Puffin Books 2002
3

Text copyright © Terry Jones, 2000
Illustrations copyright © Michael Foreman, 2000
All rights reserved

The moral right of the author and illustrator has been asserted

Set in Sabon

Made and printed in England by Clays Ltd, St Ives plc

British Library Cataloguing in Publication Data
A CIP catalogue record for this book is available from the British Library

ISBN 0–141–30737–4

THE KNIGHT AND
THE SQUIRE

WHAT HAPPENED IN
THE PREVIOUS BOOK

Tom – a poor orphan from a small village in the north of England – has been taught by the village priest, and proved to be a brilliant Latin scholar, but that isn't what he wants to do. He dreams of becoming a knight. So when the Abbot threatens to put him in his school and turn him into a churchman, Tom runs away from home.

Tom falls in with a young rascal called Alan, who is squire to an even more rascally knight, by the name of Sir John Hawkley. The three of them join Edward III's expedition to seize the throne of France.

Alan and Tom lose Sir John when he absconds with a particularly large haul of booty after the seige of Laon. Alan and Tom try to join the King's retinue but instead are arrested as spies.

The Duke of Lancaster, however, comes to their rescue. He is suspicious of all churchmen (whose allegiance is to the French Pope rather than to the English King). He therefore hires Tom to translate all the correspondence between the bishops of England and the Pope of France.

At this moment, Tom discovers that his best friend, Alan, is actually a girl called Ann, who has disguised herself in order to run away from home and escape being married-off to an old man. The moment he makes this discovery, however, both he and Ann are captured by Sir John Hawkley's arch-enemy – a mercenary soldier who goes by the name of The Priest. Unbelievably, however, they are rescued by wolves!

Tom and Ann return to the English army and the Duke of Lancaster reluctantly agrees to take Ann on as a female squire.

Edward III has meanwhile surrounded the city of Reims and is now laying seige to it.

And that is precisely where this book begins ...

CHAMPAGNE

· 1 ·

HOW TOM WAS
KIDNAPPED

If you've ever sat astride a man-eating shark and dangled bits of raw flesh in front of it as the creature starts to plunge down into the dark abyss of the sea, taking you with it, you'll have a pretty good idea of how Tom felt in his new job as a squire to Henry, Duke of Lancaster. For the time being, Tom was keeping his head above water, but he knew that, at any moment, the Duke might eat him for lunch.

Not that the Duke wasn't a charming man. He was more than charming. He never threw large objects at anyone. He never pushed anyone off the battlements for fun. He never even screamed blue murder when his porridge was served without honey. He was, in all respects, a perfect gentleman – compared to some Tom could name. But ... but ... but ...

When I say Tom had a new job as a *squire* to Henry Duke of Lancaster, that's not how Tom would have described it. As he complained to his best friend Ann, he was more like a *scribe* than a squire. Instead of being taught sword-play and armour-care, Tom was stuck in the Duke's *scriptorium* all the hours of daylight, translating and transcribing any correspondence in Latin that the Duke (or his spies) came across.

"The Pope's a Frenchman!" the Duke of Lancaster would exclaim every so often. "Goodness knows what our English bishops are writing to him about! And I can't trust another churchman to tell me! So you translate their letters for me, little Tom! You'll not hide any treachery these priests are plotting!"

"If only there *were* more treachery involved," Tom thought, "it might make the work less tedious." As it was the letters were usually pretty hum-drum. Even so, Tom often wondered how on earth the Duke's spies "came across" them, although he never asked questions. Several letters had blood-stains on them.

One day, Tom was sitting by the window copying a particularly long and dull letter from the Pope to the Archbishop of Reims into English, when the door opened and a man he had never seen before walked into the room and scowled. His scowl was black. His eyebrows were black. And he was dressed entirely in black – from his

black hood right down to his black boots. For all Tom could tell his heart was black as well.

Something inside Tom screwed itself up and became a small elastic ball of alarm in his stomach. He didn't say anything; he simply carried on his copying as he felt the man cross behind him to the window and look out.

"... with the most fatherly affection that we have always shown to our dear son and blah de blah de blah de blah ..." Tom was in the middle of writing the last "blah" when suddenly the parchment was whisked out of his hand, so that his pen slid across it and the ink flew off the nib and made a blot on the original, next to a blood-stain.

"That's torn it!" thought Tom.

"So, my little sprat, it's you who has been copying out the Archbishop's letters," smiled the Man in Black, exposing a row of teeth sharp as a wolf's. "The translation is accurate," he went on. "You have a remarkable grasp of Latin for one so young ... But what's this bit: 'blah de blah de blah de blah'?"

"Well, the Pope always writes the same rubbish at the end, so I don't bother to write it out exactly..." Tom started to say, but the Man in Black had suddenly grabbed him and put his gloved hand over Tom's mouth.

"Not a peep or I'll slit your throat," he promised, as he pulled Tom back behind the arras that hung over the small garde-robe in the corner of the room. And somehow Tom had the feeling that this was the sort of promise the Man in Black would keep.

A garde-robe was really what we'd nowadays call a lavatory. The word garde-robe was a "euphemism". Actually the word "lavatory" is also a "euphemism". Lavatory originally meant "a bowl for washing your hands in" – so when we say, "Excuse me, where is the lavatory?"

we're actually saying, "Excuse me, where is the place to wash your hands?" In the United States of America you can't say the word lavatory – so you have to pretend you're going to have a bath: "Excuse me, where is the bathroom?" It seems that for centuries people have done everything they can to avoid saying they're going to have a "pee" – which itself, of course, is an eighteenth-century euphemism – being the initial letter of the thing that you really want to do in the first place!

In the fourteenth century they used to say, "Excuse me, where is the place to keep your clothes?" That's what garde-robe meant.

So it was that Tom found himself standing in the lavatory in rather more intimate contact with a complete stranger than he would have liked.

"I suppose it wouldn't be quite so bad if he didn't have his hand over my mouth and nose," thought Tom. "At least I'd be able to ..." but he didn't have time to even think the word "breathe" because the door beyond the arras opened and he heard footsteps enter the room. At the same time the Man in Black's hand moved down, allowing Tom to breathe through his nose.

"Tom?" Tom recognized the voice. "Why aren't you here?"

"I am!" Tom's thoughts screamed, but the Man in Black's hand slid back up to his nose and he couldn't breathe again.

"I came to tell you I've got to go …!" the voice trailed off.

"What?" thought Tom. If thoughts came out of our heads as physical things – like blancmange or goulash – there would have been a terrible mess all over the garde-robe, for Tom's thoughts exploded all over the place. "You can't be going! The Duke said you could be a squire! He said you could stay as long as the siege of Reims lasts! Stop! I don't want you to go! Ann!"

But the footsteps retreated reluctantly from the room and Tom heard the door shut. The most important person in his life had just walked out of it.

Ann had been taken on as a squire at the same time as Tom. Of course it was by no means usual for a girl to be made a squire, in fact it was unheard of, but Ann was currently dressed as a boy and going by the name of Alan. Even so, both the King and the Duke knew of the deception, and would have sent her home to her father in England, if Tom hadn't pleaded for her to stay. She was, as I said, the most important person in his life.

Suddenly Tom had to do something. So he did the first thing that came into his head. Actually it didn't really come "into his head" at all – it was just instinct and never got nearer to his head than his gut. He dug his elbow into the Man in Black's stomach, threw the arras aside and jumped across the room. But the Man in Black was too quick for him. As Tom tried to lift the door latch his arms were pinned to his side, and something told him not to struggle … perhaps it was instinct that froze him in mid action – or perhaps it was the cold metal of the knife that was pressing against his throat.

"Ann can't be leaving!" Tom found himself blurting out. "Where's she going? I've got to stop her! She's my best friend!"

"You're coming with me, my little sprat," said the Man in Black. And that's what Tom did.

· 2 ·

TOM DISCOVERS
SOMEONE WORSE THAN THE DUKE
OF LANCASTER

"In some ways," Tom thought to himself as he lay bound and gagged in the back of an old wagon that stank of rotting fish, with a pile of turnips dumped on top of him, "things have improved."

I mean let's face it, the Archbishop of Reims's Latin prose style was pure torture. Having to translate it, as Tom had been doing for the Duke of Lancaster, was like having your teeth pulled out by an old English sheepdog with bad breath. As for the letters from the Pope back to the Archbishop of Reims – well – Tom thought he'd rather try to swim the Sahara than translate them. They were that dry!

"If 'dull' was something you could sit on," thought Tom, "those letters would be four-poster beds!" He could hardly keep his eyes open: "The Holy Father thanks his greatly beloved son at Reims by whose righteous actions the honour of the Mother Church is upheld throughout the kingdom blah de blah de blah de blah ... and the Holy Father grants the said Archbishop, his beloved son in Christ, the indult and dispensation as of the sixth day of the sixth month of the sixth year of sixth Pope Innocent ... more blah, a bit more de, and a lot more blah de blah de blah de blah ..."

"I ran away from home so I wouldn't be forced to join the Bishop's school and spend my life poring over books in Latin," thought Tom. "I wanted to see the world ... the land of Saladin, the deserts of Arabia, the frozen wastes of Tartary ... I wanted to become a squire to a great knight and ride into battle after him ..."

And he'd been well on the way to realizing it too! He'd got to France. He'd joined the King's army. He'd even been taken on as a squire to one of the greatest lords of England, but instead of polishing armour and practising for tournaments, the Duke had kept him stuck away in the tower, translating all the Papal letters that the Duke's spies could get hold of.

"It suits me to have someone who is not a churchman to make these translations," the Duke would confide to him, in moments of unusual openness. "So I really know what these prelates are writing to each other."

And that was another thing that being bound and gagged, crushed by turnips and battered by the jolting of a cart was better than: having to report to the Duke of Lancaster every day. Ever since he and Ann had been taken into the Duke's service, Tom had had a tight knot in his stomach. He just didn't trust the Duke one inch – which was odd because the Duke himself was King Edward III's most trusted adviser ... But then, thought Tom, he wasn't sure he would have trusted King Edward III either.

"Ow!" exclaimed the load of turnips as the cart hit a particularly deep rut. The rain had turned the roads to rivers and the rivers had cut deep channels across what used to be the highway.

"Shut up!" the Man in Black snapped at his turnips, and he cracked his whip in a futile attempt to make the horse realize that carts are supposed to go up vertical slopes. "Pull! Damn you! Pull!"

But the horse had had enough. It didn't like rain. It didn't like pulling carts. And it didn't like the Man in Black. It just stood there, and the Man in Black snapped his whip and hit the horse time and again, but it just stood there, with the rain pouring down between its ears and off its head ... mute and immobile ... the traditional stance of brute beasts and poor people everywhere who have rebelled against oppression.

Tom was to remember that horse, in the middle of some of the adventures that were to follow this bumpy ride.

By now the rain had begun to seep through to the lower layer of turnips, and as it ran over Tom's clothes and started to form little pools around his elbows, he began to think the balance was shifting in favour of the Archbishop's terrible Latin prose. "At least it's dry," muttered Tom to himself.

He could now hear the Man in Black cursing the recalcitrant horse. The fellow had got off the cart and was standing hitting the horse with a large stick. Tom suddenly realized that, just by his nose, there was a crack in the side of the cart and through it he could see the Man in Black's face – no more than six inches away from his own. Tom could see the man standing there in the black night, with the black rain falling on to his black hood, and Tom shivered. It reminded him of the tale of The Devil Dressed in Black and Going Out to Dine that Old Molly Christmas used to tell him – back home in England so long ago.

And then the man roared abuse at the horse, and Tom flinched as he saw those wolf's teeth inches in front of him.

"Whoever this fellow is," thought Tom, "he makes the Duke of Lancaster look like my best friend." The thought suddenly took Tom by the throat. "But my best friend is Ann and she's gone somewhere and I don't know where!

Come to think of it – I've gone somewhere and I don't know where either!" To Tom's surprise, he found alarm spreading back into his bones. It was as if the discomfort of lying tied up under a pile of vegetables had squeezed the fear out. Now the rain was seeping into his collar and down his back, it seemed to bring with it the realization that he had been kidnapped. Tom groaned as he remembered he was on his way to what he could only assume would be an unpleasant fate.

That is, of course, if the horse ever started moving again. "Don't give in!" Tom urged the horse. "You stand there, while I get this rope off my wrists …" Tom had discovered that the rain had made his wrists slippery. But even as he felt the cords moving ever so slightly on his skin, he also felt the cart jolt. The Man in Black had finally persuaded the horse to move a leg or two.

"Hang in there!" Tom exhorted the horse. "Don't let the oppressor break your will! Refuse to co-operate with the forces of tyranny!" But he felt the horse move at least four more legs, and the cart lurched. It was to be slow going –

wherever it was they were going – but they would get there. The only question was: would they get there before Tom had wormed himself free?

Tom had still not worked out the answer when he felt the cart stop again. He heard voices and then the sound of heavy doors opening.

"Looks like the answer is: no!" moaned Tom. He'd managed to get one little finger free, and he'd got the gag off his mouth so that he could breathe more easily. But from all the evidence he could hear from outside the cart, they must have arrived at wherever it was they were going.

Another clue that suggested they weren't going any further was the way the cart had just been up-ended so that Tom, along with several hundredweight of turnips, found himself dumped unceremoniously on to the hard stone floor of a wet courtyard.

"Classy place," muttered Tom, "but I'm not sure about the welcoming committee." He had just been pulled extremely roughly out of the pile of turnips by three extremely rough-looking men.

"Where d'you want him?" grunted one of them.

"The Bishop's Parlour," said the Man in Black.

Tom suddenly felt a wave a relief. So! He wasn't going to be dumped in a compost heap with his legs tied up round the back of his head after all (that's what he'd decided was going to happen to him). Instead he was going to meet the Bishop for a nice chat in his Parlour. How delightful!

Unfortunately, Tom was just about to discover that the "Bishop's Parlour" was yet another example of that most dreaded of all figures of speech: the euphemism.

• 3 •

THE BISHOP'S PARLOUR

"If this is the Bishop's Parlour," thought Tom, "I'd hate to see his Torture Chamber!"

Tom had just been dragged (extremely roughly) across the grandest courtyard he had ever been in. In fact, the courtyard had been so impressive that Tom had thought of asking the welcoming committee to slow down a bit so he could enjoy the view. Only the fact that his gag had been put back over his mouth stopped him.

He had then been bundled (extremely roughly) down a flight of narrow stones steps into a dank, vaulted catacomb. He had been pulled (extremely roughly) across the flagged floor and finally had been flung (extremely roughly) into a cell that had few redeeming features to offer the discerning first-time occupant. It was cold. It smelt. The walls ran with water. There was no illumination, and the heavy iron grille had just been slammed and locked shut on him with an air of such finality that Tom's heart sank to a point somewhere beneath the stone floor.

Before the welcoming committee's last torch had disappeared back up the narrow stone steps, Tom had time to register two strange machines in the cell. One was a large wheel. The other looked a bit like a mangle. There

14

were also various rings hanging from the walls ... and that was all he had time to see.

Tom lay very still in that terrible blackness. The most awful feelings seemed to creep over him – like rats climbing on board a ship, he thought. His heart started beating loudly. If he hadn't known that bishops didn't have such things ... he could have sworn that this really was a torture chamber. But surely the Bishop of Wherever-This-Is wouldn't have people tortured ... would he?

Tom began to think that perhaps he still had a lot to learn about the world. And then he noticed that one of the awful feelings that had crept over him didn't just feel like a rat – it *was* a rat! A big one too, and it was scrambling over his leg! Tom screamed and tried to kick it off – but that's a difficult thing to do when you're tied up and gagged. Besides, who would ever hear a scream in a place like this?

"Ah! You've met the rat!" said a trembly voice in the blackness. In the brief time he'd had to look around his new home, Tom had not noticed that the one other thing the cell possessed was another occupant. "He's a friendly fellow, only don't let him get too intimate with you. He bites. They do say that's where the Plague comes from." Tom's invisible companion was speaking French. "If you can worm your way over here, I'll get that gag off you," the man offered. "I'm afraid I'm chained up," and Tom heard a chain rattle against the stone walls.

Now it's an odd thing to wriggle your way across a stone floor in the pitch black toward someone you've never seen in your life, but Tom reckoned he didn't have any choice in the matter. He wriggled and rolled and his new friend the rat scampered off. Obviously, having made his acquaintance, it could now get on with more important rat-matters.

15

"Where are you?" said the voice in the dark. "Ha! Got you!" Tom suddenly felt himself grabbed and before he realized what was happening a pair of teeth sank themselves into his arm! With a gagged shriek and a super-human twist Tom managed to fling himself away across the floor. He heard the chain rattle and he knew his invisible assailant was trying to reach out for him, so he rolled a few more feet away.

"I know rat bites are dangerous," thought Tom, "but I don't suppose human bites are very good for you either!"

"I'm sorry! I'm sorry!" the trembly voice was whining in the darkness. "I didn't mean to do that ... it's only ... they haven't brought me food for days ... days and days ... d'you know what it's like to be hungry? D'you know? REALLY HUNGRY!"

Tom couldn't think when he had been more surprised in his life. He may have half expected the Duke of Lancaster to eat him for lunch, but he'd never had anyone try to take an actual bite out of him before. "And without proper cooking!" Tom exclaimed to himself indignantly. "That's how you get an upset tummy! No wonder this character has such smelly breath."

"Please! Please! Come closer!" the voice in the dark was wheedling now. "I promise I won't do that again ..." But even if there had been fifty other strangers in that pitch black cell, Tom wouldn't have trusted a single one of them. Not until he'd seen how fat their stomachs were and knew when they'd last eaten.

He decided to employ a bit of self-help, and lay there wriggling and squirming, trying to get out of his bonds, while his starving fellow-prisoner clanked his chain and tried to persuade Tom to come a little closer – just a little bit closer – so he could help him.

How long was Tom doing this? He had no idea. Two hours? Twenty hours? It certainly seemed like a lifetime. "But the odd thing is," thought Tom, "that it seems like somebody else's lifetime." It didn't seem to be happening to him at all. It was as if he was outside his own body, looking down in the blackness, watching himself wriggle and squirm, wriggle and squirm and then lie panting for breath, and then cry, and then curse, and then wriggle and squirm all over again.

And anyway, what was the point of getting free? He'd still be incarcerated in the cell, hidden away from the light of day – he wouldn't be free ... Or was "freedom" only a relative term? Perhaps "freedom" for one person would be another's prison, and perhaps ... But it was at this moment that Tom suddenly got his hand out from the rope. He didn't know really why it suddenly happened but there it was: his hands were free!

In less time than it takes to kick a rat, Tom had got his legs and mouth free and kicked the rat into the bargain! It squealed, and ran off to nibble the starving prisoner.

"Where are we?" was the first thing Tom asked. He thought perhaps the more important question was: "How do we get out of here?" But he also felt there was a sequence to be followed. First he had to get his bearings.

"This is called the Bishop's Larder," whined his fellow prisoner.

"I thought it was the Bishop's Parlour," replied Tom.

"Don't contradict me! It's the Bishop's Larder!" yelled his erstwhile assailant. "I should know what it's called! I've been here long enough! You've been here scarcely five minutes and you start trying to tell me it's called something else!"

"I'm sorry! I'm sorry!" replied Tom.

"It's called the Bishop's Larder! That's the point! They leave us in here to starve to death! Some joke – eh? The Bishop's Larder!"

"Anyway the point is which Bishop?" Tom felt he had to steer the conversation around to something useful.

"Which Bishop? What are you talking about? There's only one bishop here!"

"But where are we?"

"In his torture chamber!"

"But whose?"

"The Bishop's."

"WHAT BISHOP?" Tom had completely lost it. He screamed this at the top of his voice. There was a shocked silence and then the man muttered:

"Jean de Craon, Archbishop of Reims, may he rot in hell!"

The truth hit Tom like a sack of wet turnips: he was a prisoner in the very city which he, and ten thousand other Englishmen, were besieging. He had been kidnapped by the enemy!

· 4 ·

HOW TOM NEARLY
INVENTED THE FLUSHING
LAVATORY FIVE HUNDRED YEARS
BEFORE THOMAS CRAPPER

Before Tom had a chance to think about what it meant to be a prisoner behind enemy lines, there was a crash and a rattle as five guards burst down the stairs. Tom just had time to throw himself back on to the ground and stick his arms behind his back, so that he still looked as if he were trussed up, before they'd opened the iron grille and pulled him out.

In the flickering light of their torches he could see his companion – the would-be cannibal – chained in the furthest corner of the cell, and Tom could understand why the man had tried to take a bite out of him. He was as thin as half a stray dog, and had a hunger in his eyes that Tom had never seen before, and hoped he would never see again.

"For pity's sake!" pleaded the wretched prisoner, who was clutching at one of the guards. "A bit of bread! Please!" But the only thing the guard gave him to fill his stomach was a sharp kick.

"I'll be back! I'll get you out of here!" Tom found himself yelling as he was shoved out of the stinking cell. Although why he should feel so concerned about someone who had just tried to eat him, he had no idea.

As Tom was marched up the stone steps from the dungeon and across a hall towards what he guessed were

19

the Archbishop's living quarters, he kept up a pretty good pretence of still having his hands tied behind his back. Night had fallen long ago. Outside, rain was pouring down the gutters and turning the walls of the Archbishop's Palace into vertical rivers. The wind was banging against the wooden shutters and the shutters were banging against the catches. And the thunder was banging against the clouds.

The guards seemed to be preoccupied with a game of dice that one of them had lost the night before. Apparently he hadn't called the number he had meant to call and had consequently been swindled out of a big win that would have meant he could have lived in clover – even a bed of roses – for the rest of his life … certainly until the next game. His colleagues commiserated with him and laughed at him in equal proportions. The two who carried the flaming torches walked on either side of the loser and put their arms around his shoulders.

"Such bad luck, Jacques!" said one of them.

"It wasn't bad luck!" expostulated Jacques. "I had the right number! I just said something else!"

"You were swindled, if you ask me!" grinned one of the others, and they all laughed and ruffled the loser's hair, which made him extremely cross.

Tom was marching behind them, with the other two guards roughly pushing his shoulders and occasionally his head. They were laughing as well, and when one of them leant forward and also proceeded to tousle the loser's hair – just to annoy him – Tom thought: "This is it!"

I don't know whether you've ever been in a "this is it!" situation. It's one of those moments when you know there's no point in thinking the thing through. "This is it!" You know it. No question. "This is it!" Either you jump or you don't jump – either you land in the swimming pool and get

20

wet or you walk away from the diving board and wonder what it would have been like. Well, Tom decided to jump. This WAS it, as far as he was concerned. He didn't stop to think what would happen next, he just jumped. To be precise, he jumped up and grabbed the flaming torches from the guards in front, and because the guards all thought he had his hands safely tied behind his back, and because they were all laughing so hard at their friend, not one of them was ready for it.

One of the torches crashed to the floor and was extinguished immediately. The other – to Tom's amazement – was in his hand. He swung it round and smashed it into the first thing that came close, which happened to be the face of one of the guards who had been pushing him. The guard screamed and fell to the ground. The other leapt at Tom, but all he got was an armful of flames and in another second that torch, too, hit the ground and was extinguished.

Plunged into blackness, the party of guards seemed to disintegrate completely. The guard behind fell over the guard who'd fallen on to the floor. The two in front turned and, as luck would have it, their elbows hit the guard who'd been down on his luck in the first place bang on the nose! In that split second, all his rage and frustration boiled to the surface and he lashed out at his two colleagues, punching first one and then the other on the sides of their heads.

Tom didn't wait to sort out any of the misunderstandings that thus arose amongst these soldiers (who'd always got on pretty well up till then). He just ran – through the pitch blackness – and straight into the wall.

"Uh huh!" he exclaimed. "Never try and walk through walls!"

"There he is!" yelled the guard who had fallen over the guard who was still rolling on the floor. But he was the only one who was interested in Tom's whereabouts. The other three were too busy fighting each other to even hear. And by the time the guard had sprung at Tom and, in so doing, had also hit his head against the wall, Tom was off across the hall and lost in the darkness.

It was a brilliant get-away! Only slightly marred, perhaps, by the fact that Tom had just flung open the first door he'd come to, and walked into the Guardroom! A roomful of off-duty guards all turned to look at him.

"Whoops!" said Tom. "Out of the frying pan into the frying pan!"

The guards in the Guardroom could hear the shouts of the guards outside in the hall, so Tom decided to postpone congratulating himself, at least until after he'd kicked the soldier who'd just grabbed his arm, punched the other soldier who had lunged for his leg, backed out of the door again and sped off across the hall and round a corner as fast as his legs would take him. And by that time, he'd forgotten how pleased he'd been with himself anyway.

As he ran, a flash of lightning lit up the room just long enough for him to realize what a truly impressive room it was, and also to see a dozen soldiers now in full pursuit behind him. He also had time to glimpse a small doorway ahead of him to the left. As soon as they were plunged back into blackness, Tom made for that door. And now this is where, in my opinion, Tom was very, very clever indeed. Instead of rushing through the door and banging it shut, Tom tiptoed up to it, opened it slowly, crept through it and shut it ever so quietly ... It took a lot of nerve, but the result was that not one of the soldiers realized what he'd done, as they rushed past yelling and shouting, and Tom leaned back against the door with his heart beating.

The sounds of the soldiers had disappeared off down the passageway before Tom dared to feel his way forward in the darkness. One pace took him to a small object which he stepped in. It was an object for which there was then and still is now no decent euphemism: it was a chamber-pot. And it was not empty.

"Oh NO!" Tom tried to stop himself groaning aloud, but he couldn't help it. "I don't believe it!" He shook his foot and suddenly a strange idea jumped into his head. Wouldn't it be great, he thought, if people "kept their clothes" (he was using the euphemism that was current in the fourteenth century, remember) in a place where it could all be washed away straight into an underground pipe and so on out to sea – you know, you just pull a chain or something, and it all flushes away, without having to leave potfuls lying around the floor for people to step in! Wouldn't that be fantastic?!

If only Tom had remembered this thought, he might have invented the flush toilet five hundred years before Thomas Crapper did. But unfortunately, at that very moment, Tom made another discovery that drove the first idea straight out of his mind.

Incidentally, it's a curious fact that the flush toilet is universally recognized as one of the most useful inventions in the history of civilization, and yet look up Thomas Crapper in the *Dictionary of National Biography* or the *Encyclopaedia Britannica* and you won't find his name there. I suppose the flush toilet is just one of those things that everybody wants to use but nobody wants to talk about – hence the euphemism. If only Thomas Crapper had invented something respectable, like dynamite or the machine gun, he might have been as famous as Alfred Nobel or Richard Gatling

Anyway, back to the story! The discovery that drove Tom's happy inspiration about the garde-robe from his mind was the discovery of a solid stone ledge. He made this discovery in the simplest possible way – by stubbing his toe sharply against it.

"Ow!" Tom tried not to scream this aloud, but was only partially successful. He'd really hurt his toe the way one only does when one is trying to be really careful. Tom fell forward on to his hands and in so doing made yet another discovery. The stone ledge, against which he'd so successfully banged his toe, was actually the beginning of a spiral flight of steps.

Before you could say "Rats beware!" Tom was up those steps and had found himself in a different world.

HOW TOM WAS TRAPPED
IN A LADY'S BEDROOM

A candle was burning on a three-legged stool at the top of the staircase. By its light, Tom could see he was in a large room that contained a wooden chest, two stools, and a luxurious bed – a welcoming, beckoning, silk-covered bed with a canopy above it, draped in crimson – the most fantastic bed that Tom had ever seen.

But the most amazing thing of all, as far as Tom was concerned, were hanging on the walls. They were so extraordinary to Tom that they changed his whole world-view. He couldn't help just staring at them. Then he walked over to them and started touching them, one by one.

They were carpets: rich, velvet wall-carpets the like of which he had never seen. To tell the truth, Tom had hardly ever seen even a carpet before, let alone a carpet hanging on a wall. Carpets were simply not the sort of thing people had – even on their floors – back home in his little village in England. You might put rushes, or a bit of straw, or even – if you were well off – a bit of sacking. But a carpet? You wouldn't find a carpet in all the hostelries in London. Nor in the inns of Sandwich. Not rich, deep-piled carpets like these he was now stroking with his hand. Not carpets that were adorned with magical pictures: a lady sitting in a rose garden … a dog … two strange creatures that Tom had never seen before … He could hardly make sense of it. Pictures were yet another thing that Tom was not used to. And pictures on a carpet and a carpet that hung from the wall … It was all a bit beyond his experience.

He had heard that back home – so far away – Sir William had a carpet, but then Sir William was the Lord of the Manor. It was said that he had brought the carpet back from one of his journeys to Arabia … And suddenly everything went spinning through Tom's head, as he stood there in that strange, rich room, running his hand across the soft pile of that wall-hanging: the simple cottage he had grown up in, the exotic places he wanted to go to. Sir William's men – were they still after him? Would they try to drag him back to the village and force him to work in the fields – all day and every day? Tom smiled grimly to himself. "Well, they'll never find me here," he thought. "Not here in the enemy's town, deep inside the Palace of the Archbishop of Reims! I'm as safe as …"

The door catch rattled. Tom dropped to the floor so that he was hidden behind the bed, as he heard footsteps cross over to the chest at the foot of the bed. He heard the clink of some coins being thrown into the chest. Then the lid closing. Then the footsteps returned to the head of the bed.

He heard the rustle of clothing. "Jeanette!" It was a woman's voice. Soft as the candle-light. "Jeanette!" Liquid as the wine he could hear being poured into a bowl.

"Madame?" Jeanette had come to the door.

"Undress me," said the soft voice. "He is a brute." Tom heard the rustle of clothing dropping to the floor and the scurrying feet of the maid as she hurried about after her mistress.

Tom didn't know whether to be embarrassed or scared. "Sooner or later that maid's going to come round to this side

26

of the bed to blow out that candle," he told himself. "And then she'll see me for sure!" There was only one place to hide – and that was: under the bed.

"A true brute!" said the soft voice again, and the bed heaved a sigh of agreement, as the lady lay down upon it. "I cannot stand him." The soft voice paused to take a draught of wine. "Perhaps they'll hang him! Huh! That would be worth seeing, Jeanette!"

"I'm sure you don't wish that, Madame!" replied the tactful Jeanette.

At this moment Tom discovered that while hiding under the bed was in principle a good plan, it had one snag: there was no "under the bed" in which to hide. The bed was solid down to the floor.

He could hear the maid fussing over her mistress's pillow. Any moment now, he thought, she's going to come round the bed, pick that candle off the stool, and find one dishevelled, smelly English boy who's wanted by every guard in the Palace. Oh dear …

The maid had started to walk round the bed. Tom cowered.

"Jeanette!" The soft voice might have been as silky as the sheets upon the bed, but it had the steel of command underneath it. Jeanette stopped. "Come here, Jeanette. Kiss me goodnight."

Jeanette returned to the bed head, and Tom felt like sinking through the floor. He could not hear what was being said, for they were whispering so quietly now that it could barely have been communication. "Come on! Get it over with!" he muttered to himself. "Kiss her goodnight! Then come for the candle so you can discover me!" It was all Tom could do to stop himself standing up and saying: "Look! I know you're going to find me eventually so I'll save you the

bother: here I am!" But he didn't. He stayed pressed up into the shadow against the bed, hoping that perhaps he wouldn't be noticed after all.

At last the maid raised her voice again: "I must go, my lady!" she was saying, and the soft voice kept repeating:

"He is a brute!"

"Yes, my lady. Shall I blow out the candle?"

"Uh oh!" thought Tom. Here it comes ..."

"Why not, Jeanette? Blow out my dreams as well ..."

"My lady, whatever do you mean?"

"I'm so wretched, Jeanette."

"I am sorry, my lady, I must go – my Lord Jospin ..."

"Oh? My Lord Jospin!"

"You know it well, my lady … I have no secrets from you …"

The maid had come round the bed, by this time, and was heading for the candle where it stood on the stool at the head of the spiral staircase. Tom could now see her. In her long gown, she looked to him more like a lady than a maid! Tom pulled himself into as small and as insignificant a ball as he possibly could and shut his eyes. He wasn't quite sure why he shut his eyes – perhaps he hoped everyone else in the room would do the same thing.

Then suddenly a ray of hope lit up his dark corner. Of course! Jeanette would walk across to the candle and blow it out and then, when she turned round, everything would be dark and she wouldn't see him in any case. Phew! Tom practically collapsed with relief and opened his eyes.

"No!" murmured the sad, soft voice. "Don't blow the candle out! Let it burn. I cannot face a night so black." Tom groaned. The maid was now half-way from the bed to the stool; when she turned back again, she would see him for sure. Tom cringed.

Jeanette turned. Tom was now plainly in her line of view, but, as luck would have it, at that very moment, the door of the chamber opened and a man's voice rang out across the room: "Take care, my lady! A prisoner has escaped. We shall post a guard by your door." The maid's attention – for some miraculous reason – was riveted upon the man at the door. It was as if Tom and everything else in the room were no longer visible to her.

Tom wondered what on earth could be so interesting about the fellow at the door. He sounded ordinary enough. "Perhaps he's wearing a large pair of rabbit's ears," thought Tom. "Or maybe he's balancing a chamber-pot on his head!" Whatever the man was doing, Tom was grateful enough, for the maid's eyes never left the door, and Tom went unnoticed.

"Thank you, my Lord Jospin," said the sleepy voice of the mistress.

"Good night, my lady," said Lord Jospin. "Good night, Jeanette."

"Good night, my Lord Jospin," said Jeanette, dropping a flustered curtsey, before returning to her mistress's side. The door closed, and Tom was safe … for the moment.

· 6 ·

WHAT TOM FELT WHEN
HE SET EYES ON THE BEAUTIFUL
EMILY

Tom lay, hidden behind that luxurious bed in that luxurious chamber, for what seemed like an age. He heard the rattle of armour, down at the bottom of the spiral stairwell, and the thud of a pike-staff hitting the floor. The guard had taken up his duties by the downstairs door. Tom stole a peek at the door across the room – on the other side of the bed. "That probably leads into the private rooms," he told himself. "There's a fifty-fifty chance it's unguarded." But he would have to wait to find out.

Tom decided to pass the time by calculating his chances of getting out of the Archbishop's Palace, getting out of the city of Reims, and of getting back to the English army. He decided he had a 70–30 chance of getting out of the Palace and a 60–40 chance of getting out of Reims. He was just about to give himself more cheering odds for getting back to the English army, when he heard Jeanette, the maid, leave.

The door shut. And no – she didn't speak to any guard outside. The odds were now in favour of there not being any guard! All Tom had to do was wait for the mistress to fall asleep. It all seemed ridiculously easy.

But the great lady was not showing any signs of falling asleep. She kept sighing and tossing and turning. No position seemed comfortable for her, and the bed kept heaving and sighing as if in sympathy for her discomfort.

"How can anyone be uncomfortable in a bed like that?" thought Tom indignantly. He'd never slept on anything more comfortable than a bit of straw. And he usually fell asleep the moment his head hit the pillow – which was usually a bit of straw as well. He was willing to take an odds-on 1–99 bet that this great lady's pillow was stuffed with goose down! "So why doesn't she fall asleep on it?"

"At least," thought Tom, "the longer she takes to get to sleep, the more likely it is that the whole Palace will be asleep as well." So he reconciled himself to waiting for his moment to escape … everybody must be pretty sleepy by now … he was pretty sleepy himself … very sleepy indeed … in fact, now he came to think about it, he could hardly keep his eyes open … and he made a valiant effort to do so but found, as he opened his eyes for the fourteenth time … that the candle had burnt right down to a stub and that he had actually been asleep after all!

Tom listened. There was no sound from the bed. The great lady was breathing softly and evenly. This was his moment. He stood up very slowly and tiptoed to the end of the bed. Then he started to head for the door, but something made him pause.

"Don't stop!" a voice inside him warned. "Just go as quietly and as quickly as you can to the door. Check there's no guard. Then creep out … You'll find the way out of the Palace. And then run or steal a horse. Get back to the safety of the English army."

But no! Instead, Tom found himself turning to look at the great lady whose presence had kept him cooped up in this chamber for so many hours. He knew he shouldn't. He knew the whole history of his adventures that were to

32

follow would somehow be altered by his turning back to look at that great lady. But he couldn't help it. He turned and looked at her as she lay there sleeping in the luxurious bed and something very odd happened to him. Tom wasn't quite sure what it was, but his heart seemed to shoot up into a position somewhere in between his ears.

Lying in the bed, illuminated only by the last flickerings of soft candle-light, was the most beautiful creature Tom had ever seen. The great lady was, it turned out, a young woman of perhaps sixteen or seventeen. She was lying stretched out with her face framed by a damask pillow, white as snow, but warm and soft in the last candlelight. Her forehead was broad and her dark hair brushed back, her lips were turned up at the corners in the slightest of smiles, and her arm was smooth and perfect, lying across her breast, as she breathed easily and lightly.

"Turn around!" Tom told himself. "Get out of here!" But he just stood there glued to the floor. "Move!" he screamed inside himself. "While there's still a chance! LEAVE!"

But somehow the serenity of the girl's sleep seemed to wash away all the turmoil from Tom's mind. That slight smile on her lips held him in a captivity that was every bit as strong as the cell in which he'd been thrown when he first arrived. Tom sighed, and made a superhuman effort to stop himself reaching out to stroke her cheek.

"This is CRAZY!" He had just noticed the way her eyelashes curled together. Tom tore his eyes away for a moment, and noticed the first glimmer of daylight squeezing in through cracks in the shutters. Perhaps it was the unnatural light of day that lifted the spell. Perhaps it was something inside him, but suddenly Tom found himself turning and tiptoeing away.

It was probably not much more than ten or eleven feet across the room, but to Tom, creeping as quietly as a mouse on Sunday, the door seemed as far away as the Great Wall of China. He had just about reached the Steppes of Russia, and was heading out across the Mongolian plateau, when his blood froze. He stopped, dead in his tracks. His heart plunged back down into his ribs and then on down through his intestines until it hit the floor with a thump. A voice, commanding and yet soft, held him. If it had been any other voice, he would have simply run. But this voice settled over him like a net over a small bird.

"Where are you going?" said the voice. "Turn around!"

Tom turned around. How could a voice sound so much older than its owner? The young woman was leaning up on her elbow. Her dark hair spread over her shoulder. Her eyes were grey and sparkling, and her mouth still smiled as if the whole world were there simply for her amusement. Tom suddenly felt shabby and poor – despite the fact that he was still dressed in the livery of the Duke of Lancaster. He didn't know where to look.

"Did you think I didn't know you were there?" The

young woman was laughing at him. "I nearly told my Lord Jospin that I knew where his escaped prisoner was, but you looked so harmless, curled up by my bed with your eyes tight shut! Poor boy!"

Tom now suddenly felt not only shabby but also foolish. All his stratagems, all his waiting, and she had known he was there all the time ... And yet how strange that she didn't call for help – that she seemed to have no fear – even now ...

"Come here!" the mistress was patting the luxurious bed. "Sit down and tell me who and what you are."

HOW TOM DISGUISED
HIMSELF AS A LADY'S MAID

The truth: that he was an English boy, who had run away to become a squire (and one day – maybe – a knight) and was meanwhile in the service of one of her arch-enemies, the Duke of Lancaster, who was at this very moment plotting the destruction of her city. And yet what else could he say? So he said it.

When he had finished, he half-expected her to hit him, to shout insults at him, to call the guards and have him arrested as an enemy and a spy, but she didn't. The beautiful creature seemed amused. Her beautiful mouth curled into a beautiful smile and she leant forward and ruffled his hair – the way he used to ruffle his little sister Kate's hair, back home so far away and so long ago.

"So … little 'Tom' … is that your name? … Here you are in the stronghold of the enemy … Aren't you scared?"

Tom nodded, although he was actually thinking: "If this is 'being scared' then Heaven must be the most scary place not on earth!" for the truth was that with every curl of her smile, with every glance of her eyes, with every toss of her head, she was reeling in Tom's young heart like a fish on a line.

"So …" the commanding voice had dropped to a conspiratorial whisper. "We've got to find a way of helping you to escape."

"You'll help me to escape?" Tom was having the same sort of difficulty spitting the words out that you or I might have if we had to explain to our parents that we were getting married to a gorilla.

"Sh!" hissed the young woman. "Let me think." At this moment, she pushed Tom away and was apparently just about to slip out of her luxurious bed when she stopped and frowned for the first time. "Well?" she said sharply. "Don't just stand there gawping, boy! Turn around!" Tom turned around hurriedly – for you see in those days people usually slept naked in their beds. He heard the rustle of clothing and then that soft yet somehow stern voice told him he could turn back. By the time he did, the young woman was dressed and opening the shutters of her chamber window.

It was going to be an awful day. The sun had not quite risen, and the clouds were thick enough to make you think it never would. It was the sort of day a condemned man would walk to the gallows on. And it was still raining. When was it ever not raining?

"You can't climb down there!" she was telling Tom. And when Tom looked down the sheer drop of wet stone, he was inclined to agree. "We'd better get you out some other way!"

Tom suddenly felt nervous. The beautiful young woman was smiling again, and Tom already somehow knew that smile spelt trouble ... Why was it she made him feel so – so what? – so warm and yet uneasy ... so elated and yet terrified? By the way the corners of her mouth were curling up now, and the way her grey eyes were sparkling in the early light, he knew she'd hatched some plan and he knew he wasn't going to like it. He also knew that if she had told him to jump off the top of the tallest tower in the Palace, he'd have done it. If she'd told him he could fly, he'd have believed her.

What she actually said seemed pretty harmless: "Here! Little Tom! Put this on!" That was all she said. And yet Tom would have preferred to jump off the tallest tower in the Palace.

"But that's ..." Tom knew he was stating the obvious – he just couldn't help it – "... one of your gowns!"

"Of course, little Tom. You will be my new chambermaid. That way we can walk out of the Palace together and nobody will stop us! A good plan, eh?"

" 'We'?" exclaimed Tom. "You're going to escape with me?"

"Perhaps – perhaps not – but at least I can see you on your way ..."

Tom had to agree it was beginning to sound like a good plan – a very good plan. He couldn't see a single argument against it, except that there was no way he was going to dress up as a girl in front of this young woman, whom he

wanted to impress, whom he wanted to ride and joust in front of, with her scarf tied to his helmet – to win the day for or to rescue on horseback and do all those other things that knights were supposed to do and probably never did.

"But this gown will not look good over the top of your doublet," she was saying. "You will have to take off your clothes."

Tom was just about to ask for directions to the highest tower in the Palace, when he realized she was already unfastening his doublet and telling him to keep still. As she unloosened his belt, and started to pull the doublet over his head, Tom suddenly stopped her. "I don't know your name," he said – as if it were important not to undress in front of anyone whose name you don't know.

That mouth turned up at the corners in a mischievous smile as she breathed a word that Tom would never forget: "Emily," she said, and pulled his doublet off his back.

Tom had never tried to get into a girl's dress before. Actually two dresses, for first Emily made him put on the under-gown and then the sleeveless parti-coloured surcoat. It had deep arm-holes cut right down to the waist – so you could see a lot of the under-gown.

"These are called 'the windows of hell'!" whispered Emily with a grin, as she straightened out the arm-holes, but she wouldn't explain why, no matter how many times Tom asked. She just laughed.

Then she went to the wooden chest and pulled out a coif and some headscarves. "Now we've got to make you into a proper girl," she said, as she started to arrange the scarves upon his head. Tom almost died of embarrassment.

When she had finished, Emily held Tom by the shoulders and smiled. "Now it is all right for us to do this," she said, and her grin gave Tom butterflies in his … well, butterflies all over actually. The next minute Emily was laughing at him as he struggled to get away. "Oh no!" she was laughing. "You are my hand-maid now! It is all right for me to kiss you!"

But Tom tore himself free and stood at the other end of the room, his cheeks burning. "I think we should go," he said, "before anyone wakes up."

"A good idea, little 'Tom'," said Emily – suddenly all seriousness. And the next minute the pair of them were sneaking out of the door.

· 8 ·

HOW TOM DISCOVERED
THAT MEN ARE THE PROBLEM

You probably aren't expecting a lecture about architecture at this point, and I wouldn't dream of delivering one, except that I don't know how else to explain the situation in which Tom found himself the moment they stepped outside the door of Emily's chamber.

You see, there is an invention that we use today that didn't exist in Tom's day. It's something we walk through practically every day of our lives. We probably don't even think of it as an invention. But it is. It is an architectural invention – and an extremely useful one at that – it is called: the corridor. I don't know who first thought of joining rooms up with a long passageway, but they didn't think of it until surprisingly recently. Six hundred years ago, one room usually led straight into another. So to get from one end of a palace to the other you had to make your way through room after room, going: "Excuse me! ... I'm so sorry to disturb you ... Oh! I do beg your pardon! ... SORRY! ... Don't mind me – I didn't see a thing!" and so on.

"Sh!" whispered Emily, rather unnecessarily and, to Tom's mind, rather too loudly. They were both tiptoeing across a large room, which even in the dingy light of this dingy dawn was clearly a magnificent chamber, with wall-hangings and paintings and several beds. One was a big

41

imposing bed, with a curtain all round it. The others were single beds on which Tom could just make out sleeping forms.

About half-way across the room, a terrible growl and an explosion of angry breath made Tom freeze in his tracks. He'd been discovered! He'd be sent back to the "Bishop's Parlour" for ever. But Emily giggled. "The Archbishop's snoring for France!" she whispered in Tom's ear. "That usually means he's about to wake up." And with that she hurried to the next doorway and through it. Tom had no intention of being left behind in what was sounding increasingly like the inside of a volcano, so he followed.

Tom and Emily now found themselves in a very long room, with long windows from floor to ceiling and long tables that stretched almost from one end to the other. However, as far as Tom was concerned, the longest feature was the long guard, who was guarding the next doorway.

The guard was not only long, he was also very much awake and, what was worst of all, he was watching their approach suspiciously.

Tom tried to pull Emily back, but she just brushed him off and kept going.

"Morning, your Ladyship," said the guard, bowing to Emily. "Good morning, mademoiselle," he said as he bowed to Tom, who instinctively pulled one of the kerchiefs across his face. "It's going to be a foul day, your Ladyship," continued the long guard cheerfully.

"Thank you for cheering me up, Gaston," replied Emily, and she bundled Tom out of the room. They were finally out of the main building and walking along an open wooden gallery, that ran around the courtyard above the cloisters.

Tom was shaking like a jelly on a donkey. "I can't go through with this," he mumbled.

"Oh! Little Tom!" Emily was mocking him. "All we have to do is walk down across the courtyard, tell the gatekeeper we are going into the meadow to pick flowers, and you'll be free!"

"But he'll never believe we're going to pick flowers! It's raining like Noah's birthday!" hissed Tom from under his veil. And indeed it was. The rain was thundering on the wooden roof of the gallery like all the drums of Doomsday.

"We'll see!" said Emily, and she skipped off along the gallery and down the stairs.

By this time, the light in the east had grown a little stronger, and the first servants were stirring about their daily chores. A maid with a bundle of firewood was struggling up the stairs and dropped a curtsey to Emily as she ran down. But, to Tom's relief, the maid turned into a doorway before she reached him.

"Say to yourself: 'I'm a girl'!" Tom told himself. "Walk the way a girl would walk." He had just taken his first – what he hoped was girl-like – step, when he felt a strange sensation behind that made him jump out of his skin. He turned to find the long guard peering down at him.

Of course! How could he have been so stupid as to imagine anyone would not see that he was a boy, dressed up in girl's clothes that were too big for him anyway? Tom's knees didn't exactly knock, but they certainly seemed to huddle together for comfort. He took a deep breath and was just about to do the only thing he could think of in the circumstances – i.e. head-butt the guard in the stomach – when he noticed that the man was not scowling at him. In fact he was smiling – and smiling in the most peculiar way.

"Hello, darling," the guard was saying, "I haven't seen you here before." And Tom suddenly realized – in one of those flashes of inspiration that come to us all occasionally

– that the strange sensation that had made him jump out of his skin was the sensation of having his bottom pinched!

"Of all the cheek!" thought Tom indignantly.

"And what's your name, little darling?" asked the guard.

"Er … my name?" Tom's mind went blank. He couldn't think of a single girl's name.

"Oh, a right little shy one, eh?" smiled the guard.

"My name is … T … T …" It was no use, Tom just couldn't think of anything except Thomas and Timothy and Terence and Tancred and Talbot and Tristram and Titus and Toby!

"Tabitha?" enquired the guard helpfully.

"No!" said Tom, "I mean yes! Tabitha!"

"That's a nice name," said the guard.

"For goodness' sake! He's talking to me as if I were a five-year- old!" thought Tom, backing away from the over-friendly soldier.

"I'm off duty in a couple of hours," smiled the guard, as he cornered Tom against a pillar. "I could give you some of my breakfast beer …" Tom thought he'd never heard a more unattractive proposition in his life. And then – to Tom's complete and utter stupefaction and, I may add, indignation – the guard suddenly reached round and pinched his bottom again!

In an instant, Tom found himself getting into character! Without a second thought he slapped the guard hard on the cheek, then ducked under the man's arm and raced off (in as ladylike a way as he could muster). He glanced back to see the guard rubbing his cheek but still grinning inanely.

"Men are strange creatures!" thought Tom.

By the time he caught up with Emily, she was explaining to the gatekeeper the joys of picking flowers in the rain.

HOW TOM GOT OUT OF
THE PALACE FOR THE FIRST TIME

"… and they last longer," Emily was saying.

The old gatekeeper shook his head. "You're a wild one, and that's the truth, milady."

"And it's fun anyway, isn't it, Thomasina?" Of course! thought Tom – why hadn't he thought of "Thomasina"?

"Well you'd better wear my old coat," said the gatekeeper and he disappeared back inside his lodge. Tom looked around the Palace courtyard. Above them loomed the gigantic mass of the great cathedral of Reims, against which the Archbishop's Palace seemed to huddle as if for protection from the wrath of God. Huge brightly coloured giants gazed down from the ethereal heights on to the worldly goings-on in the Palace.

"Come on! Come on!" thought Tom. "Open the gates before somebody spots me!"

"Stop bouncing up and down, little Tom!" Emily was whispering in his ear. "Ladies' maids don't do that!"

But before Tom could stop, the gatekeeper had appeared with two old coats, and the next moment he had unlocked the great gates of the Archbishop's Palace.

Tom would have felt a surge of relief but for one thing: a figure had just emerged from inside the gatekeeper's lodge and was now standing behind the gatekeeper. Tom recognized the man immediately and he was certain that the man recognized him.

Tom pulled the old coat over his head and turned away as slowly as he dared. But he was sure he'd been spotted. It was the Man in Black.

"Come on," said Emily. Tom took two paces, and he heard the Man in Black mutter something to the gatekeeper and then start to follow. "There you are!" Emily was saying. "I actually do like picking flowers in the rain ..." But Tom didn't hear a word she was saying. His ears could only focus on the footsteps catching him up from behind ... any minute now, he knew, he would feel that heavy hand upon his shoulder ... and wait a minute! There it was! The Man in Black was literally breathing down his neck.

"Yes? What is it?" Emily had turned, but Tom just stayed frozen to the spot, with the Man in Black's hand on his shoulder.

"It's dangerous in town," said the Man in Black, but Tom didn't hear – he had already started to run. And behind him, to his horror, he heard Emily shout out: "Stop him!"

Tom ran as he'd never run before in his life, and he could run pretty fast when he tried, but today there were

three things against him. The first was the fact that the Man in Black could also run pretty fast when he tried. The second was the fact that Tom was not at all used to running in a dress. The third was the fact that today of all days was market day in the great city of Reims.

Now Reims was famous for its market, and people came from all over the region to buy and sell food and meat and fish and wine and cloth and leather and everything else you could imagine. Old ladies with aprons full of artichokes were sitting on stools, cages of chickens were stacked behind an old man who looked a bit like a chicken himself. There were stalls and tables and produce and people milling about and shouting and jostling.

Hence, as soon as Tom started running, he found himself dodging tradesmen as they set up their booths, farmers as they spread out their wares and everybody else doing the things that people do in the biggest market in the whole of France ... until – inevitably – he caught his foot in something (it happened to be a stool) and went flying. The kerchiefs and the coif that he'd been wearing also went flying and he landed up with his head in a basket of eggs that a young woman had just carefully arranged on the floor.

Now I'm not saying that every egg in that basket was broken, but if they weren't they must have all been double yolks, for Tom's entire head turned yellow. Bits of shell stuck to his hair and his eyes were glued up with raw egg. Thus he was spared the sight of the Man in Black standing over him laughing and then bending down to pick him up and carry him back into the Archbishop's Palace.

"So much for the great escape!" said Tom to himself, as he heard the great gates of the Palace slam once again behind him.

· 10 ·

THE REVOLT OF THE CITY
OF REIMS

Tom wasn't absolutely sure who stuck his head under the pump and washed all the egg out of his hair and ears, but he was pretty sure it wasn't Emily. Emily, he was certain, wouldn't have banged his head repeatedly against the pump. Nor would Emily have pulled half his hair out with the egg shells. The only thing he felt really certain about, as the Man in Black marched him unceremoniously back into the Archbishop's Palace, was that he was about to be exposed as an enemy and a spy. The best future he could look forward to, as far he could see, was being tortured and then executed. Not exactly what he'd been hoping for in life – but there you go …

So it was a mild surprise to Tom, as he picked himself up off the floor of the main audience chamber, where the Man in Black had thrown him, to find himself in front of a smiling face. The smiling face belonged to an elaborately dressed man seated on a throne, who – he could only assume – was Jean de Craon, the Archbishop of Reims.

"Uh oh!" thought Tom. "When great men like this smile at me, it usually means something unpleasant is about to happen …" Then – as if to make matters worse – the great man laughed, and so did the throng of people standing around.

49

Tom went from "indignant" to "bright red" as he suddenly remembered he was still wearing Emily's dress. So, as the court laughed at him, he heaved a sigh and bowed low to everyone in turn, which, of course, made them laugh all the more. Finally the Archbishop raised his hand.

"So," he said, "this is the little sparrow who has been translating our messages for the Duke of Lancaster?" Tom thought of denying it for approximately one thirtieth of a second. "Come here, little sparrow," smiled the Archbishop, crooking his finger. Tom approached the great man, and waited for those smiling lips to form the words: "Take this little sparrow away and put him in a pie!" or some such thing.

But the smiling lips kept smiling. And the Archbishop's voice remained unnervingly calm. "How is it that such a little sparrow is able to write and read with such remarkable facility?" Tom suddenly noticed the Archbishop had been speaking to him in Latin.

"Er ... I ... I was taught by the village priest ..." replied Tom, as he realized he himself was also speaking in Latin. "I just happen to be good at languages. I don't know why."

"Remarkable," murmured the Archbishop, reverting to French. "My spies told me the Duke of Lancaster was employing a young boy to translate the Papal correspondence ... I wanted to know if it was true."

"But I'm not a spy!" Tom blurted out – this time in French.

"Ah! The sparrow sings in French too!" The Archbishop's smile was starting to look dangerous again.

"I've only picked up a bit," muttered Tom, tugging at his dress, as if he felt now was the moment to get out of it.

"Apparently enough," snapped the Archbishop. "I am

sorry to deprive my lord of Lancaster of his song bird, but I prefer that his translations are done by someone in Holy Orders – someone who is sensitive to the needs of the Church. You will therefore remain here – perhaps I can find another use for you," and he smiled a smile that curdled the little food that sat in Tom's stomach.

The Archbishop clapped his hands and two guards stepped forward. So did Emily. "Your Lordship," said Emily, sinking a generous curtsy. "May I ask a favour?"

"Yes, my child? What is it?"

"Let the boy remain with me. It amuses me."

"But he will be nothing but trouble ..." replied Jean de Craon, Archbishop of Reims. "He has already stolen your clothes!" The gatekeeper had kindly refrained from implicating Emily herself in the escape.

"Please, your Lordship," and Emily smiled at the great man in such a mischievous way, and the corners of her mouth turned up so impishly, that Tom fell head over heels in love with her all over again.

And when his Lordship, the Archbishop of Reims, finally said: "Very well, Emilia, do with him as you wish", Tom began to think that perhaps captivity was not the worst thing in the world ... Or he would have done, had he had time to think anything, but at that moment something quite extraordinary happened ...

A white-faced herald ran into the audience chamber. "My Lord Archbishop!" he shouted. "They're attacking the Palace!"

A buzz of words went up like a swarm of bees, stinging the ears. The Archbishop raised his hand, and the swarm settled back into silence, as he shouted: "Call the guards!"

Tom's first thought was: "The English! They've started the siege of Reims without me!"

51

The Archbishop looked round at his court. The faces he saw had become frightened and tense. The Archbishop smiled at them. "So ... one of you cannot be trusted ... I wonder which one it is ...?" But at that moment, the noise of shouting in the courtyard pulled everyone to the windows.

Heads were appearing above the parapet of the outside wall – and here and there a man was climbing over. Strange, thought Tom, that there aren't any helmets or English banners ...

Men began to drop down into the courtyard ... but wait a minute! They weren't English soldiers ... they looked more like townsfolk – but that would be crazy! Why would the townspeople of Reims be attacking the Archbishop's Palace at the very moment the English army was camped outside their city?

Suddenly the old gatekeeper was running across the yard waving his hands and yelling ... and the great gates were shaking and trembling and then suddenly there was a terrible crack as the bar split. The next moment the gates swung open and an immense crowd of townspeople fell and rushed and jumped into the courtyard. The shouting and crashing had now become a continual roar that seemed to shake the air. And yet the odd thing was that – even though it was so loud and earth-shaking – it all seemed to be happening far away ... in another land ... in another world ... An avalanche of townsfolk, with their weather-beaten faces and their unwashed bonnets, engulfed the Archbishop's Palace ...

Tom looked around the faces of the aristocrats, but those blank expressions of horror gave him no clue as to what was going on. At that moment, Emily grabbed his hand and started pulling him across the audience chamber. No one seemed to take any notice of them. The Archbishop was sitting on his throne, rocking himself back and forth with his hands round his knees. "That's it!" said Jean de Craon, Archbishop of Reims, as he caught sight of Tom. "Fly, little sparrow! Fly!"

"Where are we going?" asked Tom. Emily had pulled him through a small doorway and up a narrow spiral staircase.

"Hurry, little Tom!" she shouted.

"What on earth are you doing?" yelled Tom. They had arrived back in Emily's bedchamber, and Emily was pulling clothes out of the great wooden chest. Down below Tom could hear the whooping and hollering of the invaders. "We're not going to a wedding!" he exclaimed.

Emily was busy stuffing dresses and under-gowns, kirtles and coifs, hose and slippers and sandals and shoes into a bag. "Little Tom!" she was saying. "I am never coming back! I have waited for a moment like this!"

"But ... we're as good as dead if we don't leave now! They're in the Palace!" And it was true! The yells and hollers were now echoing through the halls below.

"If I have no clothes – I may as well be dead!" retorted Emily, throwing the bag at Tom. "And I suggest you get your clothes as well, little Tom!" And with that Emily was off down the back staircase, and Tom suddenly remembered he was still wearing one of her gowns!

It was probably the biggest dilemma Tom had had to face since he'd arrived in Reims: should he do the sensible thing and just GO, or should he do the very thing he'd just been criticizing Emily for doing – i.e. worry about his wardrobe? He could already hear townspeople coming up the stairway. At any moment now they would burst through that door – exactly where his doublet was lying!

In a split second, Tom was across the room and had

snatched the thing up. The next moment he was back again and hurtling down the other staircase after Emily. Even as he did, he heard the townsfolk burst into the bedchamber behind him, and he heard their whoops as they ran about pulling the hangings off the walls and the silk sheets from the bed.

"How could you think about clothes at a time like this?" panted Tom as he caught up with Emily.

"I see you've got your doublet," was her only reply.

"Well … I may need that," said Tom.

"And you think I should walk around naked?" she retorted. Tom couldn't think of any reply, which was probably just as well, because he and Emily had just run into a Large, No.1-Size Problem. They'd also just run into the kitchen, which was all part and parcel of the Large, No.1-Size Problem.

The kitchen was empty; the cooks had already fled; pots and cauldrons were still swinging on their hooks; mixing spoons were still sticking up out of bowls of half-beaten batter, and dough was still settling where it was being kneaded on the long boards. None of this, of course, was the Large, No.1-Size Problem.

The Large, No.1-Size Problem was the fact that the double door that led to the outside, and which had been carefully locked, was now behaving in a very undoorlike fashion. It was shuddering and creaking and bulging – and it was doing this because a large crowd of townsfolk were in the process of breaking it down.

The only other exit from the kitchen was the one Tom and Emily had just come in by, and Tom could already hear the raiders coming down the spiral staircase behind them. To put it crudely: they were trapped! And that, as far as Tom could see, was indeed a Large, No. 1-Size Problem.

The door shuddered again as the townsfolk heaved against it. The feet on the staircase clattered closer.

Emily looked at Tom, as he stood there clutching her bag of clothes and his doublet, dishevelled and bareheaded, and still of course wearing her gown. Suddenly the corners of Emily's mouth twitched and then – to Tom's utter astonishment – she burst out laughing. It was all so frightful, she just couldn't help it.

Now I don't know whether it was being laughed at, or whether it was the fact that the doors of the kitchen suddenly began to splinter, and the Large, No. 1-Size Problem turned into a Mega, 22 Carat-Gold "Jam" (possibly even a "Pickle'), but I do know that at that very moment an idea leapt into Tom's head.

"Emily! Look!" he shouted, and he dropped to his knees and plunged his hands into the warm ashes around the edge of the kitchen fire. He then began rubbing the ash over his head, face and gown. The door of the kitchen cracked open at this point and they could see the townsfolk outside.

"What are you up to, little Tom?" asked Emily. By way of a reply Tom simply threw the next handful of ashes over her. "WHAT THE …!" Emily exploded. The next minute, Tom was tipping more ashes down her back. "Ow!" she yelled. "That was a HOT one!"

"I'm sorry!" Tom kept yelling "I'm sorry!" – and indeed he was – to throw ash over the beautiful Emily felt like an act of vandalism – like painting a moustache on the Madonna! It truly hurt Tom to do it – it hurt him even more, of course, because Emily was kicking him. "It's a disguise!" he explained. Outside, the townsfolk were preparing for one last heave against the splintered wood … "We mustn't look like we belong in the Palace …" And that was where his explanation had to stop, as the double doors burst open and a dozen filthy-coated townspeople, wielding knives and poles, burst into the kitchen.

Tom hitched up his skirts, leapt on to a table, and yelled: "The Archbishop's hams are as tasty as anyone's in the kingdom!" And with that he started pulling down the hams that hung from the ceiling and tossing them at the intruders.

The townsfolk, who had fallen into a stunned silence at the sight of this strange, cinder-covered girl prancing about on the kitchen table, gave a whoop and a cheer and began swarming over the kitchen, grabbing bags of meal and sacks of flour, bowls of lentils and jars of precious spices, hams and joints of beef, loaves of bread and skins of wine …

Tom was reaching for yet another ham from the ceiling when Emily tugged at his gown: "Tom! That was brilliant!" she hissed. But the thrill of pride that Tom was just about to enjoy, evaporated as Emily turned on one of the raiders who had snatched up her bag of clothes. "Hey! Leave that alone!" she yelled. "You dirty, scab-picking, louse-ridden peasant!" and she began clouting the man over the head with an iron soup ladle.

"Uh oh!" muttered Tom to himself, "there goes all my good work!" Tom jumped down hurriedly with a ham in each hand. "Here you are, my friend!" he said to the man, who had just fallen over backwards under Emily's assault. "You'll find this more nourishing than lady's clothes!" and he thrust one of the hams into the fellow's hands and grabbed Emily's bag. Emily herself had by this time turned on her heels and was making for the doors. "Wait for me!" shouted Tom. His own doublet was being trampled under the feet of the crowd, and what with

Emily's bag and the ham he was still holding, it was with some difficulty that he finally managed to retrieve it. He then set off after Emily.

Emily was threading her way through the mêlée with her nose in the air and a handkerchief in her hand with which she shooed away anyone who got too close. "Oh dear!" said Tom to himself, "I don't think Emily's quite got the idea about being inconspicuous!"

He could see their whole brilliantly planned escape foundering under Emily's upturned nose. The next moment, however, it was Tom who brought their escape to a sudden halt. They had just reached the main gates of the Archbishop's Palace, and were about to step out into the town for the second time that day, when Tom stopped dead. "Bother!" he said.

"Hurry, little Tom!" called Emily. "And mind you don't drop any of those gowns in the mud!"

"Emily!" Tom called. "I can't leave!"

"Why do you talk nonsense, little Tom? All we have to do is to just keep walking ..."

"No! There's something I said I'd do ..." moaned Tom. "I've got to go back!"

"GO BACK!" exclaimed Emily. "After we've just escaped?! NO!" She almost howled this last word.

"I'm sorry ... I promised someone ..." muttered Tom.

"You can't go back!" Emily commanded him. "I won't let you! You have to stay with me."

"You wait here," said Tom. "I won't be long!" And, with that, he dumped the bag of clothes and his doublet and the ham into Emily's arms.

"Hey!" shouted Emily. "I'm not carrying these!" Tom hesitated. He couldn't bear Emily being annoyed with him. To tell the truth, Tom was rather annoyed with himself. He wasn't annoyed with himself for having made the promise in the first place, but he was annoyed with himself for remembering it!

"All right!" he yelled. "I'll take this!" and he grabbed back the ham and plunged back into the mayhem of the Archbishop's Palace, brandishing the joint of meat as if it were a mighty weapon!

By the time he reached the Great Courtyard, it was engulfed in black smoke and men clutching silver candlesticks and velvet gowns lined with ermine, treasure chests and bags of fine food, skins of rare wine and carved chairs. From within the building, screams could be heard.

Tom held the ham above him, hoping and praying that he looked like a respectable looter, and raced alongside the cloister. Suddenly a small man with a bald head and a red nose ran up and lobbed a burning torch into one of the windows of the Great Hall. At least, that is what the small man with the red nose had intended to do. But unfortunately for his career as an arsonist, the torch failed to reach the high window, and fell on to the roof of the cloister, from where it rolled and dropped harmlessly into the courtyard at Tom's feet.

"Thanks!" yelled Tom. "Just what I needed!" and he picked the torch up and disappeared through the door by which he'd first entered the Archbishop's Palace.

"Hey!" said the small man with the bald head and the red nose. "Thass ... thass ... mine!" But by the time he'd managed to get these words through the swamp of red wine in which he'd just soaked his mind, Tom was down the spiral staircase and standing at the door of the Bishop's Parlour. The stench and the cloying dampness hit him in the stomach like an old friend he didn't want to see again.

"You!" he called. "Cannibal!" A chain clinked in the

darkest corner. "I don't know why I'm doing this," muttered Tom.

"I'm dead," came the Cannibal's voice from the darkness.

"No you're not!" yelled Tom. "You're talking to me! So you're still alive!" The Cannibal went silent – the way people do when they've just been soundly beaten in logical argument. "I promised I'd get you out! And here I am!" But how? That was the only question.

Tom glanced around the stone vault. To his left there was a small recess, which was where the jailer normally sat, and on the wall, hanging from a large nail, was a bunch of iron keys. In a flash, Tom had them off the wall and was unlocking the grille which swung open with a creak that could almost have been a sigh of relief.

Tom then did something which he never thought he would ever do again in his life – at least not of his own free will. He stepped back into the Bishop's Parlour – the torture chamber of the Archbishop of Reims. A chill shivered up his spine, and he suddenly felt curiously vulnerable, wearing only Emily's light, loose-fitting gown. The Cannibal cowered in his corner, as if trying to avoid the inconvenience of being rescued.

"I'm not coming near you!" said Tom as he threw the bunch of keys at the wretched prisoner. They landed in the filth and straw in front of him – and there they lay. Freedom was within the reach of his fingertips and yet he just stared at Tom blankly. "You're free!" said Tom. "I told you I'd come and get you out! And now I have!"

But still the Cannibal made no effort to take up the keys. He simply stared at Tom – his eyes narrowed and his tongue flicked out from his parched mouth and suddenly Tom realized what the man was looking at. "Oh! Yes! I forgot! I brought you something to eat too!" And he threw the ham at the Cannibal. Before it could even touch the floor the emaciated creature had leapt up to the full length of his chain, plucked the joint of meat out of the air and – before you could say "Christmas pudding!" – had sunk his teeth into it.

"That could have been my shoulder!" thought Tom with a shudder. "The sooner I get out of here the ..." and there he stopped, for he had just turned to discover, standing in the doorway, the two people he least wanted to see in the Bishop's Parlour – though for different reasons.

"I'm sorry!" Emily was saying. "I came to find you!" Emily was the first person he didn't want to see in such a ghastly place as the Bishop's Parlour.

The other person currently had his arm locked round Emily's beautiful neck. "So! – the 'little sparrow' turns out to be a homing pigeon."

The man's mouth was full of wolves' teeth. It was the Man in Black. Tom didn't want to see him in the Bishop's Parlour for the simple reason he didn't want to see him anywhere! A feeling that was immediately justified as the Man in Black produced a key, slammed the door of the torture chamber, and locked it.

· 11 ·

HOW THE CANNIBAL
SAVED TOM AND EMILY

The turning of that key in that lock sounded to Tom like the first shovel-full of soil must sound as it hits the coffin of someone who is being buried alive. Emily screamed. Tom yelled and threw himself against the grille. And the Man in Black just stared at them with cold eyes.

But there was something wrong. The Man in Black had locked them in the Archbishop's torture chamber all right, but – wait a minute! – he had locked himself in with them! Before Tom had the chance to ask why, his question was answered.

"This is the safest place to be right now," growled the Man in Black. And with that he dowsed both the torches and they were in blackness.

Tom felt Emily's hand slip into his. And somehow – even though he was once again a prisoner in the stinking confines of the Archbishop of Reims's darkest dungeon – he felt like the luckiest boy in the world …

Time passed. Neither Emily nor Tom spoke a word. They sat there huddling up together for warmth.

Finally Tom whispered: "How can you w-w-w-women wear so l-l-l-little?" He was shivering in the thin gown that Emily had made him wear.

"We don't usually sit around in freezing cold dungeons," said Emily.

"Shut up!" growled the Man in Black. "Pretend you're prisoners!"

"We *are* prisoners," pointed out Tom.

"There's someone coming!" snapped the Man in Black.

They could hear footsteps on the stone stairway and see the flickering light of a torch, as several young townsmen appeared wearing aprons and little white caps on their heads. They must have been apprentices. All of them were excited and out of breath and grinning.

"Hey! Look!" said one of the youths in an apron. He looked like a carpenter's apprentice. "The old fox's got some chickens in his den!"

They all came over to the grille and peered in by the light of their torch. "Look! A scarecrow and two little white doves!" grinned the smallest apprentice. "And that one in black must be the Devil! The Archbishop's got the Devil in his dungeon!"

They all seemed to find this immensely amusing. The Man in Black emitted a low growl that was definitely the sort of growl Tom could imagine the Devil making. As the amusement died down, however, one of the apprentices peered in between the bars of the grille and shuddered.

"Look!" he whispered. "A rack and a wheel!" The others went quiet as they gazed on those instruments of torture. Then the smallest apprentice suddenly smiled at Tom and Emily. "Don't worry!" he said. "We'll soon have you out of there!" and he tried the door handle of the cell.

Tom found himself thinking (rather ungenerously): "Oh yes! Good idea! We might have sat here for months without thinking of trying the door handle!"

"It's locked!" observed the carpenter's apprentice.

"Gosh!" Tom couldn't help saying aloud. "I've never been rescued by a real genius before!"

The young man in the leather apron and the cap looked at Tom in a slightly bemused way, then he laughed and said: "Have you got the key?"

Again Tom tried to bite his tongue, but he couldn't help saying: "Oh yes, this gentleman here has a key – he can let us out any time he wants." Of course this happened to be quite true, but he made it sound really ironic.

"Shut up!" snarled the Man in Black, and his wolves' teeth were bared for just a moment. But the apprentice hadn't taken offence; he simply laughed again and then nodded to the others. The next minute they were all putting their shoulders to the grille and starting to heave. They heaved and they shoved, but it was no good.

"There'll be a key somewhere," said the smallest of the apprentices, and he took the torch and started searching the rest of the dungeon. He found the nail where the jailer's keys had been hanging but, of course, nothing else. For a short time the rest of them joined in the hunt, then they seemed to lose interest. The smallest returned to the grille.

"We'll find the key!" he grinned. "Then we'll come back for you! Promise!" And with that the apprentices turned, laughing and whispering, and hurried back up the spiral stone staircase to the light of day.

The Man in Black snorted. "We'll not see them again," he muttered. And he was right.

Several hours later, Tom was woken up by a rather peremptory kick in the side. "Ow!" he exclaimed.

"Get up!" The Man in Black was standing over him. Emily was shivering miserably by his side. "I have some business to finish with the Archbishop," the Man in Black told him.

"I will never go back to him!" snapped Emily.

"Open the door!" The Man in Black tossed his keys to Tom.

"Take your filthy hands off me!" Emily was yelling as she kicked and hit the Man in Black.

"Let go of her!" Tom knew it was a pointless thing to say, but he said it anyway. At least it made the Man in Black laugh. Tom hadn't realized the fellow had a sense of humour.

"Open the door, little sparrow, before I break every bone in that little body of yours!" It was the sort of sense of humour that made Genghis Khan overrun Asia, India and most of Arabia.

"Let go of her!" Tom couldn't believe he'd said it a second time.

"Perhaps you didn't hear what I said, little sparrow ..." The Man in Black gripped Tom's neck with his free hand as if Tom had been a chicken on the way to market. "You don't tell me what to do. I tell you what to do." Tom was beginning to think that perhaps Genghis Khan had been overrated as a humorist.

Emily, who had gone rather quiet, suddenly let out an ear-piercing scream and started kicking the Man in Black again. Tom joined in. The next minute the Man in Black had them both pinned against the wall of the cell, and then, before Tom could see how he did it, he had a knife pressed against Tom's throat. "Uh oh!" thought Tom. "I've been here before!"

"I advise you to do as I say," growled the Man in Black, "if you want to stay ..."

"Alive?" croaked Tom. He didn't know why he felt it was so important for the Man in Black to finish his sentence, but the Man in Black never did finish that

particular sentence. He just glared at Tom, and bared his wolves' teeth.

"You're not going to scare me like that!" thought Tom, who had some experience of being glared at. On the other hand, he'd never seen anyone glare in quite the way that the Man in Black was now glaring at him. The man's eyes were bulging so much that Tom thought they were going to fall out of his head. The next moment Tom realized that the Man in Black had dropped the knife and was clawing at his throat.

It was then that Tom saw a hollow-eyed face peering over the Man in Black's shoulder; the Cannibal had one of his chains around the Man in Black's throat as the fellow dropped to his knees, choking, grasping at his neck, his eyes bulging more and more.

"What are you waiting for?" asked the Cannibal. "Run!"

In the next second Tom and Emily were racing up the

stone stairs as fast as their legs could carry them. But before Tom turned the first corner, he glanced behind and caught sight of the Cannibal dropping the Man in Black face downwards on to the filthy floor. Tom could not tell whether the Man in Black was alive or dead – but I'll tell you a terrible thing: at that particular moment, Tom didn't really care.

· 12 ·

HUE AND CRY

"What d'you mean – you're coming with me?" asked Tom, sticking his head out from under one of the market stalls.

"Just find my clothes!" Emily hissed.

"I'm going back to the English army! Your enemies – remember?"

"Stop talking nonsense," replied Emily, "and get the bag!"

"Are you sure you hid it under here?"

"Of course I'm sure. It's with your doublet."

"Well I can't see either of them," said Tom.

"I suppose I could have hidden them under that stall over there." Emily pointed at another market stall.

"A fish-stall?!" exclaimed Tom. "They'll stink!"

"Perhaps that one then," suggested Emily helpfully. Tom heaved a sigh; his knees were getting quite sore with diving under all these stalls ... But again there was no sign of either the bag of clothes or his doublet.

It was late in the day by the time Tom found the right stall. It was selling linen and fine cloth. "Got them!" yelled Tom.

"Got you!" A gruff voice suddenly grabbed him by the collar, and Tom found himself looking up into the face of a large woman with (rather surprisingly) a beard. "What are you doing with my stuff?"

"It's not your stuff," said Tom, who couldn't take his eyes off the beard. "This is my friend's bag of clothes and that's my doublet. She left them under your stall ..."

"She did no such thing!"

"She did!"

"Little thieving liar!"

"It's true!"

"I bought them things this morning off the man who runs the fish stall!" said the bearded woman.

"You see! I said I left them under the fish stall!" exclaimed Emily triumphantly.

The bearded woman had grabbed Tom's chin in her hand, and was squeezing it in her thick fingers. Tom couldn't help noticing that her hand looked (and smelt) remarkably like one of the hams from the Archbishop's kitchen. It was all he could do to stop himself taking a bite out of them.

"Wait a minute!" said the beard. "You're not a girl!"

"Well done! You have won first prize for observation!" exclaimed Tom. "Look!" And he pointed over her shoulder.

"A prize?" The bearded woman couldn't stop herself turning to look where Tom was pointing. Whereupon Tom grabbed Emily's bag of clothes and his own doublet, and bolted.

The bearded woman yelled. Emily laughed. And all the other traders turned to look at them as they ran as fast as they could through the throng.

"Stop them!" the bearded woman was shouting. "They stole my things! Thieves! Robbers!" A ripple of disapproval ran around the market-place. But by that time

Tom and Emily had disappeared round the corner and were running, hell for leather, down an alley that turned a corner and ran alongside the wall of the new cemetery.

As they ran, however, the big bag of clothes started to fall apart and Tom kept tripping up over his doublet.

"I can't run with these!" gasped Tom. He could hear the stall-holders in the market square shouting and the sound of feet pounding on the cobblestones. Before Emily could stop him, he'd thrown the bag over the wall of the cemetery.

"My clothes!" yelled Emily.

"You too!" yelled Tom.

"What d'you mean?" yelled Emily.

"Over the wall!" said Tom.

"I can't!" said Emily. The hue and cry had started in earnest.

"You've got to!" exclaimed Tom, and he put his hand out so she could place her foot in it.

"No!" she said.

"Please, Emily!" Tom pleaded, and at that moment the hue and cry burst into the alley-way and the noise of it seemed to echo off the roofs and double in volume. The effect on Emily was instant. She put her foot into Tom's hand, grabbed the top of the wall, pulled herself up and over and dropped down on the other side.

"Thanks for the help!" muttered Tom as he looked up the high wall. He glanced back down the alley-way. Once the hue and cry reached the corner, they would see him, so he flung himself at the wall, found a hand-hold and pulled himself up. Before he was two seconds older, he was on top of the wall, and, as the first pursuers rounded the corner, he dropped into the cemetery below.

"You're standing on my best gown!" hissed Emily. The bag of clothes had come apart as it flew over the wall and Tom had landed on a particularly delicate silk surcoat of blue and gold.

"Sh!" whispered Tom, as the crowd of angry stall-holders surged towards them on the other side of the wall.

"Thieves! Robbers! Stop them! Stop!" The thunder of their footsteps shook the ground. Tom expected a face to appear over the top of the wall at any moment, and to hear the cry: "Here they are!" But nothing happened. Emily and Tom listened with bated breath as the noise of the mob raced on down the alley-way ... until eventually the shouts and yells mingled with the barking of all the dogs of the city, who seemed to have joined in the hunt.

Tom and Emily were safe. At least for the moment.

· 13 ·

A NIGHT IN THE GRAVEYARD

"What d'you mean – you're coming with me?" asked Tom.

"That's what you said at the beginning of the last chapter," replied Emily.

"This isn't a book!" exclaimed Tom. "This is our lives! This is actually happening!"

"My life is a story," smiled Emily. "I tell myself what's going to happen next."

"And does it?" Tom was quite intrigued despite himself.

"More often than you'd think," replied Emily. "For example, I told myself that a brave knight would steal into the Archbishop's Palace and help me escape."

"But I'm not a …" Tom began.

"You can tell yourself you are, little Tom!" said Emily, and that mouth of hers crinkled up at the corners into that smile of hers that did indeed make Tom feel as if he were a knight in shining armour riding on a white horse. "Anyway you've certainly helped me to escape," she added.

Tom felt himself glow inside. He felt as if he could sit there for ever listening to Emily telling him nonsense about life being a story. Nonsense is fine if it's beautiful. But the sun was now setting and there was other nonsense – uglier nonsense – queuing up to gain entry into Tom's head.

"And was spending the night in a cemetery part of the story you were telling yourself?" Tom asked.

Emily shivered and shook her head.

I don't know whether you've ever spent a night in a cemetery, but it's not something I would recommend – unless, of course, you happen to be dead. (In which case, you shouldn't be reading this. So stop it! This is not a book for ghosts!)

At least Tom and Emily had found a small hut, in the corner of the cemetery, and there they made themselves a nest of dead leaves and Emily's bundle. Now they were watching apprehensively as the last remains of light faded from the sky. The graves began to look like black bodies lying on the ground. The yew trees became monsters guarding the dead – waiting to pounce on anyone foolish enough to spend the night there ... Tom felt a chill run up his spine – a chill that seemed to freeze his common-sense, and allow a carnival of icy fears to take over his mind.

The only object of hope was the moon, that had stolen silently up the sky as the light faded. But even that was elbowed aside by blustering clouds that smothered the world beneath in fearful darkness.

"If this is one of the stories you're telling yourself," whispered Tom, "couldn't you lighten it up a bit? At least make the clouds go away ..." But Emily didn't reply. She lay there gazing straight up. In the few moments of moonlight, when Tom could glimpse her, she looked serene and calm. Her delicate nose was straight and her mouth still twitched slightly at the corners as if the whole world somehow amused her. Tom thought she was the most beautiful creature in the world.

What he didn't know was that as Emily lay there in that damp hut she was too busy trying to be brave herself to think about anything else. That was when the rain started to fall. In a curious way, the rain helped.

"They don't come out in the rain," said Tom.

"Who don't?" Emily tried to whisper, but her voice was so very very small it could hardly even count as a whisper.

"Ghouls and ghosts," replied Tom. "Rain makes them all go soggy. A soggy ghost can't float around in the air, can it? And nobody would hear you going 'Booooooo!' in the middle of a thunderstorm! Very frustrating for any self-respecting ghoul."

Emily gave a snort, which Tom thought was probably a laugh, and she put her arm around him. Tom didn't dare move. He just lay there feeling unbelievably lucky – even though he was cold and damp and hungry. And that was how they fell asleep, with Tom muttering silly nonsense about ghosts getting breadcrumbs in their sheets, about bugaboos catching colds and sneezing because they've been out in the rain all night, and about a demon who was afraid of thunder.

And meanwhile the thunder – the real thunder – roared over the cemetery, and the rain crashed down on the roof of their little hut, and gushed off the eaves, and lashed the graves of the dead as if punishing them for even having thought of coming out tonight to haunt these two young people – or at least that's what Tom said ... or perhaps it's what he thought he would say but somehow never did because he had finally fallen fast asleep. And so had Emily. But the smile never left her lips.

· 14 ·

THE POWER OF CLOTHES

When dawn broke, the cemetery looked such a sorry sight that you could never have imagined it to have held any fears at all. The night's thunderstorm had brought down branches. The rain had turned the earth into puddles and rivulets, and the pathetic handful of gravestones were leaning at comical angles. By way of a compensation, however, the sky had shaken off the clouds, and now stretched above them blue and bright.

Tom was thankfully wearing his own doublet again, but he was still cold and a little damp from where the rain had trickled through the thatching of the hut. He looked at Emily, who was still fast asleep. At least she looked as if she were fast asleep, but you could never be too certain with Emily. "Emily!" he whispered. "Emily! Wake up! It's daylight!"

Emily's lovely face frowned, then her smooth forehead wrinkled as her brows arched together, and she opened one grey eye. "I've got to go to the garde-robe!" she said, and stood up and stretched. As she glided out of the hut she called out to Tom: "Lay out my grey gown with the fleur-de-lis on the sleeve."

"I'm not your chambermaid!" Tom didn't actually shout this back, instead he sorted through Emily's clothes until he

75

found the grey gown with the fleur-de-lis on the sleeve. When Emily returned he handed her the dress.

"No! no! no!" she exclaimed. "Lay it out so I can see it's all right to wear!"

"But!" exclaimed Tom.

"And when you have done that you may dress my hair. I will take the plain linen gorget."

"We're trying to escape!" cried Tom. "It doesn't matter what we look like!"

"It always matters – what you look like," returned Emily. "We are what we wear."

Tom sighed.

Some time later, Emily and Tom found themselves approaching the main gate of the city of Reims. "I still don't see how you can come with me and join the English army," Tom was saying. "I mean they are your enemies?"

"Who said the English were my enemies?"

"Well, we're doing a pretty good impression of it!" exclaimed Tom. "We're besieging your city!"

"Little Tom!" Emily was laughing at him. "You are so sweet I could eat you ..." He didn't know why, but Tom hated it when Emily was nice to him like this. "You know nothing about these things, do you?"

"What d'you mean?" replied Tom indignantly. "I know that our King Edward has a better claim to the throne of France than your King John, whom we captured at the Battle of Poitiers and who now lies in an English jail! I know that King Edward has come here to force the city of Reims to crown him King of France!"

"But how do you imagine he can force a great city like Reims to crown him King of France?" asked Emily.

"He's got an army of ten thousand men!" Tom explained patiently. "It's the largest army ever to leave England!"

Emily's laughter echoed among the still-shuttered houses, and Tom was afraid she'd wake all the townsfolk who had been chasing them only the night before. "Ten thousand men!" she said. "And you know the snag about having ten thousand men, little Tom?"

"How can there be 'a snag'?" exploded Tom. "It's a huge army – it can force the city of Reims to do what it likes!"

"But ten thousand men have to eat," replied Emily. "And this countryside has been picked clean by the war. Outside the city there is scarcely enough for ten men to eat – let alone ten thousand. Your King Edward cannot stay here or his ten thousand men will all starve to death."

"But when we defeat you we will take everything in the city!" cried Tom.

"But how can you defeat us?"

"In battle!" Tom simply could not believe how naïve Emily was in these matters.

"You'll never get the chance to do battle," she said.

"Why not?" Tom couldn't help smiling … but then so was Emily.

"The city will just wait for your King and his ten thousand men to get hungry and go away," laughed Emily. "Look at the walls!" They were at that moment passing through the gates of the city of Reims, and Tom could indeed look at the walls. And when he looked at them, he could see why the people of Reims had no need to fear even an army of ten thousand men. Perhaps Emily was not naïve at all … "You know the only chance your King Edward has of being crowned King of France?" asked Emily. Tom shook his head. "His only chance is that my uncle – the Archbishop – will let him into the city and do it for him."

"The Archbishop is your uncle?" gasped Tom, but

before he could think what this meant, they were hailed by the gatekeeper.

"Hello! And where are you two young people off to on this cheap and cheerful morning?" said the gatekeeper.

"Oh, Mr gatekeeper!" Emily had taken the man's hand

in hers. "You know what it is to be young ...? You know what it is to love?" And here she made a grand gesture with her arm so that the gatekeeper found himself staring straight at the fleur-de-lis embroidered on her sleeve. The effect was instantaneous.

"Oh! I'm sorry, your Ladyship, I didn't recognize you!" The gatekeeper whipped off his hat and fell to his knees before Emily. "I am the servant of the Valois always."

"God be with you," said Emily, and she floated out of the city of Reims, whispering to Tom as they went: "You see, little Tom? We are what we wear!"

They walked away from the city gates in silence. Tom hitched Emily's bag of clothes on to his back and turned all that Emily had said over in his mind. Eventually he said: "But why on earth would our King Edward expect the Archbishop of Reims to let him into the city?"

"Why shouldn't he?" Emily smiled at him. "They are cousins."

"Cousins?" said Tom – kicking himself for lapsing back into repetition.

Emily laughed. "The Archbishop does not like the French King Jean – the Archbishop thinks he would be better off under the King of England. That is why the townspeople stormed his Palace yesterday – to stop him handing their city over to the English."

"But wait a minute!" exclaimed Tom. "If King Edward is your uncle's cousin ... Then you're King Edward's ..."

"I just call him uncle," said Emily sweetly, and she skipped off down the muddy road that wound between the ruined vineyards of Champagne.

It was not the first time since his adventures began that Tom had had the feeling that he had a lot to learn. And he had a strong suspicion that it was not to be the last.

• 15 •

HOW TOM GOT EMILY'S
LUNCH

It is amazing how heavy a bundle of clothes can get when you've been carrying them for six miles. Even Emily's clothes, which were no more than silk and taffeta, began to feel like a lead weight on Tom's back, as he tried to keep up with their light-heeled owner. Emily was walking in front as usual, with her head held high and her nose in the air. His attempt at dressing her hair had not been totally successful, and strands were now falling out from under her coif, but to Tom's mind there was nothing he would change about the way she looked as she picked her delicate way through the mud.

Tom kept wanting to apologize for not having supplied her with a horse. He couldn't think why he should feel it was all his fault, but he did. Emily had that effect on people.

They had reached the village of Verzenay. Beyond it lay the Forest of the Mountain of Reims, within which they would find the Abbey of St Basle, where the English King had made his quarters.

And yet despite the proximity of the English army, a few were still working diligently among the pitiful handful of vines that had not been burnt or broken or trodden underfoot by the soldiery. From the way the men worked, you could not tell that their crops had been destroyed and their lives ruined by the presence of the English. They seemed to be working on as if everything were perfectly normal – perhaps because they had no alternative.

By now, however, the morning was well advanced, and one or two wives could be seen struggling across the tortured land, bearing whatever scant rations they could find for their menfolk.

"I'm hungry," said Emily. Tom knew exactly what she meant. She meant he had to find her a clean, dry place to sit, and then run off to get her some food – nothing too oily – and making sure that the bread was not too coarse and that there was some meat but that it was fresh and that it had not been heated up more than once …

And that was exactly what Tom found himself doing a few moments later. The first housewife he met scurrying down the main street, with her man's meal in her hands, shook her head and scowled. "Only a little broth and a piece of bread," ventured Tom. But the woman was off down the road, as if she'd just met the devil himself, begging by the roadside.

Once among the small, thatched cottages that bordered the street, Tom spotted a half-open door. He knocked and waited but there was no reply. So he stuck his head in and saw the smoky interior of a humble house, with a meagre fire burning in the hearth and a cauldron hanging over it from a chain.

"Hello?" Tom called out. "Anyone here?"

Silence.

Just the crackle of the fire and the slight chink of the chain as the cauldron swung in the draught from the door. "Anyone mind if I come in and steal a few things?" Tom called.

Silence.

"Righto! If you're sure you don't mind than I'll just creep in and take a few things to eat and then be off."

Still there was no reply. So Tom slipped through the door and tiptoed across to the fire. Hanging in the cauldron was a small pudding wrapped up in a cloth. Tom hauled it out of the broth. "Hmm," he muttered to himself, "not quite cooked." Then he noticed several dry sausages and the remains of a ham hanging from a beam. So he grabbed a couple of sausages, and turned to look for the bread. Instead of bread, however, he found an elderly man holding a pitchfork.

"What are you doing?" growled the old man with the pitchfork.

Tom nearly lost his sausages. He certainly lost his appetite. "I told you before I came in. Or didn't you hear me?" Tom didn't know why he said this, but that's what he said.

"What's that?" growled the old man, jabbing the pitchfork under Tom's nose.

"I came in to steal some food," replied Tom, wondering why jokes always sounded feebler when you repeated them. "I asked if it was all right."

"What're you saying?" growled the old man.

Tom was not going to repeat it a third time, so he shouted very loudly: "YOUR WIFE VERY KINDLY TOLD ME TO COME AND HELP MYSELF TO WHATEVER I NEEDED!"

"What d'you say?" growled the old man.

"I KNOCKED AT THE DOOR" Tom yelled.

"Don't you threaten me!" growled the old man and he jabbed the pitchfork towards Tom's left ear. Tom ducked away from it, tripped over a log and fell with a clatter into the corner. The old man took another step towards him, so Tom yelled as loudly as he could:

"YOUR WIFE TOLD ME TO HELP MYSELF!"

"I got no wife!" growled the old man. I'd like to be able to apply a word other than "growl" to the old man's way of speaking, but there really isn't one. "Ululate", "bark", "bellow", "yap", "snort", "churr", "grate", "pule", "gruntle", "howl", "miaow" – none of these gives the sense of how the old man communicated. I suppose he did "snarl" a little – but even that doesn't quite do his speech patterns justice. It was a "growl", and there's no other word for it.

The old man lifted up the pitchfork and was about to plunge it down into some portion of Tom's body – although exactly which portion Tom had no idea, because the old man's hand was shaking all over the place.

"Look out!" yelled Tom. "Behind you!" It was an old trick and it might have worked, but unfortunately Tom didn't yell it loud enough.

"It's a pitchfork!" growled the old man.

"I DIDN'T SAY: 'WHAT'S THAT?' " yelled Tom. "I SAID ... oh, never mind ..."

Tom had noticed the pitchfork was about to descend

towards him, so he threw a sausage at the old man's head and rolled to one side, just as the pitchfork landed in the earthen floor beside him. The old man fell backwards under the sausage attack, and Tom leapt to his feet. Or he would have done if the pitchfork hadn't pinned the edge of his doublet to the floor.

"Sausage-feathers!" exclaimed Tom, as he pulled the pitchfork out.

"Mercy!" whined the old man. Miraculously he had stopped "growling" and the hard-pressed author was able to apply another word to his way of speaking. Tom was now standing over the old man, brandishing the pitchfork himself. He grabbed the sausage back.

"WHERE'S THE BREAD?" he shouted.

"NO! NO! NOT MY HEAD! Don't cut off my head!" whimpered the old man – not a hint of a "growl" left in his speech.

"I DIDN'T SAY ... oh!" Tom gave up, and looked quickly round. There was a cupboard on the other side of the room, and Tom had it open before you could say "Thief!" or, rather, before the old man could say "Thief!" Inside was a half-consumed loaf of black rye bread. It didn't look very appetizing but at least it was bread. Tom stuffed it into his doublet.

"Thanks!" yelled Tom. "I'll pay you back if ever I get the chance!" And he bolted out of the cottage, pausing only to jam the pitchfork through the handle of the door.

"Thief!" yelled the old man at last. "Thief!" And he sprang to the door and rattled it helplessly, as Tom sprinted off down the village.

· 16 ·

TOM WISHES HE HAD
MORE THAN SAUSAGES

Tom found Emily on the edge of the vineyards looking, he thought, like a princess. She sat with her back straight and her nose in the air. Her throne was nothing more than a large boulder, but nonetheless she was holding court. Five peasants had left their vines, and were now lined up in front of her. Not a single mouth was shut – even though not one of them was eating his lunch right then. Instead they were all proffering their lunch-boxes up to Emily for her inspection. Emily, for her part, gave each a perfunctory glance; once or twice she might deign to dip her delicate finger into the thin pottage. When she did, the proud owner of the lunch in question held his breath, nudged his neighbour and stared at this beautiful creature who appeared to have fallen out of the blue sky into their muddy world, hoping against hope that she would choose his lunch to eat.

It's the elderly man's turn. His toothless mouth is gaping like the pit of hell ... No! The princess does not even choose to dip her delicate finger into his gruel! His face falls as he receives back his rejected lunch-box. He gazes sorrowfully into it – how could he ever have imagined a princess would eat such sorry food? But now Emily is smiling up at the tall young man with the broad shoulders and the mop of fair hair that falls over his eyes. Yes! She has chosen him! His lunch is hers! He is the happiest mortal in the wide world, and his reward will be to gaze upon the lovely Emily as she fastidiously picks her way through his cheese and bread.

Emily smiles at the young man. He is overcome with shyness. He doesn't know where to look. The other country courtiers gawp at Emily, as if waiting for the miracle that will surely happen when a creature from another sphere descends among ordinary mortals.

Tom stood there, some way off, and looked at the hard fought-for provisions in his hands. Suddenly he noticed the sausage was bent (presumably where it had hit the old cottager's head) and the bread had a trace of mould on one corner. His world went into shadow. Actually everybody's world went into shadow, for the clouds were hurrying to cover the naked blue of the sky from the sight of men.

Tom sat down on a milestone, took out his knife and cut off a slice of sausage and a hunk of bread. They tasted of smoke and shadows.

"Why! Little Tom!" Emily's voice suddenly lit up Tom's day again. "What are you doing sulking over there?" Tom hadn't realized that was what he was doing, and said so. "Yes you are too!" smiled Emily. She was now standing over him. Her courtiers were still transfixed, gaping by her throne. "Look at you!"

Tom stood up. "Perhaps we should get on our way. We've still two or three miles to go," he said.

"Little Tom!" teased Emily. "I do believe you're jealous!" Tom had no idea what she was talking about. "And look! You had brought me a beautiful sausage ... and some delicious black bread ..." Tom tried to hide the sorry offering. "We can present them to my uncle, the King!"

said Emily and, laughing, she skipped off down the puddle-strewn road, turning only to wave at the mortals who still stood in their muddy field in their muddy boots gaping helplessly at the vision that had so briefly touched their lives. Only the fair-haired youth waved back.

Tom stuffed the sausage and the bread into the bundle of clothes, and followed, full of contradictory emotions. In some strange way he felt he was no longer himself when he was with Emily. His whole life became eclipsed by her presence and her needs. In one way it was a wonderful feeling. But in another way Tom wasn't at all sure he liked it. And yet, he asked himself, wasn't this what being a knight was all about? Every knight – every squire – had to have a lady whom he served until death. Perhaps Emily would be his lady to whom he would dedicate all the deeds of derring-do and all the adventures that still lay ahead.

Stepping in a puddle brought him to his senses. Before night fell, he reflected, they would reach the English encampment and then it would be all over. Emily would be welcomed into the King's household, and he would be sent back to the Duke of Lancaster's scriptorium. And there, he told himself, he would forget all about Emily and the corners of her mouth turning up …

Meanwhile, as they approached the great Forest of the Mountain of Reims, the clouds took over more and more of the sky. And as they got nearer the English camp, the thought of someone else began to take over Tom's mind. He was alarmed to find the bright image of Emily being jostled aside by the memory of Ann … or should he be calling her Alan …? What on earth had happened to her? How could he have forgotten to think about her? How could he have let Emily eclipse his best friend in all the world? Suddenly, Tom felt quite ashamed.

• 17 •

HOW TOM AND EMILY
DON'T FIND THE ENGLISH ARMY

When Tom and Emily finally reached the spot where the English army was encamped, the first thing they noticed was that it wasn't there. The large swathes of forest that had been cut down by the pioneers were still there. The vast areas charred by fires and flattened by thousands of feet were still there. But of the English army itself there was not a single trace ... not a single buckle ... not a single boot ... not a single scrap of stale bread ... not a single nothing.

"What did I tell you!" exclaimed Emily. "I said they'd have to raise the siege sooner or later!"

"They can't have gone!" muttered Tom.

"Well if they haven't they must be World Hide-and-Seek Champions!" laughed Emily.

It was getting cold as night edged its way through the forest. Tom shivered. There is nowhere on earth so lonely as a place that has just been vacated by ten thousand men. "Let's get on to the Abbey," said Tom. "Perhaps the Duke of Lancaster's still there."

But he wasn't. Nor was the King.

Nor, indeed, was anybody. When they reached the great Abbey of St Basle, they found it empty. Really, truly empty. There were no people. There was not a stick of furniture.

There was not a thread of cloth. Worse still, there was no food. It was stripped as clean as if a plague of locusts had swarmed through it – which wasn't far from the truth. The rooms, that had been full of talk and business when Tom had last walked through them, now echoed with silence. The rich wall-hangings and the silver chalices and golden plates were all safely locked up in King Edward's coffers (wherever they were), and the Abbey itself was as shorn of ornament as a priest at bath-time.

But the odd thing is that when the monks returned to the venerable Abbey some days later, they were overjoyed. For, you see, King Edward III of England, in his munificence and out of respect for the magnificent old building (which even then was six hundred years old) had forbidden his men to do what they normally did to magnificent old buildings – i.e. burn them to the ground. So the monks of the Abbey of St Basle had a lot to be grateful for. The same could hardly be said for Tom and Emily.

Tom could scarcely see Emily in the gathering gloom. "I think we should light a fire," he said. "As quickly as possible."

Emily said nothing, but she went and sat down in a corner, with her back against the wall, put her face into her hands and didn't move for another hour. By which time, Tom had got a fire going and the smoke was curling up into the high ceiling of the hall. He spread out a feast of dry sausage and dry bread on a dry board beside the fire. He had found some fresh water in a nearby stream, but he couldn't think of any way to carry it, so he told Emily where to go if she was thirsty. Then they sat down and ate and wondered.

Well, that's not quite true. Emily ate and Tom wondered. Somehow, even though he'd only eaten a slice of bread and

89

sausage all day, he wasn't hungry. And somehow, even though she had had her pick of the vineyard workers' lunches earlier, Emily was.

TOM AND EMILY MEET A
STRANGE KNIGHT

"You must have seen them!" exclaimed Tom. "There were ten thousand of them!" But the old man just shook his toothless head and carried on carving the piece of wood in his hand as if his life depended on it – although as far as Tom could see he had no talent as a sculptor whatsoever.

Emily gave Tom a dig in the ribs. "Hit him," she said. "He knows which way the army went – he's just not telling."

"But how is hitting him going to help?" Tom really didn't understand Emily sometimes.

She shrugged her delicate shoulders. "You've got to show these people who's in charge."

"Well I'm not going to hit him," replied Tom.

"Then I'll have to do it myself," said Emily and she squared up to the old man, who had, by this time, finished carving the piece of wood. As she pulled back her hand, however, the old man raised the piece of wood above his head. And Tom suddenly realized that what he had been carving was not a piece of fine art at all! In fact it had a very precise function, which the old man was just about to test!

"Look out!" cried Tom and he charged head first at the

old man's stomach just as the old man brought the cudgel (which is what he'd been making) crashing down towards Emily's fine-boned skull. It missed and instead hit Tom hard across his back. He and the old man both crashed to the ground and the club itself dropped into a convenient puddle of water. By now Tom was sitting astride the old fellow, pinning his arms to the floor. His toothless mouth was opening and shutting like a trout out of water. "Now listen," said Tom, "we don't mean you any harm. But we must know which direction the English army took!"

Now you might think that the direction in which a vast army had just marched would be quite obvious. After all, ten thousand men are bound to leave a bit of a trail. And you would be right; the English army had left a vast trail of destruction behind them. If you had been looking down from the clouds, it would have been as plain as a peddler's pack-staff. But Tom and Emily were standing right in the middle of it. All they could see around them were ruined houses, broken fences and smoking ashes, a devastated and burnt-out countryside – stretching as far as the eye could see – to the north, to the east, to the west, to the south. As far as Tom and Emily were concerned the army could have gone in any direction.

The inhabitants of Ambonnay had all fled with the first distant sounds of the army's approach: the shrill fifes, the sounding drums and the rumble of wagons and of ten thousand voices moaning about the weather and how much their feet hurt …

How the old man came to have been left behind was a mystery. But here he was, as alive as a fish, twisting about in Tom's grip – trying to grab back his cudgel. "Now stop that!" said Tom, as the old man tried to bite his wrist. "I've given up doing food impersonations!"

"Zkxrtght!!!!" said the old man – or something along those lines. Emily had just hit him on the head with his newly carved cudgel. "Next time I'll do it with the heavy end!" she shouted. "Tell us which way they went!" The old man twisted round and pointed his sharp nose towards the south. "They were on their way to Burgundy!" he gasped. "May God punish them!"

"You see!" said Emily some time later and much further down the road. "You have to hit these people to show them who's in charge." Tom sighed. The beautiful Emily, who was so unmannish in her behaviour, never ceased to surprise him. But before he could even shake his head, there was a crash and the thud of hooves – and a magnificent white stallion burst out of the woodland ahead and came clattering up the road towards them.

It was an extraordinary and alarming sight. But perhaps the most extraordinary and, in some ways, alarming part was the fact that loosely attached to the magnificent white stallion was a knight in full armour. His leg was caught in the stirrup and he was being dragged along the road.

Tom's first instinct was to dive out of the way, but he caught sight of Emily out of the corner of his eye: he could see her standing her ground. So Tom stayed where he was, and as the horse thundered past he grabbed the loose reins. The horse reared and Tom was jerked off his feet and thrown down on to the knight, as Emily grabbed the horse's bridle from the other side.

Tom picked himself up, while Emily tried to calm the stallion. The knight who had looked like a metal sack of potatoes as he was being dragged along the ground, suddenly came to life. He struggled frantically to get his foot out of the stirrup and then leapt up – or rather struggled up as quickly as the cumbersome coat of plates and greaves would allow him.

Once he was standing he turned and looked at Tom, and Tom felt the most odd sensation. The knight's visor was down and Tom could see nothing of the man inside, and yet … he had the most uncanny feeling that he knew him!

· 19 ·

THE SILENT KNIGHT

"Are you all right, sir?" asked Tom. The knight didn't reply. Tom shifted from one foot to the other. "Is there anything we can do?" he asked. Emily was stroking the stallion's muzzle and making soft cooing sounds into its ears. The knight turned to look at her and then looked back at Tom. And once again Tom was gripped by the strange certainty that he knew this man.

The knight was of average height. He wore greaves on his arms and legs and a coat of plates over a mail shirt. Over this he was wearing a silk tunic emblazoned with a red hand holding a bolt of lightning. His tunic, however, had been streaked with mud when he was dragged unceremoniously along the road, and his greaves and helmet had been scored by stones. Standing next to Emily, he cut a sorry figure.

"One of the most remarkable things about Emily," thought Tom, "is that she never gets dirty. How does she do it? Last night we slept rough in a deserted abbey, this morning we've walked something like ten miles and yet she looks as if she'd just been dressed by her chambermaid – as fresh and bright as the daisies in the meadow over there."

Tom found himself slipping back into "squire mode". Before you could say, "Coming, sir!", he was at the knight's side, rubbing mud off with his sleeve, but a metal-coated arm pushed him away.

"Let me just clean you, sir!" exclaimed Tom. "Your back's filthy …"

The knight didn't reply. He simply turned and tried to swing himself back on to his horse – but that is not an easy thing to do when you're wearing plate armour, and his leg would never have made it over the horse's back, if Tom hadn't leapt forward and given the knight a push in exactly the right place, at exactly the right time.

The knight, however, did not thank him. Instead he beckoned to Emily. She hesitated. Then she jumped up behind him on the horse and put her arms around the knight's waist. She looked down at Tom. The corners of her mouth turned up into that smile of hers, and she murmured, "Come, little Tom", as the knight pricked his horse, and they started off along the road to Chalons.

Tom trotted behind. "At least Emily's got what she wanted," he said to himself. "He may not be in 'shining armour' but at least he's a knight and he's certainly carrying her off … somewhere …" And Tom's mind started to run ahead of them, down the road and round the corner … and round the next corner and round the next corner … And try as he might, Tom just couldn't see what was going to happen next.

They travelled in this manner for some miles – Tom running behind, and his thoughts running ahead, and Emily keeping up a one-sided conversation about her family: her brother Guillaume, who had been captured at the battle of Poitiers by the English and was still waiting for his ransom to be paid; her father, who had been killed in the uprising of the common people in Paris; her mother, who had died many years ago, and so on and so forth.

By nightfall, the little party had arrived at the town of Chalons-en-Champagne, and found themselves standing outside an inn. Although nobody said anything, Tom clearly got the impression that he was expected to do something. So he put down his bundle and went in to organize rooms for the night for the knight. "It's not often you get to repeat the same three words in the same order and mean totally different things," he muttered to himself, as he approached the large, bull-headed man who appeared to be running the place.

"Where's his money?" growled the innkeeper. "I've had it up to here with so-called nobility sponging off us! They think they're so high and mighty they own everything! Well they don't own me, and if your master wants to stay here he's got to pay me first – understand?" Tom nodded and trotted back to communicate this joyful news to Emily and the knight.

Emily had given up chattering to her taciturn escort some miles back, but when Tom relayed the innkeeper's message, she burst into a voluble tirade against peasant-tradesmen getting above their station and how the whole lot of them should be hanged by the devil! The knight showed no reaction at all; he offered neither advice nor money, and eventually it was Emily who pulled out a bag and handed a coin to Tom.

"I'm not sleeping in the hedge for another night!" she said.

When Emily had been installed in the best room the inn had to offer, the knight nodded to Tom to follow, and they were shown into a large room – simply furnished with a large bed, a small bed and a stool. There was a small window which overlooked the main courtyard of the inn, where horses were having their harnesses removed for the night. The mysterious knight neither spoke nor gave any indication of what he wanted. "Perhaps he's waiting for me to remove his harness?" thought Tom. But when he went to unbuckle the knight's coat-armour, he was brushed away unceremoniously. So, instead, Tom hung out of the window and watched the to-ings and fro-ings in the torch-lit yard below.

There was certainly something afoot. Perhaps someone important had arrived? Maybe, thought Tom, the King of France himself has returned from captivity in England, and has come here in disguise ... maybe that's who this mysterious knight is ...? And Tom turned suddenly to look at the man, only to find that he had already raised his visor and was now looking at Tom with a sort of quizzical smile.

"I'm sorry about the silence," said the knight. "I didn't want you to give anything away."

And certainly Tom would have given everything away if the knight had spoken before. His mouth would have dropped open a mile wide (as it was now), his eyes would have popped out of his head another mile (as they were doing now) and he would have gasped: "It's YOU!" Because it was! The knight was Ann.

• 20 •

THE TROUBLE WITH
BEING A WOMAN

"Not Ann," said Ann. "I'm Alan – in fact at the moment I'm officially Sir Geoffrois de Bernay. But it's all right to call me Alan." She could have been pretending to be Sir Wotnot of Notwot, as far as Tom was concerned. He simply hugged her and danced around her, laughing and punching her armoured sides.

Yes, it really was Ann! Ann who had run away from home disguised as a squire, who had become Tom's best friend, who had led him through so many scrapes before they reached the English army camped outside Reims, where they had talked themselves into the service of the Duke of Lancaster. Ann – who all that time Tom had thought was a boy called Alan! Ann – who had come into the scriptorium when he was being kidnapped by the Man in Black.

"The Duke said he'd let me be a squire, but you can't believe a word these people say, you know, Tom," said Ann. Tom nodded. They were lying sprawled on the bed. Ann had now taken off the armour and was once again dressed in the tunic and hose of a squire. "One of the maids-in-waiting told me she'd overheard the Duke say I was to be sent back to England, to my father – whether I liked it or not. And you know what would have happened then!"

"What?"

"I told you! He'd have married me off to that revolting old man! So I decided not to wait. I thought you might come too, but I could not find you – and you mean to say you were in the garde-robe all the time?"

"I tried to yell, but the Man in Black had his hand over my mouth!" said Tom.

"I looked for you in the great hall and everywhere," Ann continued, "and then I got a summons from the Duke. I knew that was it – if I didn't leave I was done for! So I took food for a couple of days and just walked out of the camp and kept walking."

"Where are you going?" asked Tom. "What are you going to do?"

"I'm going west to join Sir Robert Knolles' army – in Brittany. They say there is plenty of opportunity with Sir Robert's outfit."

"But why isn't Sir Robert fighting over here for the King?"

"Oh ... Sir Robert doesn't fight for anyone else – he only fights on his own account ... That's why there are so many opportunities," said Ann airily.

Tom was quiet. He wanted to say: but then what's the difference between Sir Robert Knolles and a bandit? But he somehow felt he couldn't – so he changed the subject.

"Where did you get the armour and the horse?" he asked.

"Ah!" said Ann. "I borrowed them!" And she told the tale of how she'd come across Sir Geoffrois de Bernay swimming in the River Marne.

"He didn't seem to be using either his armour or his horse," said Ann, "so I borrowed them, but they were both a bit big for me as it turned out. Lucky you two came along."

Tom looked at his friend. She was always so unpredictable and yet somehow always the same. He felt safe to be back with her, and yet her hair was cut short again and she was wearing boy's clothes – he couldn't work out whether he was back with Ann or with his old friend Alan.

"Do I have to call you Alan?" he asked.

"Absolutely!"

"Why can't you just be Ann?" asked Tom after a pause.

"Too dangerous!" replied Ann. "It's all right for high-born young ladies like your Emily ..."

"She's not 'my' Emily!" said Tom. Ann smiled.

"It's all right for her to go around as a girl, but for someone like me – well I'd be walking into trouble every time I stepped into an inn."

"But why?" asked Tom.

Ann thought for a few moments and then replied: "You've been taught by churchmen," she said. "What do they call us women?"

"The daughters of Eve?" said Tom.

"Why?" asked Ann.

"Women are all descended from Eve – like men are descended from Adam."

"And what happens in the story?" she asked.

"Adam eats the forbidden fruit ... and they're thrown out of the Garden of Eden," said Tom.

"But it's Eve who persuades Adam to eat the fruit ..."

"So?" said Tom.

"So," Ann went on, "she's to blame for all the woes of the world, according to the churchmen, and since all women are the daughters of Eve, we're to blame for ... well ... everything that's wrong!"

"But that's stupid!" exclaimed Tom.

"It gives a lot of men an excuse to treat women badly," said Ann.

"But not if you're a knight!" exclaimed Tom. "A knight must …" But before he could elaborate on the duties of a knight, the door flew open and Emily burst in with her black hair flying loose over her shoulders.

"We can't stay here!" she exclaimed. "Who's this?" Emily had stopped short and was staring at Ann.

"Sir Geoffrois de Bernay at your service," laughed Ann and she gave a low bow. "Although you can call me Adam."

"She said – I mean he said – Alan!" Tom couldn't bear the idea of having to remember yet another name for Ann. "His name's Alan," he repeated, although he couldn't believe for a moment that Emily wouldn't see straightaway that Ann was a girl.

"Alan," said Emily. "So you are our knight in shining armour?"

"Slightly rusty armour," replied Ann, "and I'm really only Sir Geoffrois's squire, but why have we got to leave, Emily?"

"Leave?" It was as if Emily's mind had been wiped clean for a second, but now it was suddenly full again. "My uncle!" she exclaimed. "The Archbishop! He's here! In the inn!"

Tom glanced out of the window at the commotion in the courtyard. But before Tom could exclaim: "She's right!", there was a knock on the door and the landlord stuck his bull head round it and roared: "You'll have to give up these rooms. Important guests have arrived."

Tom couldn't remember when he'd ever felt so indignant – perhaps when his sister Katie had put a spider in the soup, or maybe when he saw the village priest kicking his dog.

But Emily was already on the attack. "That's all right,

102

my man," she said, "we'd just decided this inn isn't good enough anyway. Louse-ridden, filthy hovel! Come get my clothes, Tom!"

"You'll find nowhere else tonight!" shouted the landlord as Emily flounced out of the room.

Tom glanced at Ann. "We'll have to get her out of here!" he whispered. "Trouble is Emily's useless at being incognito – someone's bound to spot her!"

Ann had a mischievous grin on her face. "I wonder how she feels about wearing armour?" she said.

· 21 ·

HOW EMILY BECAME A KNIGHT AND TOM DID A HANDSTAND

The one thing about armour is that if it doesn't fit – it really doesn't fit. I mean if your trousers are too loose you can always tighten your belt, or if your blouse is too long in the sleeves you can turn the cuffs up, but you can't take in a steel cuirass or shrink an iron helmet. Sir Geoffrois de Bernay was not a particularly big man, but his chest was a good ten inches wider all round than the delicate Emily's, and his shoulders were at least four inches further apart. Dressed in his armour, Emily looked like a snowdrop in a man-trap.

"Ow! it hurts!" she complained. "The greaves are rubbing on my shins!"

"Just try not to think about it," said Ann (a.k.a. Squire Alan).

"Let's get out of here!" whispered Tom.

"You look very attractive like that," Ann chuckled in Tom's ear. Tom's face went as bright red as the gown of Emily's he was now wearing.

"Shut up," he said. He didn't know why, but he would rather have jumped off the moon than wear Emily's clothes again. Perhaps it was the way Ann made fun of him as he slipped the velvet gown over his head – perhaps it was the way she laughed as she arranged the kerchiefs about his neck – but it was the best disguise they could think of.

"Now walk as if we own the place!" hissed Ann, as she led the way down the wooden stairs. Each step creaked as if it were calling everyone in the inn to come and watch them escape. The creaking of the stairs, however, was as nothing compared to the clanking of Sir Geoffrois' armour, around the slender Emily.

"Try to keep quiet!" whispered Tom from behind Emily.

"Yerspry culeek kwark win eberisints doo pig!" retorted Sir Emily. It was a speech that might have baffled many, but Tom, with his gift for languages, immediately recognized it as the Illfittingarmourese or Visorinthefacespeak for: "You try to keep quiet when everything's too big!"

By this time, Tom could see the Archbishop's retinue milling about the hall of the inn. He was sure everyone must be able hear his heart banging against his ribs, but there was no going back. He hitched the bundle of Emily's clothes higher on to his shoulder and just tried to look like a lady's maid. Ann – or rather Alan the Squire – was striding confidently towards the door. Sir Emily the Extremely Uncomfortable clanked and clattered behind her, and Tom's heart was now beating so loudly he couldn't even hear his knees knocking together.

"Blimey!" muttered a servant, who was manhandling an iron-bound chest across the hall. "It's His Honour the Duke of Dustbins!"

"The Prince of Pan-lids!" yelled another wag. A titter spread round the room, as everyone stopped their work to look at Sir Emily.

"Hey! Sir Saucepans!" called out another.

"Don't you know it's the Count of Clanking!" grinned another.

Tom shut his eyes. It was a nightmare. But at least there was no sign of the Archbishop, thought Tom, and he lifted his gown so that he could walk a little bit faster. At which very moment there was a commotion at the other end of the room, as the Archbishop of Reims himself strode into the room wearing a riding cloak and a wide hat. He appeared to be staring straight at Emily. "It's all up!" thought Tom. "Here we go back to the Bishop's Parlour!"

The nightmare turned into a living horror story as the Archbishop's voice rang out across the room: "Sir Geoffrois de Bernay!" he exclaimed. Squire Alan froze, but Sir Emily, not realizing it was she who was being addressed, carried on, collided with Squire Alan, and collapsed backwards on to the floor in a clatter of armour. Whereupon the entire room exploded into laughter.

During the general uproar that followed, the bull-headed landlord leapt forward to lift Sir Emily to her feet. "That's odd," thought Tom, "it's not like that landlord to be helpful." He looked across at Ann, Squire Alan, who was also looking at the landlord in surprise. She caught Tom's eye and gave a nod towards the landlord as if to say: "Why's he suddenly being so friendly?"

"And another thing," thought Tom, "why's he finding it so hard to pick Emily up? She's only a little thing ..." But there wasn't time to think any more about it. The Archbishop was striding across to the unfortunate Emily. As things were to turn out later, it would have been better for the three of them if Tom and Ann had spent a little more time thinking about what the landlord was up to, but we mustn't get ahead of ourselves ...

The whole plan had seemed so fool-proof, and yet even the best thought-out enterprises may founder against the jagged spike of one simple but unforeseeable snag. In this case how could any of them have guessed that of all the people in the world the only one for whom Jean de Craon, the Archbishop of Reims, felt the slightest glimmer of warmth was the man he had grown up with as a child, and that man happened to be none other than Sir Geoffrois de Bernay? The man in whose armour Emily was now encased!

Before Ann could take a step through the door, the Archbishop had grabbed Emily by the arm.

"What a stroke of Fate, Sir Geoffrois!" he cried. There was a note of desperation in the churchman's voice. "To have encountered you at this very moment! But what's the matter? Are you ill? You seem frail and feeble?"

If the truth were known, Emily was feeling extremely frail and feeble. The presence of the Archbishop of Reims, whom she thought she had seen for the last time, turned her insides to a mixture of sour cheese and stones, and made her head unaccountably keen to be where her feet were. A gasp went up from the crowd as Sir Geoffrois de Bernay swayed and slumped into the arms of his squire.

"My master has suffered grievously in his last encounter with the English!" explained Squire Alan quickly. "He has lost a lot of blood and I must get him to a physician quickly! Perhaps you will excuse us!"

"Whatever do you mean? 'Excuse you'?!" exclaimed the Archbishop. "I do not recognize you, sir, but you clearly do not know how dear Sir Geoffrois is to me. I will have him treated in my own chambers. Take him up there at once!"

Squire Alan heard a groan from inside Sir Geoffrois' armour. "He's bad!" exclaimed Ann. "I'd better get him to the physician!"

"He shall have mine!" insisted Jean de Craon, Archbishop of Reims. "Take him to my rooms!"

"The physician is just outside ..." mumbled Squire Alan desperately. The Archbishop, however, appeared not to hear him.

"Sir Geoffrois! It is so long since we gazed on each other ... let me see your face!" Another groan – or rather a squawk – came from the middle of the armour, as the Archbishop attempted to open the visor.

"Please! Your Highness!" exclaimed Squire Alan (a.k.a. Ann), brushing the Archbishop's hands away. "Sir Geoffrois has asked me to keep his visor closed at all times!"

"What nonsense are you talking?" The Archbishop looked suspiciously at Ann. "You aren't Sir Geoffrois' squire."

"That is the tragedy!" said Ann as Squire Alan. "Sir Geoffrois' squire was killed in the same action! Sir Geoffrois himself was wounded in the face, and has sworn no one shall look upon him until he is recovered."

"Sir Geoffrois! Wounded in the face?!"

"It was only by the actions of his brave squire that Sir Geoffrois' life was saved!" Squire Alan was inching his way through the door.

"What was the name of Sir Geoffrois' squire who was killed?" The Archbishop had his hand on Ann's arm; she wasn't going anywhere, until the great man was answered.

Now I firmly believe that Ann would have come up with a totally convincing answer, but she was spared the trouble, because at that very moment a remarkable thing happened. As the Archbishop peered suspiciously at her, there was a gasp and yet another burst of laughter from behind him. The Archbishop span round, glaring.

The moment he turned, Ann grabbed Sir Emily's hand and ran. The Archbishop half-turned to stop her but was too surprised by what he had just seen across the hall to do anything else.

You have to remember that in those days, six hundred years ago, people behaved slightly differently from how we behave now. For example, nowadays if you want to show how rich you are, you can drive around in a Rolls Royce or a Lamborghini, you can travel First Class from one expensive hotel to another, and you need never walk in the street; in this way you are spared the awful experience of mingling with people less wealthy than yourself. Six hundred years ago, however, you couldn't hide away like that. People – whether rich and poor – either walked or rode a horse. Even the King would have to ride a horse through the streets of London to reach the Abbey or go to his country home. And neither walking nor riding insulates you from the *hoi polloi* in the way a chauffeur-driven limousine with shaded windows does.

In other words, in the fourteenth century, rich and poor rubbed shoulders together in a way that we can often avoid doing nowadays. And since a rich aristocrat in Tom's day couldn't show off by driving a Lamborghini, he tended to show off by wearing flashy clothes. What you wore was so important, it was even laid down by law: in England, for example, a mere craftsman – like a carpenter or a wheelwright – was not allowed to wear gold or silver or embroidery! People's appearance reflected their station in life.

Another way you could demonstrate how wealthy or high-born you were, without the aid of a Porsche, was by the way you moved: holding your head up high and strutting around would mark you off from the cowed peasant, staring at the ground.

So, with all this in mind, imagine the Archbishop of

Reims's surprise when he turned round to find a lady's maid, dressed in an expensive red silk gown with gold trimming, walking upside-down on her hands through the assembled throng!

Gasps came up from the crowd like the air from a dozen blacksmith's bellows. The bull-headed landlord gasped. A dozen servants and a dozen chambermaids gasped. The Archbishop himself gasped. They all gasped.

At which point, the lady's maid jumped back on to her feet, jammed her wimple back on her head, snatched up a large bundle and then swept out of the hall. And, for some inexplicable reason, the retainers of the Archbishop of Reims and the servants of the inn simply fell back and let her through.

"Phew!" thought Tom as he reached for the door-handle, "I thought I'd create a diversion, but I never thought it would be as easy as ..."

At that moment, however, the voice of the Archbishop of Reims thundered out across the hall: "Stop her!" Tom flung the door open, threw his wimple at the first person who tried to grab him, and fell flat on his face into the mud of the courtyard.

And that was how, for the third time, Tom found himself the prisoner of the Archbishop of Reims.

· 22 ·

THE ARCHBISHOP'S
PRISONER AGAIN

The filthy straw of the stable was certainly better than the last accommodation the Archbishop had provided for him, but on the whole Tom would have preferred to be sleeping in the second best bedroom in the inn – as previously arranged. Given the choice, Tom would also have preferred not to have his hands tied behind his back. All in all, thought Tom, the Archbishop had no idea how to treat a guest – especially since the place was alive with rats. There was one now – scratching at the bottom of the wall just behind his ear! It must have been a pretty big rat too, for it was banging one of the planks as if it were trying to break in!

"Sorry!" Tom whispered to the rat on the other side of the wall. "Me and the other horses have just had a discussion and we've decided we don't want to share this stable with any rats tonight."

By way of answer the rat banged harder and the plank juddered. A cold draught of air hit Tom's nose as the nail holding the plank gave way. Tom jumped out of his skin! A rat that could do that must be the size of a horse! And then – to top it all – he heard the rat whisper: "Is that you, Tom?"

The next minute the grinning face of Ann appeared in

the crack in the wall. "Help us get this board loose!" she whispered. "We've got to be quick!"

And before Tom could say: "I can't! I'm tied up!" Ann had her hands through the gap and was freeing his wrists. The horses stamped their feet and whinnied, as if they too wanted to be set free.

"What's that?" It was the voice of the guard outside the stable door.

"Hurry!" whispered Tom. They could hear the cross-bar being slid away from the stable door. Ann redoubled her efforts to free Tom's hands.

"He's coming in!" exclaimed Tom in the quietest voice he could manage under the circumstances. But his hands were now free. Ann kicked at another board and Tom tore it away from the wall. He could now see Emily standing behind Ann, still in her suit of armour.

"Where are my clothes?" she hissed. But before Tom could apologize for having lost the bundle when he'd been overpowered by the Archbishop's men, he heard the stable doors opening. Next moment, the light from a torch surprised the horses and they reared and pulled against their halters. In a flash Tom had covered the hole in the wall with straw and lay back against it pretending to be asleep.

The guard frowned. He knew there was something wrong. In his experience, there was always something wrong. It was a condition of life. There had been a lot wrong when he was a child: poverty, cold, hunger. Then he had become a soldier and some things had improved a little, but still poverty, cold and hunger had dogged him. There was always some nasty surprise round every corner, in his experience. And there was also something else, but he could never remember what it was.

The guard stepped cautiously into the stable and looked

towards Tom. Tom kicked himself as he realized that he'd got his hands in his lap instead of behind him. The guard was approaching warily – his eyes searching out dark corners for whatever unpleasant surprise lay in wait for him. If only he could also remember the other thing that he always forgot ...

As the guard's eyes left Tom for a moment, Tom hurriedly stuck his hands behind him and his feet into the straw. Suddenly the guard was standing right over him.

"Big rat!" muttered Tom.

"What did you call me?" growled the guard.

"I said there are big rats in here," said Tom.

The guard shivered. "I hate rats!" he said. (Could that be the unpleasant surprise that lay waiting for him?)

"A really big one ran over my leg just now!" said Tom.

"Shut up!" said the guard. "Don't talk about it!" And he was just about to administer a judicious kick to Tom's stomach, when he stopped. "Why! They didn't tell me you was a lady!" he grinned. Tom's stomach turned over. "Don't you look sweet lying there in the straw in your silk gown and all!" said the guard. For the briefest of moments, he had forgotten that there was a nasty surprise lying in wait for him and that nothing good ever happened to him.

"Here we go again!" thought Tom, and before the guard could say another word of flattery, Tom kicked the man's legs from under him and he crashed down into the straw. The torch went flying and fell into the next stall.

As the guard fell backwards, he suddenly remembered what it was that he always forgot: that the nasty things that happened to him always happened when he'd forgotten they were going to happen. Like now.

And it was precisely because he was taken so unexpectedly, that when he fell his head whip-lashed back and cracked on the stone floor. At the same moment, Tom heard Ann kick another plank out of the wall. Without hesitating, he shoved his way – bottom first – through the hole.

"Let's get out of here!" exclaimed Ann, but Tom grabbed her sleeve.

"Why is it," he said, "that whenever I escape from anywhere, I always have to go back again?"

"What are you talking about?" asked Ann.

"Listen!" said Tom. The silence of the night was broken by the clanking of Emily running out of the courtyard, but another sound was left behind. It was only a slight sound, but it made Tom's blood run cold. It was a sound that he remembered only too well: it was the crackle of flames.

"The guard! The horses!" whispered Tom. "We can't leave them in there!" And before Ann could stop him he'd rushed back into the stable, and was discovering just how difficult it is to drag the body of a concussed guard across a stable floor with horses on either side of you kicking and bucking.

Ann looked round at the dark windows of the inn. The flames were already casting a jumping light across the cobbled courtyard. Ann and Emily had deliberately waited until everyone was asleep before returning to rescue Tom. They had tiptoed across the yard, silent as mice, past the sleeping guard and round to the back of the stable. But now the time for keeping quiet was over. "FIRE!" she yelled as loud as she could. "Fire in the stables! Wake up, everyone!" Then she plunged into the stable.

"I can't move him!" said Tom. The guard, however, was beginning to come round.

"He can look after himself!" said Ann, and she turned her attention to the horses in the stalls beyond. There were three of them, and she tried to pull them towards the entrance, but they shied and refused to go past the flames. "Help, Tom!" she cried.

"Sorry!" said Tom to the guard, as he dropped him and ran over to Ann.

"You've got to save yourselves!" Ann was shouting at a grey mare. And whether the grey mare understood or not, it suddenly bolted for the stable door and in an instant the other two followed. The flames by this time had spread to the stalls on either side, and the whole stable had become a chaos of fire-crazy horses.

The guard opened his eyes, but before he could remember what the nasty thing was that had just happened to him, there were shouts and screams from the yard, and the face of the bull-headed landlord appeared at the stable door.

"The horses!" he yelled.

"Time to go!" shouted Ann, and she and Tom leapt over

the guard, and out through the broken wall.

The courtyard, meanwhile, had turned into a pandemonium of screaming figures running hither and thither, lit by the red glow from inside the burning stable. In among these stood other static figures – men and women in various states of undress, who blinked as bleary and unready as dead souls facing damnation. Tom and Ann dodged among them and, before the last of the horses and the unfortunate guard had been dragged to safety, the two friends had disappeared into the darkness of the night.

· 23 ·

TOM HAS HIS FUTURE
TOLD

From several miles away, the red glow in the sky above the town looked really quite attractive. But Tom's ears were still ringing with the shouts and screams of men and women, and the neighing of horses, and the stamping and clattering and chaos of the inferno they had left behind. He couldn't shake off the feeling of having done something dreadful – it was a feeling he remembered from long ago when he and Alan (a.k.a. Ann) and Sir John Hawkley had left England behind them with the town of Sandwich burning in their wake. He also remembered the dreadful moment when Sir John had deliberately set fire to the great library at Laon.

"Where d'you think Emily is?" asked Tom.

"She ought to be here somewhere," replied Ann. "We agreed that if we got separated we'd meet up at the first village to the south."

"Why did she have to go running off anyway?" muttered Tom.

Ann smiled. "You sound very concerned about her," she said, in a way that made Tom feel quite indignant, though he wasn't sure why.

"Well ... I feel sort of responsible for her," he said. Ann laughed. "I do!" Tom insisted. "I promised she could come

118

back with me to join the English army. She wants to ask the King's favour."

"She's got a hope!" snorted Ann.

"He's her uncle," replied Tom.

Tom and Ann had discovered an old shed full of broken carts, and had decided to spend the rest of the night there.

"Well, I've got to get a night's sleep," said Ann, as she curled herself up into a large coil of rope that lay on the floor under one of the broken carts. "I've got a long way to go tomorrow, if I'm going to reach Sir Robert Knolles' army before he packs up and goes home."

"Won't you come back with us?" asked Tom.

"No fear!" said Ann, and she shut her eyes. "If Emily's not here by daylight," yawned Ann, "we can go and look for her." And she lay back in the coil of rope with her head sticking out one end and her feet sticking out the other, like a cuckoo in a nest.

Tom tried to make himself comfortable on a pile of straw, but he was shivering in Emily's thin dress, which still was all he was wearing. He attempted to shut his eyes, but they just wouldn't stay shut. "Supposing she's been captured by someone?" he found himself murmuring.

"Then there won't be much we can do tonight," muttered Ann.

"Supposing she's lost?" said Tom.

"Then you can find her tomorrow," said Ann.

"Supposing she's hurt herself! Supposing she's lying somewhere injured!" Tom was suddenly on his feet ...

Ann groaned. "You'll never find her in the middle of the night," she grumbled.

"At least I ought to check out the village – you know

– just make sure she isn't lying ill somewhere," said Tom, slipping his shoes on.

"I need some sleep," grumbled Ann. But, all the same, she heaved herself up from her rope nest and followed Tom out of the shed.

The village was eerily quiet. The houses and cottages were shuttered and silent. Not a dog stirred. Not a mouse squeaked. Not a cat blinked in the night. The occasional door swung on rusty hinges, and creaked in the darkness like a lost bullfrog.

"I can't believe anyone's living in this graveyard," murmured Ann.

"Just what I was thinking," said Tom. "This place gives me the creeps!"

Ann was peering into a narrow alley where some overhanging houses actually seemed to touch each other overhead, and where no smatter of light penetrated. "I suppose we've got to look everywhere," she sighed, and slipped in between the buildings. Tom followed and the alley seemed to swallow them up like a lizard's throat swallowing a couple of mayflies.

As soon as they stepped into it, the narrow passage seemed to come alive. Doorsteps seemed to shift across the ground to trip them up. Latches and catches caught at their sleeves. And every window seemed to be watching them as they made their way through the gloom.

"Emily?"

"Emily!"

Tom had stuck his head through an unshuttered window, which seemed to call out to be investigated. "This is just the sort of place she might be resting for the night," he thought, and – as if in answer – a voice croaked: "She's not here." Tom froze in his shoes.

120

In the gloom, he could just make out the shape of an old, old woman sitting by the window-sill. "We're looking for a friend – she was wearing armour. Have you seen her?"

"I have never seen anyone," whispered the old woman. "I have been blind since the day I was born." Tom must have gasped, for the old woman continued. "Do not feel sorry for me; I see other things – things that those with eyes cannot see."

"Can you see where Emily is?" asked Tom.

"Yes," replied the old woman. "She is beneath the grass ..."

"Is she dead?!" exclaimed Tom.

"But she is dry."

"I said 'is she dead?'" Tom felt like shaking the old woman, but he didn't. In the dimness she looked so frail that she might just fall apart like burnt paper.

"And you, young man," the old crone continued, "you have enemies in high places. Important men who would like you out of the way ..."

"Does one of them look like a tortoise with stomach ache?" asked Tom – he was thinking of the Archbishop of Reims.

"But remember that you possess something they do not have ..." croaked the old woman.

"Tom!" It was Ann hissing from further down the alley. "What are you doing?"

"What do you mean?" Tom asked the old woman. "What do I possess?" He could no longer see her across the window-sill, but he could still hear her voice ...

"It is something they cannot make and something they cannot take ... and something ..." the voice was scarcely audible now ... as if it were disintegrating into the darkness of the room, "… something … they will never understand …"

"Tom!" Ann was next to him, shaking him. "What are you staring at? It's just a shutter!" And Tom suddenly realized he wasn't peering across a window-sill into a darkened room at all! The window shutters were closed, and he was staring with his nose right up against a wooden cross-piece.

"Uh oh!" said Tom. "The wood-worm around here must talk funny!"

"Let's find Emily if that's what we're doing!" said Ann, and she pulled Tom after her down the alley.

But Tom found he couldn't pull his mind away from the old woman. Had he imagined her? Or had she really been there? And in any case, what did she mean? What could he possibly possess that the Archbishop of Reims didn't? As far as Tom was aware he didn't possess anything apart from the clothes he stood up in. Besides, he was still wearing Emily's dress – goodness only knew where his own doublet and hose were.

· 24 ·

HOW TOM AND ANN DISCOVERED EMILY BENEATH THE GRASS

Tom and Ann (a.k.a. Squire Alan) found themselves in an odd little square – it was actually more of a yard than a square – which was bounded on each side by blank walls, as if the cottages and houses of the village had all turned their backs on it. The little square enclosed a tree and a well in the middle.

"CLANK!" said Tom – at least that's what Ann thought he said.

"Did you say 'CLANK!'?" asked Ann.

"No, of course not," replied Tom, a little irritated by the idea that anyone should assume he would say "CLANK!". "But," he continued, "I thought I heard a clank!"

"Aha!" said Ann.

"It was coming from the other side of the square," Tom added with an air of authority – just to show that he was not the sort of chap to say "CLANK!" at random.

They hurried across the open space and as they reached the other side they heard it again: CLANK!

"I didn't say a thing!" exclaimed Tom.

"That CLANK came from the side we just left!" said Ann.

CLANK!

"Hold on!" said Tom, "I think we're missing something here!" He walked across to the middle of the square.

CLANK! GROAN!

"We've been chasing the echo!" he said and he peered fearfully down into the well that stood at the centre of the square. At that very moment, as it happened, the moon came out and shone down as if it were doing an audition for daylight. CLANK! GROAN! GROAN! CLATTER!

A heap of scrap metal at the bottom of the well glinted as it shifted in the moonlight, and a white face looked up at Tom. For a moment he thought he was looking at the moon reflected in the water of the well, but then he saw the delicate features blinking up at him.

"Emily!" cried Tom.

"Little Tom!" she cried. "You've found me!"

"What a great hiding-place!" said Tom. "Congratulations!" But Emily didn't feel like joking.

"Get me out!" she called up. She was lying in a twisted heap some fifteen feet below ... and the old woman had been right about something else: the well was dry. "My ankle hurts," said Emily.

"Situation, Alternatives, Action!" Ann had suddenly become Squire Alan again. "Situation: we've got to get you out of there, Emily ..."

"Or we could just jump in and join her," suggested Tom helpfully.

"Shut up, Tom!" said Ann.

"Hurry!" said a small voice.

"Alternatives: none!" said Squire Alan. "So ... we have to pull her out!"

"Then let's do it!" said Tom.

"I was just coming to that ..." replied Squire Alan. But Tom was already leaning over, reaching into the well. Emily was trying to stand up and touch his hand, but it was obvious that they would never be able to connect.

"We need something to lower down to her," said Ann, looking around.

"You were sleeping on it!" exclaimed Tom.

"What?" asked Ann, but Tom was already sprinting back down the narrow alley.

"Don't leave me, Alan!" shouted Emily from the bottom of the well. There was a note of panic in her voice.

Ann looked down into the well. "Don't worry," she answered. "The firm of Tom And Alan is noted for its well-rescues. So what happened?"

Tom, meanwhile, sprinted back to the shed of broken-down carts and grabbed the coil of rope which had been going to be Ann's bed. He arrived back at the well-side, just as Emily finished explaining to Ann how she had run off to rescue her bundle of clothes from the inn, how she'd found some servants about to divide them up among themselves and how she'd given them all a severe scolding, before hurrying to this village as arranged; but she'd been unable to remove the armour. As she had staggered around in the dark, she'd failed to notice the well and fallen into it. She must have been lying there knocked out or shocked until Tom had called out her name.

"Please get me out!" she cried.

Tom lowered the rope into the well, but try as she might, Emily didn't seem strong enough to hold on to it.

"You've got to hold on!" exclaimed Ann.

"I can't hold on!" wailed Emily. "The armour's too heavy!"

"Hang on!" said Tom.

"I JUST SAID I CAN'T!" yelled Emily.

"I didn't mean that!" exclaimed Tom. "I meant 'Hang

125

on!' in the sense of ... oh, never mind!" Tom had just had an idea. He was tying the rope around his waist.

"I thought you were joking about jumping in to join her!" muttered Ann as she lowered Tom into the well.

"You know me! I never joke!" Tom shouted back up.

"And the Pope never says his prayers!" said Squire Alan.

"It's lucky you had the bundle of clothes to break your fall!" Tom said as he joined Emily at the bottom of the well. "A drop like that could have ..." but he never said "could have broken your neck" or whatever it was he was going to say because Emily had just planted a big kiss right on his mouth. Tom was so surprised he couldn't speak for several moments. Instead he set to work undoing the clasps and buckles that held her armour. Working away in the dark and in the close confines of the bottom of the well, it took Tom quite some time to free Emily of the cumbersome armour, but eventually there she was standing in her undershirt – unencumbered by greaves or cuirass or sabatons. Tom tied the rope around her waist and Ann was soon hauling her up to the surface.

Once Emily was safe, they pulled the armour out, piece by piece, and then Emily's bundle of clothes – but not before Tom had fished out his own doublet and hose and thankfully put them on. Finally Tom tied the rope around his own waist again, and Ann and Emily struggled and strained to pull him up.

Unfortunately, in the dark neither Tom nor Ann had noticed that the rope had started to fray. And they didn't discover just how badly it had frayed until Tom was half-way up. He heard a sound like somebody putting their foot through a lute. "What was ..." But Tom didn't need to finish the question – the answer became all too obvious: the

sound was the rope snapping. A fraction after Tom heard it, he found himself plummeting to the bottom of the well again.

"So this is what it's like to fall down a well!" thought Tom. "I often wondered." And then it hit him – that is to say the ground hit his backside. "OOOOOWWWWWW!" was the only thing he could think of yelling under the circumstances. Then something else struck him – this was the rope as it landed on his head. "OOOOO-WWWWWW!" he repeated. He wished he could have been more creative, but somehow "OOOOOWWWWWW!" summed up his innermost feelings at that moment.

"Are you all right?" It was Ann who was the first to peer down at him. Then Emily's face appeared.

"I'm fine," said Tom, "apart from the fact that I've just fallen down a well and our only means of getting me out has just snapped in two." If Tom had thought that his companions' attention was not focused on him one hundred per cent during this outburst, he would have been quite right. To tell the truth neither Ann nor Emily was listening to a word he said. They were both listening to the sound of horses' hooves approaching fast.

"What's that?" whispered Emily, her face turning even paler than its normal shade.

"What's going on?" called Tom from the bottom of the well.

"Tom! We'll come back!" That was all Ann said before she and Emily both disappeared. A dozen horsemen had just ridden into the village.

If you've ever sat at the bottom of a well and tried to work out what's going on in the world above, you'll have some idea of how little idea Tom had of what was happening. At first he started yelling at the top of his voice: "Ann! I mean Alan! What's going on?" But then he thought better of it, for by now he was beginning to hear the horses' hooves himself.

"Uh oh!" muttered Tom. The bottom of the well suddenly didn't seem such a good place to hide after all. If anyone looked down into the well they'd be bound to see him. That's just how wells are. So Tom kept his mouth shut and just listened and waited.

The horses had come to a halt. Then he could hear voices – shouts – and next thing he heard running feet. Then it went quiet again. Then he heard them again. And this time the voices were louder. Yes! He could hear quite clearly now ... Two men were standing close to the well – and they were speaking English ... He had an urge to shout out to his fellow countrymen: "I'm down here in the well! Help me!" But he stifled the cry in his throat.

"The whole blasted village is deserted!" said one.

"Not a stick of furniture even – nothing!"

"These good-for-nothing peasants get wind of us and vanish! Damn their cowardly souls!"

Tom could hear the rattle of swords being returned to their scabbards. He heard the chink of armed men moving about. One of them sat on the wall of the well. Tom could see the man's backside silhouetted against the moon.

Again Tom had to resist the urge to call out to them. "There are no rules on a raid," he told himself. "They'd be as likely to kill me for my doublet as help me. And from the sound of it, pickings have been thin!" No sooner had he thought all this than he heard a third voice, and his blood ran cold. By all the unfortunate gods of war! it was a voice he recognized:

"Well, boyos! We're wasting our time here, good and proper!" It was the Arch-Priest – the only man in the world who had already tried to kill Tom twice over! If Tom had thought it wise to keep quiet before, he now wished the well were three times deeper. "Come on clouds!" he thought. "Just when you want it dark the moon has to shine like this!"

"Call the rest of the boys to assemble in the main street," the Arch-Priest was saying. "You two fill that skin with water!"

"It's all up!" thought Tom. "They'll see me for sure!" And indeed as the Arch-Priest made off, he could hear the other two approaching the well. It would be only a matter of seconds before they discovered him. No matter how small he curled himself up, or how he lay, they would see him – lit up by the moon – at the bottom of the well.

And then the most extraordinary thing happened. It was so very extraordinary that for a moment Tom thought he must be dreaming and that this whole adventure was just a nightmare from which he would soon wake up, to find himself back home in his cottage in England, with Katie and Old Molly and the familiar smell of the animals and the baking of bread and the sun coming through the open doorway.

But he didn't wake up. It was all real. And the footsteps above were getting closer and closer to the well. Just as the two armed men reached the edge of the well, Tom heard a sort of rustle close to his left ear. He then heard the fall of soil and when he turned to look he saw, to his complete and utter astonishment, a hole appear in the wall of the well – and out of the hole there appeared a hand!

Tom would have screamed if he could, but luckily he was so astounded he couldn't find his voice – and he was mouthing soundlessly as the hand grabbed him by the collar and yanked him violently through the thin wall of earth and into a narrow underground passageway.

A second later, the two soldiers peered down to find the well both dry and empty. One of them spat into it.

• 25 •

ANN AND EMILY ESCAPE
FROM THE MARAUDERS

Like Tom, Ann and Emily had known better than to stick around to say "Hi, chaps! How are you?" to armed men in the middle of the night. Mounted men-at-arms were dangerous customers at the best of times, but in the middle of the night you could be sure they were only interested in four things: murder, plunder, rape and mayhem. Ann and Emily had therefore taken to their heels.

"Give me that!" panted Ann. Emily was making heavy work of carrying her bundle of clothes, but she held on to them for grim death.

"No!" was all she'd say.

Glancing over her shoulder, Ann could see the light of torches coming and going among the houses. The marauders were systematically searching the village, and the crashing of doors and shutters being broken down shattered the night.

"I can't run!" complained Emily. "My ankle hurts!" It was true she'd been limping since they got her out of the well.

"Just keep going until we get out of the village. If we can make it to the wood we'll be safe. They'll never find us there." Ann was trying to sound less panicky than she felt.

"I can't!" moaned Emily.

By this time they had reached the graveyard of the church. Ann glanced over her shoulder. Two riders, brandishing flaming torches, were heading towards them. "Look out! They've seen us!" she whispered and pushed Emily behind a gravestone.

"Ow!" sobbed Emily as she collapsed in a heap behind the stone.

"Sh!" said Ann.

"What was that?" The tall rider, with his hair tied in a knot behind his head, suddenly reined in his horse. "Did you hear something, Sampson?" Sampson, who was small and thin, shook his bald head.

"I bet they've emptied the church as well." Sampson sounded as if he had a terrible cold, and there seemed to be a permanent stream coming from the end of his long nose.

To the girls' relief, the men rode past the gravestone behind which they were shivering, headed for the church and were soon putting their shoulders to the church door. The door, however, had clearly been designed to withstand an assault by the Devil himself and all his legions.

"Ow!" Sampson sniffed a runner back up his nose, and rubbed his arm. "I hurt myself."

"Once they get inside," whispered Ann, "we'll make a run for it!"

"I can't," replied Emily. "Ow! My ankle!"

"Shut up!" hissed Ann.

"It hurts!"

"Do I hear voices?" The tall marauder was now attacking the church door with an axe, but he stopped and listened. All he could hear was silence. That is, if it's possible to hear silence. In fact, there was a slight rustle behind one of the tombstones, but it sounded like the wind

132

blowing the nettles. Ann had her hand over Emily's mouth, and although Emily struggled for a moment, she suddenly went limp and allowed Ann to hold her like that, while the small marauder with the runny nose sniffed the air and said:

"This is a waste of time. I know they'll have emptied the church." Then he wiped his nose with the back of his hand and rubbed it down his greasy jerkin.

"Give me a hand!" mumbled his companion – although why he should have wanted a hand that had been anywhere near Sampson's nose I have no idea. Sampson produced another axe and joined in the attack on the door.

The crashing of the axes and the splintering of the wood gave Ann the chance to hiss in Emily's ear: "Now listen, you selfish creature! Stop thinking just about yourself. I'm in danger too! And I say we run to the wood as soon as those men get into the church. It's our only chance! And you'll come with me, and you'll run as hard as you can even if your ankle hurts! And you'll stay quiet. Understand?"

Emily nodded her head. Ann still had her hand over her mouth and was pinning her arms to her sides.

"Got it!" yelled the tall marauder, as the church door finally gave up its resistance and the two men – or perhaps they really were the Devil and his legions – pushed the splintered wood aside and entered the empty church.

"I told you so!" said Sampson, and a large dollop fell from his nose and splatted on the stone threshold.

"Now!" said Ann, and she and Emily scrambled to their feet and bolted across the gravestones towards the wood.

It was unfortunate that Sampson, the small marauder, was such a sceptic. His scepticism led him to question many things, and he was – irritatingly often – proved right. He

133

was thus considered, by his fellow marauders, a bit of a know-all. In his own view, he was simply the person whose opinion he valued most. He knew he would be right about the church being emptied of valuables, and he was. Thus, the moment he saw the vacant interior he didn't bother to investigate any further (as did his companion, Frank). No, Sampson simply turned on his heel and stepped back outside. And so it was he happened to spot two figures stumbling across the graveyard – one of them carrying a large bundle.

"Well well well," said Sampson the marauder. "Look'ee here, Frank!"

But Frank had found something. Something had been left behind in the church after all. It wasn't a gold cross, however. It wasn't even a jewel-encrusted cope or a silver chalice. In fact it wasn't worth very much at all in terms of hard cash, but it did do something that neither a silver chalice, nor a jewel-encrusted cope nor a gold cross could ever have done – it leapt up and licked Frank's nose.

"Aw! Look!" said Frank. "They left a little dog in here!"

"Frank!" said Sampson, sticking his dripping nose round the broken-down church door. "There's someone in the graveyaa … Oh! Look! A little dog!"

"How cruel can you get, eh?" asked Frank, holding the pathetic animal close against his armoured chest. "He must be starving! Aren't you, poor feller?"

"They shut him up in the church?" asked Sampson. "That's really cruel. He must be missing his master … eh? eh? Are you missing your master, little chap?"

Sampson and Frank had no qualms about razing villages, and about killing old men and small children, but show them a stray dog and they both became St Francis of Assisi.

And so it was that Ann and Emily made it across the graveyard, out of the village and into the wood before the two wicked marauders emerged from ransacking the church.

"Let's give him a bowl of milk when we get back," said Frank.

"Yes," said Sampson, sniffing a long thread of mucus back into his nose. "And brush his coat ... I may even have a bit of chicken ..."

· 26 ·

THE UNDERGROUND
VILLAGE

Tom spat earth out of his mouth. His arms had been pinioned to his side and his hands had been bound. Then in the suffocating darkness of the underworld he felt himself being dragged along a tunnel. His mind went spinning in all sorts of directions. What on earth – or rather what under the earth – was going on? He kept thinking: "Perhaps I've been kidnapped by the dead!" But that was pretty unlikely.

On the other hand, he found himself reasoning, maybe people are always being kidnapped by the dead, but we never hear about it because they never return to tell their tales … His kidnapper, however, showed little sign of being dead … in fact he was extraordinarily strong even for a living person.

"Where are we go …" Tom began, but he received such a sharp crack on the head from his captor that he decided to save his questions for the time being.

At length, the narrow tunnel opened out and he saw the dim light of tallow lamps winking in the underworld gloom. His captor pulled him into an underground chamber that was high enough to sit up in; the roof was shored up with wooden planks and timber supports. From out of the cramped darkness, six dirty and emaciated faces peered at Tom. They were far from friendly.

"Why didn't you slit his throat, Anton?" was the first question. Anton shrugged his broad shoulders.

"He is a pig of an English dog," was the next helpful suggestion.

"Why have you brought him here, Anton?" This last question came from a thin, tired woman with a pallid face.

"He was in the well – if the English raiders had found him they might have found the tunnel," explained Anton.

"Then you must take him out into the forest when all is clear and kill him. Do you understand, Anton?" said the old man who had not yet spoken. "We cannot afford to keep prisoners here."

Anton nodded. "Very good, Father Michael," he said, and pulled Tom across the chamber towards another tunnel.

"Hey! Wait a minute!" exclaimed Tom in French. "Don't I get a chance to say something?"

"Why should we listen to you?" asked Father Michael. He was old and thin and weary. "You English come to our country and destroy it. You kill our sons and fathers and rape our daughters and wives. You commit the most dreadful sacrilege, desecrating our churches and destroying our homes and lives. You take our food from our mouths and leave us to starve. Do you give us the chance to speak when you do all this?"

"But!" Tom actually had no idea what he was going to say, but he felt he ought to contribute something. "But! I'm not a robber or a pillager! I was hiding from the English marauders!"

"That is true," said Anton.

"That is enough," said Father Michael. "Anton, you will dispatch him as soon as you are able." The old man shut his weary eyes, and Tom realized it was useless to plead any more. He might as well save his breath. So that is what he did, while Anton led him off through another tunnel.

· 27 ·

TOM EATS THE
CONDEMNED MAN'S SUPPER

This tunnel was marginally wider and higher than the first, and at the end of it was a rough sacking curtain. When Anton pulled this back, he revealed a most extraordinary sight: in front of them stretched a vast human burrow. It was perhaps only four feet high and, at most, nine or ten feet wide, but it was as long as a village high street. The air was thick with the smell of the tallow lamps whose feeble light sputtered and flickered in the close darkness. The whole place was propped up with whatever timbers had come to hand. Down the long wall, on both sides, were holes which presumably led to other chambers and passageways.

The burrow itself was packed with people. In the dimness Tom could just make out white-faced families – all packed in together – their pinched and hungry eyes staring at him. Some slept the sleep of undernourishment. A few ragged and emaciated men were playing cards. Women tried to feed starving babies with empty breasts. It was as if an entire village had sunk beneath the ground and – at the same time – beneath the level of humanity.

As Anton pushed Tom forwards across the crowded floor, a silence fell. Each emaciated creature stopped whatever it was they were doing and looked at Tom. And what looks they gave him! If looks could kill, Tom was a corpse before

he even took the first step across that strange underworld.
He could feel those looks as if they were physical blows.

At last, Anton pushed him through one of the holes in the
long wall, and then growled a curse at him. Tom curled up
into a corner of the small hollow in which he found himself,
and tried to pretend he wasn't there. He was, however,
surprised to hear Anton repeat the curse, and then he
realized it wasn't a curse at all: "Are you hungry?" Anton
was saying – but he was saying it as if he were wishing Tom
in the darkest pit of Hell ... which as far as Tom could see
might very well be where he was!

"A bit, I suppose ..." said Tom, although he wasn't at all
certain he wanted to take food from these starving people
who seemed to bear him such ill-will. But it was too late,
Anton was holding out a couple of roots ... turnips ... Tom
wasn't particularly fond of turnips, and these were still
covered in dirt, but even before Anton had wiped most of the

soil off them, they had begun to look to Tom like the grandest feast in the world. The only snag was that Tom's hands were tied behind his back.

Anton squeezed himself into the cramped hole and held a turnip up to Tom's mouth. When Tom had managed to eat most of it, Anton sat back against the other wall and proceeded to eat the second one himself.

"Do you hate the English very much?" Tom asked.

"Yes," said Anton. Anton was a big man. He was not the sort of man you would want to hate you – even a little. His wide shoulders hardly seemed to fit into this underground world; his hands hung too far away from his body; his head was too high from the ground. He looked like a giant among a nest of rats. His face was also big. The eyes were set wide apart. The mouth was a deep crevasse; when it open it revealed a broken alpine range of cracked and yellowed teeth. His nose was thick and misshapen. But Tom looked again: there was a gentleness in Anton's eyes that told the world this man was no ogre.

"Do you find it easy to kill the people you hate?" asked Tom.

"No," replied Anton, and he cast his eyes down on the ground.

"You're going to have to kill me," remarked Tom. Anton gave a sort of bellow and made as if to cuff Tom round the head. So Tom decided to steer clear of that line of remark. Instead he asked the one question he was burning to ask. "What is this place?"

"Too many questions!" roared Anton and he heaved his great bulk up and hurled himself out of the chamber. A few moments later a rough wooden trap was battened across the hole. Tom had no illusions: wherever and whatever this place was, he was in prison.

· 28 ·

TOM IS TAKEN TO HIS OWN EXECUTION

Tom managed to sleep only fitfully. His dreams were full of evil Englishmen in ladies' smocks and unaccountably light horses that floated in the air and wouldn't put their hooves on the ground. Besides which, his waking thoughts were occupied with wondering what had happened to Ann and Emily. Had they managed to escape from the English raiders? Or ... well, to tell the truth Tom didn't dare think about the alternative. At least he spent several hours trying not to ... and he only realized he had been asleep at all when the sound of the trap being removed suddenly woke him up.

Anton stuck his head in the hole. He seemed in a bad mood. Nonetheless he dug his hand into his pocket and pulled out a carrot, which he held out for Tom to gnaw at. When Tom had finished, Anton grunted and pulled Tom roughly out of the hole and back into the main burrow. Tom had a sinking feeling in the pit of his stomach. He knew he was now acting a role – the role of the Condemned Man. Perhaps that was why Anton was in such a bad mood.

Life, it suddenly seemed to Tom, was unbelievably arbitrary – arbitrarily given and arbitrarily taken away. Some folk live to ripe old ages, some die in their cots before they have even had the chance to be anyone, and some, like himself, are just beginning to become the people they're meant to be when – out of the blue – the chance is snatched away. He suddenly wanted to cry – not with sorrow or fear but with the unfairness of it all.

They were stumbling through the burrow, and once again a silence had settled over the human moles. The power of all those eyes, fixed on him, suddenly made Tom's knees go wobbly, and if Anton hadn't been holding his collar in quite such a tight grip, Tom was quite sure he would have crashed to the floor long before they made it to the tunnel that led to the world above.

Once again they were working their way along a narrow tunnel. Tom found it almost impossible to wriggle his way along, because his hands were still tied behind him, but Anton kept pushing him from behind into the pitch black tunnel. Each time he pushed, Tom would get a mouthful of dirt, but they kept moving forward and then, after what seemed like an eternity, the tunnel turned into a vertical shaft and Tom's head hit something hard. It was a wide flat stone across the entrance to the tunnel.

"Ouch!" said Tom. As if this had been the signal he'd been waiting for, Anton pushed Tom to one side and began to strain against the stone hatch. Carefully he raised it and daylight cracked down into the tunnel. Anton took his time. He waited with the hatch raised an inch, as he looked and he listened. Finally he seemed satisfied that no one was about and he moved the stone slab to one side.

It was only then that Tom realized the daylight only seemed like daylight in contrast to the subterranean world from which he was emerging. It was more subdued than real daylight – more ethereal – the sort of light you might get in the middle of a deep forest ... where the sun's rays

arrive at second hand – strained through branches and diffused through leaves.

But it wasn't a forest. Tom felt for a moment that perhaps he was indeed rising from the dead, for he saw now that the stone slab was in fact one of the tombstones that paved the nave of the church. He scrambled up beside Anton and looked around the bare interior.

Anton didn't look at Tom. He pushed him roughly away, as he replaced the gravestone, then he marched Tom out of the church and into the real forest. The time had arrived: both of them had to face an execution that neither of them wanted – Tom least of all.

· 29 ·

ANN AND EMILY
DISCOVER TOM HAS GONE MISSING

Emily refused to go another step. Ann could not cajole her into so much as another toe-length.

"It's all right for you!" Emily complained, as she sat herself down on a milestone. "You're a man!" Ann had almost forgotten as she seamlessly slipped back into her role as Squire Alan. She simply sat down, and leaned her back against the stone. If the truth were told she was just as tired as Emily, but she didn't have the excuse of a sprained ankle.

Instead she muttered: "Do you think Tom's all right?"

"Well, there's nothing more we can do about it, Alan, whether he is or he isn't," said Emily. They had hidden in the forest, and as soon as they had heard the marauding party making its noisy way out of the village, they had hurried back to rescue Tom, armed with a thatcher's ladder they'd found.

"Tom!" Ann whispered. "Are you all right?"

At first, they thought they could see Tom lying motionless at the bottom of the well, but then the moon re-emerged from behind a cloud and they saw – to their dismay – that the well was empty.

"The soldiers must have got him out," murmured Emily.

Ann had no better suggestion. "Then they must have taken him with them!" she said.

"Or ..." shrugged Emily.

"Or nothing!" exclaimed Ann fiercely. "Tom!" she called out, and a note of desperation had come into her voice as she started to run among the empty houses. "Tom! Are you here?" But there was no reply. He wasn't sleeping in one of the deserted cottages; he wasn't tied up in a dog kennel; he wasn't lying half-dead under a stair; that wasn't his foot sticking out of that compost heap nor his hand dangling from that hayloft ... Tom wasn't there – anywhere.

"They've taken him all right," said Ann, and she felt suddenly cold.

· 30 ·

PLANS

Ann didn't sleep a wink all that night. She felt as if a piece had been taken out of her. All through the thin hours of darkness, the same thought kept tramping through the inside of her head: Tom had gone ... they didn't know where or with whom ... or even if he was still alive ... and no matter how hard she thought about it she couldn't think of any way of finding him.

As the morning began to show in the east, the deadly certainty overtook her that she would never see Tom again. She was shocked to discover that it was as if a part of her had died ... and she knew she would carry his loss around like a dead weight inside her.

Suddenly Emily was shaking her. "Come on, Alan!" she was saying. "We've got to find the English army!"

Ann instantly turned back into Squire Alan again. "You may be. I'm not," she replied.

"Yes, you are! You're my escort now!" said Emily, as if she were announcing the final decision. "It's your duty!"

"My duty's to find Tom!" said Squire Alan. "I'm heading for Brittany."

But Emily was no longer listening – she had laid out her clothes on a flat stone, and was now carefully examining each one, and holding it up against herself. "I think – today – I'll take the blue," she suddenly announced.

"Emily," said Ann, "it doesn't matter what you wear or what colour you wear."

"That's where you're wrong, Alan!" exclaimed Emily. "The colour affects the way I feel all day – so I have to get it right. Blue will keep me calm and sensible ..."

"Well I'm going to find Tom and then we're going to join Sir Robert Knolles in Brittany," said Squire Alan. "You can come with us or not – it's up to you."

Emily shook her head. "You can't go and join up with a bandit! You're coming with me."

Ann couldn't help smiling – Emily seemed so decided. "Sir Robert is no more a bandit than any of them!"

"Yes, he is."

Ann decided to change the subject. "So the King of England is your uncle?" she asked.

"Yes. Please button up my back," replied Emily.

"And why do you suddenly need to see him?"

"It's none of your business," retorted the Lady Emilia de Valois.

"Then it's none of my business to get you to him," replied Squire Alan, and she finished buttoning up Emily's dress in silence.

"Alan," said Emily. "You have such nimble fingers for a boy ... You're faster at doing those buttons than my maid!" Emily had turned round and taken hold of Squire Alan's hand. "And your hands are so soft!" Ann quickly extracted her hand from Emily's grasp and walked over to the door of the cottage where they'd been spending the night. The rising sun was just lighting a bank of low cloud with warning flares of red.

"Look, I'm afraid you'll have to find your uncle on your

147

own," she said without turning round to Emily. "I can't go back to the Duke of Lancaster's retinue …"

Emily was looking at Squire Alan curiously. "Why not?" she asked.

Squire Alan sighed. "I injured the young Earl of Grossmont in a practice tournament, and the Duke wants me put in irons."

Emily came up close behind Ann. "Have you really fought in a tournament?"

Ann shook her head. "It would have been my first."

"Weren't you frightened?" breathed Emily.

"Yes … but we men do these things … it's exciting!" said Squire Alan. "But you understand why I daren't go back to the English army."

"But I need your help, Alan!" said Emily and she laid her hand on Ann's shoulder. "You see … there is someone in trouble … My uncle … King Edward is the only one who can help."

Ann turned and looked straight at Emily. "This person … is it someone you love?"

"Yes," said Emily, and a tear suddenly sprang to the corner of her eye.

"Is it a boy?"

"Oh, Alan!" said Emily, suddenly flinging her arms around Ann's neck. "He's in such danger! He was captured by the English at Poitiers and now three years he's been in prison in England – waiting for his ransom – but my lord the Earl was murdered during the rising in Paris and my uncle, the Archbishop, means to have the whole inheritance. I have proof that he plans to have Guillaume murdered in prison in England … That is why I must speak to King Edward!" And she threw her head on Squire Alan's shoulder and sobbed.

Ann patted her back and murmured comforting noises. "There! There!" she said. "I know what it's like to love someone. There is someone I love … but whether I see them again … who knows."

Emily looked up at Squire Alan. "Is she beautiful?" she asked.

Squire Alan shook his head. "Look … from what I hear the Duke of Burgundy made the mistake of offering the English a lot of money if they guaranteed not to enter Burgundy. So – naturally – the English gave up the siege (which wasn't going to get them anywhere anyway) and moved down into Burgundy to try and persuade the Duke to improve his offer. I'll go with you as far as the English camp but that's all! I'm not going to risk my neck …"

Emily sniffed. "Thank you, Alan," she smiled at Squire Alan. "You are so different …"

And so it was that Ann found herself setting off with the Lady Emilia De Valois to rejoin the English army from which she had fled such a short time before. Her one consolation was that among the English she was more likely to hear news of Tom.

· 31 ·

ON THE WAY TO TROYES

Squire Alan and Emily crossed the sweet-smelling River Marne by a wooden bridge that the English had flung together on their march towards Burgundy. They could see the scorched earth where the army had camped for several days, unable to cross because the Burgundians had destroyed the old bridge.

Then they walked for what seemed like an eternity, over the high chalk hills where the River Somme takes its source – a strange empty country with few farms or habitation – a countryside with its elbows up, shielding itself from the view of the world. They spent the night in a lonely barn, with only a barking dog and their own gnawing hunger for company.

Then on they tramped the next day, until finally the flat rolling tops suddenly came to an end and they could see for miles and miles. Below them ran a river and beyond that was a different world – an inhabited country of woods and fields and farms and villages. It was a world that held out the prospect of food.

The River Seine flowed briskly through the home-spun countryside of Champagne, in a hurry to get to the great metropolis of Paris. The banks were thickly wooded and overhung with willows that formed a natural arch over the water. Birds flew through this tunnel of green, and the air was soft with the cooing of wood pigeons.

Emily and Squire Alan crossed the Seine at a village called Méry, where they had hoped to buy something to eat, but the inhabitants had all fled before the advance of the English army, and not a living thing nor a scrap of food had been left behind – just the blackened fields and the empty homesteads of a vanished people.

It was at this point that Emily refused to go another step. The milestone on which she was sitting read: "Troyes 16 miles".

"Is Troyes a big city?" asked Squire Alan.

"Yes," mumbled Emily.

"Then come on!" pleaded Squire Alan. "If we can get there before dark, we'll be able to buy lodging and food and everything!" But Emily would not budge.

"It's all right for you – you're a man," she mumbled. "I'm exhausted."

"To tell the truth," Ann wanted to say, "I'm exhausted too." And she suddenly had an urge to tell Emily who she was and why she was disguised as a squire. But she bit her tongue. If the lovely Emily didn't know her secret, she couldn't give it away.

Squire Alan sighed, and spread the bundle of clothes on the ground – arranging all the dresses neatly on the blanket … "Might as well let your clothes air while we're waiting for your Ladyship to recover," Squire Alan said. Emily frowned. Then she stretched out herself on the blanket, shut her eyes and fell asleep, with the slightest of slight smiles playing on her lips.

· 32 ·

HOW TOM WAS NOT PUT
TO DEATH BY A GIANT

Meanwhile, Tom followed his executioner, the giant Anton, into the depths of the forest until they reached a glade. It was the kind of glade you might expect to choose for a picnic, or for a musical recital, or where lovers might meet, dressed in bright colours and with flowers in their hair. The branches formed a natural roof above them, and moss formed a carpet beneath their feet. It simply wasn't the sort of place where you'd expect to be killed.

Anton threw Tom down on the ground and then paced around the glade, as if looking for the perfect spot to do the deed. Tom did not feel exactly scared – although he was – he was more aware of feeling numb. "I suppose this is how a mouse feels when the cat's playing with it," he thought. "Too scared to feel scared." Suddenly Anton lurched towards Tom, grabbed him by the collar, and jerked him on to the tree stump. Tom immediately felt scared.

Anton's knife seemed to jump out of its sheath and into his hand, as he pulled Tom's head back to expose his neck and the cold steel slid noiselessly across Tom's throat. Tom felt no pain but he saw the bright blood spill out across the forest floor, gushing from Tom's gullet, in an unstoppable fountain that flooded the glade until there was a red lake as deep as a man. Tom found himself struggling for air and drowning in his own blood – except that he suddenly realized that his mind had raced ahead of events. Anton's knife was still in its sheath. Tom's throat was still mercifully intact and Anton was speaking to him.

"Who are you?" Now Anton sat himself on a moss-covered stone and looked earnestly at Tom. "Are there wars and killings where you come from?" he asked.

Tom had never quite believed that Anton was going to murder him, and now he was almost certain. Nobody would murder someone who's just told them his life story, he reasoned. So – as quickly as he could – Tom told the giant Anton his adventures, from leaving home to meeting Alan the Squire to the siege of Laon to joining the English army and discovering that Squire Alan was really a girl named Ann and finally to being set to work in the Duke's scriptorium translating the correspondence of churchmen and writing letters to the Pope and ... well, he was just going to outline his escape from the city of Reims, when he found Anton leaping to his feet and undoing the cords that tied his wrists.

"We must tell Father Michael!" Anton was saying in a state of some excitement.

"But I haven't even got to the bit about how I was nearly murdered by a giant ..." Tom began, but Anton didn't seem to be interested in anything else that Tom had to say. He was off and away, dragging Tom with him.

By the time they reached the village, many of its inhabitants had emerged from their underground hide-out, and were starting to go about the duties of the day – fetching water, scavenging in the ruined fields, cooking what little food they could find, and so on.

Father Michael was doing his bit – in the church on his

knees before the altar. Anton dropped beside the old man, and without waiting for any invitation he gabbled all he could remember of Tom's life story. As he came to the part about writing letters to the Pope, Father Michael turned to stare at Tom.

Now Tom could not have realized, of course, but this was a response that expressed intense excitement on the part of Father Michael. Normally, a slight quiver of the left eyelash was about as much reaction as you'd get out of the old man – even if you'd just told him his house had burnt down. But then, as he used to say himself, he had seen so many things in his day that nothing surprised him any more ... except, for some reason, this information about Tom writing to the Pope ... Father Michael had actually struggled to his feet ... He was clearly beside himself with excitement! And yes! His left eyelash was definitely quivering!

"But one so young ..." he murmured. "Can we really believe that one so tender of years could command the trust of the Holy Father?"

"Maybe that's why they trust me," said Tom. "The Duke wanted someone who was not a churchman, and the churchmen seem to prefer my Latin prose style."

Father Michael's reaction to Tom's words was one that no one who had known him over the long years had ever seen before – to put it simply: his jaw dropped. Tom had spoken in perfect Latin – the kind of Latin that Father Michael had not heard since his early days as a student in Paris. Anton looked at Father Michael in open astonishment. He was astonished to see Father Michael astonished. It was all astonishing!

Before the old man could say anything, however, there was a commotion outside the church. They could hear horses and raised voices, and a hungry-looking dog of a man poked his head into the church and stuttered:

"F-F-F-Father M-M-Michael! My Lord d-d-de Courcy's men are here!"

"Damn his eyes," said Father Michael, as he crossed himself before the altar and hurried out of the church. Anton followed.

Tom looked around him. Everyone seemed to have forgotten about him. They certainly seemed to have forgotten about putting him to death, for which he was duly grateful. He was suddenly free to escape – and yet he didn't. He had no idea why, but – instead of climbing out of a window or running into the forest – he simply followed Anton and Father Michael out into the churchyard.

A knot of emaciated villagers were huddled before a

dozen armed men on horseback. They were clearly not marauders, for they were all dressed in the same livery: an inverted V and a griffin's head. Marauders would have been dressed in old rough tunics and would never display badges. These were retainers in the retinue the Lord de Courcy – the greatest local land-owner.

One of the men-at-arms, however, was holding a lighted brand, and the leader was shouting at Father Michael: "I know you are paying fees to the English who hold the Tower of Rollebois!"

"But we have nothing to pay them with!" replied Father Michael.

"Don't tell me that!" screamed the knight. "You peasants have always something salted away! You live like pigs off the fat of the land!"

"Do we look as if we eat well?" asked Father Michael, indicating the starving faces and stick-like bodies of the villagers. "Do we look as if we possess anything?"

"You are paying dues to the English! Damn you! And my Lord de Courcy will have his dues by the month's end or we will leave not a roof standing over your heads!" And with that the knight nodded to the henchman who was carrying a lighted brand. The man wheeled his horse around, and rode up to the nearest cottage.

"No! NO!" screamed a young woman in a blue surcoat and a white headscarf. "My father's in there! NO!" But she might as well have been screaming at a bolt of lightning or at the raging sea, for the man rode around the cottage sticking his burning brand under the eaves until each part of the thatch had burst into flames. He roared with satisfaction as the roof suddenly caught, and the flames roared as well as if in reply.

The woman, however, broke away from the group and

rushed into the cottage. She was still in there when the roof seemed to explode into flame. It would soon collapse. The other villagers stood looking on, dumb-faced. Tom suddenly found himself remembering the road to Reims and the cart-horse that stopped in the pouring rain as the Man in Black flogged its sides – how it stood there obstinately, in mute rebellion, as if there was nothing more its tormentor could do to it to make its life worse. Just like these silent, sullen villagers now.

Anton, however, sprang into action. He sprinted towards the cottage and, by the time he had dived into the blazing interior, Tom, almost without thinking, followed.

It was the second time in as many days that Tom had rushed into a burning building to save someone. It seemed to him that fire and the sword had become just as much a part of everyday life in France as coughs and itches. And he was right. Since the English had begun their war twenty years before, the country had suffered until it seemed it could suffer no more; and then it had suffered even more – so much more that it had seemed impossible that the poor people could support any more suffering – and then it had suffered even more and then it had suffered still more until it seemed that suffering had become the only way of knowing that you were still alive.

In the blazing cot, the main roof beam was still holding, but the thatching straw had collapsed into the cottage. Anton was kicking it out of his path, and, as Tom joined him, he glanced across but said nothing. They could see the woman huddled in one corner, clutching an old man to her. As Anton kicked the last of the blazing straw aside, she rose to her feet. In a second, Anton had picked the old man up, placed him on his broad shoulders and was heaving himself out of the building. The woman didn't move,

157

however; she just stood with her back against the wall as Tom pulled her arm.

"Come on!" he cried. "We'll get cooked!" But the woman gazed at him stupidly as if she didn't understand a word – as if she didn't understand what was happening – as if she didn't understand that her life and his life were in danger. "Come on!" pleaded Tom. But she did not move.

One of the roof timbers fell with a crash into the blazing thatch in the middle of the room, sending up a shower of sparks and loose flame. Tom pulled the woman and pulled her and pulled her and still she held against him. "Please!" cried Tom. "For my sake!" But she looked at him blankly. "For your father!" he yelled.

"He's dead," she said. And then, is if speaking the words had released her from a spell, she took to her heels, crashed past Tom and out into the open air. In his surprise, Tom toppled over backwards, and fell among the burning straw, but he was up on his feet again in an instant, and in the next moment he had charged out of the developing inferno, just a second before the main roof timber collapsed across the doorway.

The moment Tom appeared, Anton grabbed him, threw him down to the floor and began banging his head against the ground. Tom fought back, but it was no use against the giant.

"What've I done?" Tom yelled in surprise. But the giant kept banging his head on the floor and suddenly the other villagers were gathered around him kicking him, and Tom found himself thinking: "The world's gone mad! I try to help them and they beat me up!" But a minute later they had all stopped and were looking at him oddly. It was at that moment that he smelt the sickly smell of singed cloth and felt a strange feeling up his spine.

"Your back!" gasped Anton. "It was on fire!"

Lord de Courcy's men had hung around long enough to enjoy the conflagration and to be quite certain that the cottage would be reduced to ashes, but then they had turned their horses about and ridden out of the village. They wanted to find somewhere they could get a decent lunch and some good wine. The villagers could still hear their laughter a mile down the road. It was all in a day's work for the men-at-arms of my Lord de Courcy.

Anton, the giant, stood up, and Tom got unsteadily to his feet. The woman in blue was hunched over the body of her father, sobbing. The rest of the villagers stood, blankly staring at what had probably become for them a daily scene of suffering. The dumb rebellion of the horse.

Father Michael turned a world-weary eye on Tom. "We have a task for you," he said.

· 33 ·

EMILY AND SQUIRE ALAN
SUFFER A FINANCIAL
EMBARRASSMENT

Ann and Emily had reached the great city of Troyes
shortly before lunch. There they discovered that the
English army had been in the neighbourhood for
some time, but, finding Troyes too well defended for their
liking, the English had turned their attentions to the much
smaller (and therefore less hostile) town of Tonnerre not far
away to the south.

"You'll like Tonnerre, Alan," said Emily. "It's a beautiful
town. And the wine is very good."

"Maybe," replied Squire Alan, "but I'm not going
anywhere until I've eaten. I'm starving." And so, feeling very
cheerful and that their quest was nearly at an end, the two of
them went straight to the best tavern Troyes had to offer, and
there they ordered the best meal the tavern had to offer. It was
half-way through this feast that Emily made the fateful
discovery.

"When did you last see it?" asked Squire Alan.

"I had it in the inn in Chalons," said Emily, "when I was
wearing the armour."

"Then you couldn't have lost it!" exclaimed Squire Alan
… "Unless it came off while you were down the well or …"
And then suddenly she gave a whoop. "I know! It was the
landlord! D'you remember – in the inn – when you bumped

161

into me, and you fell backwards on to the floor – the landlord helped you up – I thought he was being unduly friendly! But of course! He was just helping himself to your money bag!"

"That boil-ridden flea-sack! I'll tear his tongue out and put his eyeballs in vinegar! I'll disembowel him on a spit and have him roasted for breakfast!" And there is no doubt, that Emily would have done all of those things, if the wretched man had been to hand. But, luckily for him, he wasn't.

"The problem is," said Ann, "I haven't got a sou!"

"WHAT?" Emily turned on Squire Alan. "You dare to tell me you've dragged me all this way to sponge off me?!"

"What are you talking about!" exclaimed Squire Alan. "I haven't 'dragged you' anywhere! At your request and out of the goodness of my heart, I'm escorting you to the English army – so you can ask the King to release your lover-boy – remember?"

"He's not my ..." Emily began, but Squire Alan interrupted her.

"As far as I'm concerned – I don't want to go anywhere near the English army! I want to go to Brittany! I'm just doing this for you!"

"But I didn't know you were just a beggar tricked out in a doublet and hose!" exclaimed Emily.

"Emily!" replied Ann. "You are a selfish, spoilt, rich, little brat! Now just pipe down or the landlord will know something's up." And to do Emily justice, she saw the point at once.

"I'm sorry, Alan," she said. "You're right." And she looked into Squire Alan's eyes.

"Situation, Alternatives, Action," said Ann, turning away. "Situation: we've no money and we've just eaten a big meal ..."

"Thank goodness for that at any rate," murmured Emily.

"By the way, how do you manage to eat so much without getting fat?" asked Ann.

"I don't swallow," said Emily.

"But ..." said Ann.

"Just joking." Emily's mouth turned up at the corners.

"Alternatives," Ann continued. "One: tell the landlord and throw ourselves on his mercy. Two: get some money. Three: do a bunk."

"Three," said Emily, without hesitating.

"Exactly!" said Ann.

"But let's finish eating first," suggested Emily, and she carried on demolishing the mutton chop in front of her.

Ann glanced around the tavern. It was busy and the landlord was sitting at table drinking with some cronies. He was in fact celebrating the fact that he had finally – at great expense – achieved the main ambition of his professional life by laying a stone floor in the main public room, thus bringing the inn up to the quality of those high-class establishments in other great cities. He was pleasantly unaware that two of his apparently best customers were at that moment planning to "do a bunk".

Ann considered the Two-Stage Bunk, in which one partner leaves to go to the garde-robe (remember the euphemism) and the other waits for a suitable moment to do the bunk. Then there was the Total Bunk, in which, if the chance arose, both made a dash for it. Then there was the Diversion Bunk. This was a variant on the Two-Stage Bunk, in which the one who is excused to go to the euphemism creates a diversion, which enables the one still at table to make their escape.

"Here's what we do," said Ann in a low voice. "I'll get up to go to the garde-robe and you carry on eating ..."

"So far so good," smiled Emily. The fact is Emily had never been truly and utterly without money before, and instead of feeling vulnerable or frightened at this moment, she felt a thrill of adventure. It's odd how different situations affect different people.

"Now then, I'll create a diversion ... I'm not quite sure what it'll be ... but you'll know when it happens, and then you choose your moment to do the bunk – got it?"

"I like being with you, Alan," said Emily. "You make things exciting."

"Yes ... well ..." said Squire Alan, and couldn't think of anything else to say. Which was odd for Ann.

Some moments later, Squire Alan stood up. He strolled casually across the room to the door that led to the backyard. As he did, Emily suddenly jumped up and made a bolt for the door! The landlord, who was getting intimately acquainted with a pint pot of ale, most of which was just then half-way down his throat, spluttered and leapt to his feet. The pint pot crashed across the table and the remaining ale splashed across the straw-covered floor. But Emily was out of the door and had disappeared into the myriad narrow streets and alley-ways of Troyes, before the landlord had even so much as swayed, fallen over a bench, picked himself up, rubbed his head and sat down again among his cronies.

Ann had been watching all this with dismay. Her carefully worked-out plan lay in ruins ... except ... that nobody seemed to be paying any attention to her at all. The landlord was vacillating between a new pint pot which had miraculously appeared the moment the first went flying and complaining to his drinking pals about young high-born ladies trying to ruin poor honest, inn-keepers like himself. The rest of the customers were equally pre-occupied discussing Emily's sudden departure. In effect, Emily had created her own diversion, and Ann was able to simply turn around and walk to the back door unnoticed. It couldn't have been easier!

Ann had just put a foot across the threshold, however, when she realized the snag. Of course there was always a snag! Emily's bundle of clothes was still under the bench where they had been eating. Ann groaned. She'd have to go back for them. After all they were worth more than a dozen mutton chops – in fact, if the truth were known, Emily's bundle of clothes was probably worth more than the whole tavern!

So Ann turned around, and strolled back to the bench. Curious eyes watched her sit down again. The landlord struggled to his feet, still rubbing his head, and lurched over to her.

"Hey!" he said. "Young gentleman! Whiz yer frind in susha urray?"

There was a sudden silence. Everyone it seemed, was waiting for Squire Alan's reply. What could a young squire say that could possibly explain the strange and sudden departure of his mistress? It was the sort of situation Squire Alan relished.

"My Lady suddenly realized she'd left a purse with ten gold sovereigns somewhere in the market hall," said Ann. "It could be anywhere, and she's offering half a sovereign to anyone who finds it and returns it to her ..." Ann had hardly finished, before the entire room rose to its feet and made a rush for the door.

"'Ere! Lemme first!" the landlord was shouting. "I was the one who asked!" But he tripped over another bench, fell heavily and – as luck would have it – knocked himself senseless on his brand new stone floor.

Ann picked up the bundle of clothes, and strolled out.

Some time later, Ann had still not found Emily, and neither had the landlord nor any his customers found a purse with ten gold sovereigns.

· 34 ·

THE SECRET OF THE UNDERGROUND VILLAGE

"You see how we live?" said Father Michael. Tom swallowed another mouthful of cabbage soup. It was hot but it was poor, thin stuff – more cabbage-flavoured water than soup.

"We are like beasts ..." Father Michael went on. "No! worse than beasts! ... If we were beasts we would be fattened up ... not starved ... The English have destroyed our homes, they have stolen our goods and our cattle, and they have burnt our crops."

"Why don't you seek shelter in that tower I saw down the road? Or there's the Lord de Courcy's castle!" exclaimed Tom.

Anton laughed. He was watching Tom eat as if watching could make him fat. "The Tower of Rollebois is half our problem!" he said.

"English brigands took the Tower last October," said Father Michael, "and now they use it as a base from which to plunder and destroy us whenever they choose. They even demand taxes from us – taxes to use our own roads, taxes to use our own rivers, taxes to use our own forests, taxes to grow our own food ..."

"Surely it's the Lord de Courcy's responsibility to drive the English out of the Tower?!" exclaimed Tom.

Anton laughed again. "The Lord de Courcy is the other half of our problems!" he said.

"The Lord de Courcy doesn't want to miss out. He hears that we have paid taxes to the English, so he sends his men to demand that we pay him what we have paid the English. He takes from us the last coins in our coffers. If he hears we still have blood left, he will come and take that too!" said Father Michael.

"But at least you have his castle to shelter in, when the English attack," Tom didn't quite know why he seemed to be taking the Lord de Courcy's side – maybe it was just that he couldn't quite believe what he was hearing.

"Of course we do!" chuckled Anton, as if it were an old joke. "So long as we pay my Lord de Courcy! A hundred sous for every soul that passes through his gate! Otherwise, the English can do to us what they please."

"But that's …" began Tom.

"Not all!" said Father Michael. "To protect ourselves we have been forced to live underground – like wild animals – you have seen it for yourself. But if the Lord de Courcy knew we had such defences he would come and tear them down – he does not want us to defend ourselves – so keen is he to take our last sous!"

"But how can I help?" asked Tom. "You don't want me to attack the Tower of Rollebois single-handed or something?"

Anton roared with laughter and poured a tiny drop more cabbage water into Tom's dish. "I should like to see that!" he said.

"No, my son," said Father Michael. "We need you to deliver a message for us … we need you to plead our cause, if you will …"

"But the King of England won't listen to me!" exclaimed Tom.

"We don't want you to speak to the King of England," said Father Michael.

"Nor will the Lord de Courcy!" said Tom.

"Or the Lord de Courcy!" said Father Michael. Tom looked from him to Anton's grinning giant's face.

"There is no use talking to my Lord de Courcy! Oh no!" said Anton happily.

"Then who do you want me to take a message to?" asked Tom

Father Michael put his hand on Tom's shoulder. "We want you to go to His Holiness the Pope!" he said.

Tom nearly choked on his cabbage water. "The Pope!" he exclaimed.

"I shall come with you!" said Anton, as if that explained it.

"But what business could I have with the Pope?" asked Tom.

"The Pope is the third half of our problems," said Anton.

"You can't have three halves ... oh, never mind," said Tom.

"We are robbed and taxed by the English, we are robbed and taxed by the Lord de Courcy, till we are too poor to feed our own children, and yet still the Holy Church demands her portion too. I am expected to collect the tithes of all my flock – one tenth of all they possess – just as if there were no war ..." Father Michael never showed his feelings, but nevertheless Tom thought he could see tears in his eyes.

"What would happen if you simply didn't collect the tithes?" asked Tom.

"The Holy Father would put us under a curse – he would expel us from the Holy Church and leave us without

168

even the protection of God," said Father Michael simply. "He has already threatened as much. By the feast of Corpus Christi we must pay a tenth of all the goods and cattle we had before we were robbed by the English, or the Pope will excommunicate us – declare us to be no longer Christians – we shall be shut out from the love of Christ!"

"You said you write to the Pope! You translate his letters! That's what you told me!" Anton was quite excited. "You could tell the Holy Father of our troubles. He would understand and forgive us!"

Tom looked from Anton to Father Michael. Both men were looking at him as if he were the Philosopher's Stone that could turn lead to gold.

"Will you go?" asked Father Michael. "Will you put our case before the Holy Father?"

"No!" thought Tom. "I can't! I have to find Ann and Emily again! I must get back to the English army!" His thoughts span on to the tournaments he wanted to win, to the banners and trumpets of the battles he wanted to prove himself in, and to all the distant lands he was going to

travel to. But at that moment, the door of the church opened, and a thin-faced young woman – almost a girl – came in with a bundle of rags in her arms.

"Father Michael!" she said, and Tom realized that the bundle of rags was a small baby – a little scrap of a thing, that lay still and silent in the girl's spindly arms. The young woman didn't cry. She simply stood there, before her God, with her dead child and her empty belly and her aching heart. Anton got up, and put his arm around her.

Father Michael bent his head in prayer.

"Yes," said Tom. "I'll go."

TOM AND ANTON SET OFF
ON THEIR QUEST

Tom had nothing to pack. Anton wrapped up some cheese and some bread in a cloth, and tied them on to the end of his long staff. He hung a large knife from his belt and a small pan, and pushed a spoon through his hat as usual. Finally he very carefully and ceremoniously placed the letter to the Pope, which Tom had written to Father Michael's instructions, inside his doublet. Then he was ready to leave.

It appeared that Anton had no wife to say goodbye to, no mother, no father, no girl-friend. He did say goodbye to the other villagers, but they just stood silently watching them go. Nobody cheered. Nobody waved. Father Michael might have done, had he been the sort of person who expressed any sort of feeling at all, but since he wasn't he didn't. It was, thought Tom, a poor sort of send-off for an expedition that hoped to stop the village being excluded from Heaven!

He quickly put all these thoughts aside, however, and concentrated on matching his pace to the giant strides of his companion. It was four hundred miles or more to the great city of Avignon, home of the Pope – the head of the Catholic Church and God's representative on Earth. He hoped Anton would slow down soon.

"Hey! Anton!" Tom called out. "I don't want you getting to Avignon a week ahead of me!"

And even when they got to Avignon, Tom thought, he wasn't at all certain how they were going to get in to see the Pope. He hoped Father Michael was right, and that when the Pope's people heard Tom speaking Latin, they would take him to the Supreme Pontiff at once. But that was a hurdle they'd cross when they got there.

Anton had stopped and was grinning at Tom. "I'm glad I didn't have to kill you," he said.

Tom caught the giant up. "Would you actually have killed me, if you'd really had to?"

The giant screwed up his eyes and looked into the distance, as if trying to see the road ahead. Eventually he said quietly: "In war we cease to be a human beings. War turns us into wild beasts. We must choose to become either a tiger or an ox. The tiger stalks its prey and then tears it to pieces, the ox grazes – meaning no harm – until it is torn to pieces."

"But …" Tom wanted to say: Surely there is good in war too? What about all the gallantry and bravery, and the excitement – the crested helmets and the flying banners, the trumpets and the drums, the victories and the prizes … Surely men wouldn't have been waging war for all these centuries if there weren't some good in it? But other images started to crowd these thoughts out of his mind: a monk cut down by an armed man on a horse – the burning library at Laon – the suffering written on the faces of the underground villagers – the girl holding her starved baby …

He would have to keep up with Anton the giant.

· 36 ·

ANSELM THE MONK

Ann had found getting out of the inn easier than she expected; finding Emily, on the other hand, was more difficult than she had anticipated. Troyes, she decided, was an excellent city for hiding in. The wooden houses were crammed together in a maze of tight streets, that leaned against each other at odd angles and in bewildering confusion. Only the great stone-built cathedral of St Peter and St Paul stood vertical and correct.

"I've got as much chance of finding Emily here as I have of becoming Chancellor of China!" Ann muttered to herself. So she decided to make her way to the cathedral: there, she told herself, she would be able to find a quiet spot, out of the wind, where she could settle down to wait for Emily. She pushed open the massive oak door and stepped cautiously in. The interior was dark, in the gathering dusk, but it was illuminated by a myriad of candles and the air was filled with the sweet sound of monks at prayer. And, of course, exactly in the spot where she decided to sit down and wait for Emily, she found Emily.

"What kept you?" asked Emily. "I've been waiting for you for ages."

"Why did you bunk off like that?" exclaimed Ann.

173

"QUIET!" said a monk who was about to sing a psalm to the glory of God. "Who is that chattering at the back of the chapel?"

Anselm the Monk was a proud man. He was proud of his Abbey, he was proud of his position as cellarer, he was proud of his ability to make terrific bargains when buying wine (which he bought for the Abbey in great quantities), he was proud of his cellar and he was proud of his new shoes which were made of the very finest leather. But most of all – absolutely most of all – Anselm the monk was proud of his singing voice.

"Who is that?" his voice hit its most imperious and unmonk like tone.

To Ann's surprise she heard Emily reply in an equally loud voice: "I am the Lady Emilia de Valois! And who may you be?"

There was a silence. Anselm the Monk was at a loss for what to say. You see, as well as being proud of his Abbey, his position, his business sense and his shoes – oh yes! and, of course, his singing voice – Anselm the Monk was also very, very proud of his family. It was rumoured that his great great great great step-uncle once removed had been a butler in the household of Charlemagne the Great! So, as you can imagine, Anselm was tremendously impressed by anyone of good breeding and he was anxious to please anyone socially superior to himself. The family of the Valois was currently about as high as you could go in the social hierarchy of France. So Anselm the Monk was: (a) dumbstruck to find himself addressing such an illustrious personage as the Lady Emilia de Valois, (b) confused by the fact that such a high-born lady appeared to be crouching at the back of the side chapel in which he was about to sing vespers and (c) mortified to find that he had actually been

174

shouting at such a full blue-blooded aristocrat.

"My name is Anselm," he quavered. "I am a poor monk, cellarer to the Abbot Gregory here at the Abbey of St Peter and St Paul."

"Then get on with your office," said Emily without a single quaver in her voice. "And mind your own affairs in future."

"Yes, your Ladyship! Of course, your Ladyship!" said Anselm the Monk and burst into a florid rendition of the 32nd Psalm: "Happy is the man whose disobedience is forgiven".

Tour de force though it was, Emily and Squire Alan had heard enough.

"Uh oh!" said Emily.

"Uh oh!" said Ann. They were now standing on the steps of the cathedral. Night had fallen while they had been inside. They could see the soft light of candles burning behind the shuttered windows of the houses, but down the alley-ways there now lurked a darkness so solid you could almost touch it. Each narrow lane seemed to have become a black corridor of unimaginable evils. Emily glanced at Squire Alan. Of course it wouldn't worry him, but even so she was not surprised when he said: "Well, we're not going to find the English army tonight! Let's stay where we are."

Even the thought of finding a space among the beggars at the back of the church was a relief, and Emily squeezed Squire Alan's arm in gratitude. As they turned to re-enter the house of God, however, they were confronted by the shining face of Anselm the Monk. He was holding a church candle, and the light flickered over his scrubbed features.

"My Lady de Valois, please, please excuse me, I should never have shouted like that if I'd known to whom I was talking ... It was most unfortunate ..."

"What do you want?" said Emily coldly.

"Well ... was wondering ... if you'll forgive the impertinence ... but ... how shall I put this? I see you and your squire here ... How do you do ..." – here he turned to Squire Alan – "I see you ... well ... what shall I say ... you are here in the cathedral ... at this late hour ..."

"Obviously we're here in this cathedral at this late hour," returned Emily tartly, "otherwise you wouldn't be talking to us."

"Quite, quite so ..." Ann could see sweat breaking out on the monk's forehead and starting to run down his plump cheeks – even though a cold breeze had sprung up – "but I was wondering ..."

"Spit it out!" said Emily.

"Well ... I don't wish to intrude ... but am I right in thinking that you and this young gentleman, how do you do ..." – once again, the monk turned and bowed to Squire Alan – "are without lodging suitable for so illustrious a personage as ..."

"You're right!" Squire Alan cut him off. "We were promised rooms at the best inn ... the er ..."

"The Golden Cross?" said Anselm the Monk without hesitation and he licked his lips. He had enjoyed many a tasty (though illicit) meal at the Golden Cross.

"But they had given our rooms away, and every other hostel in town was full ... And now I fear to take my lady into such dark streets at night," continued Squire Alan.

"Quite right too!" exclaimed the monk. "These streets are full of thieves and dangerous women ... so I'm told! That was why I wondered if I might be so bold as to ..."

"We'd be most obliged!" said Emily.

"... to offer you lodging in our humble house ..." Anselm the Monk trailed off. He knew he was doing something that would – eventually – get him into trouble.

The reason he knew this was quite simple. The Abbot Gregory disapproved of anything he did. Yet he could not imagine why Abbot Gregory would object to his inviting the Lady Emilia de Valois and her squire to stay in the Abbey hostelry – after all, they were duty bound to offer lodging to weary travellers. Then again it was not as if he were inviting a pauper or a penniless widow to stay – the Lady Emilia de Valois must be rich beyond imagining – she might even show her gratitude to the Abbey by a donation of hard cash (which was always welcome) ... No! Anselm the Monk was convinced that Abbot Gregory would – for once – applaud his act of generosity. The only trouble was that he knew he wouldn't.

And then a thought suddenly struck him. "Where are your horses?" A note of anxiety had crept into his voice.

"They are already stabled at the Golden Cross," replied Squire Alan without batting an eyelid. "We insisted they look after our horses even if they couldn't look after us."

"But it is outrageous they could not find room for your Ladyship!" murmured Anselm. "It is almost beyond belief!"

"Isn't it just?" agreed Squire Alan. And it was – but it was the best story she could come up with on the spur of the moment.

And so Anselm the Monk took the Lady Emilia de Valois and her squire, Alan, into the Abbey hostel, still filled with misgivings about what the Abbot Gregory would say – especially since they did not have horses.

• 37 •

THE ABBOT'S
HOSPITALITY

The Abbot Gregory looked down his nose – and there was plenty of nose to look down.

"What did you say they had done with their horses?" he asked.

"They said they'd left them at an inn ... I forget which one ..." Anselm the Monk was always anxious to convey the impression that he was not at all familiar with places like the Golden Cross.

"Stuff ..." said the Abbot Gregory very slowly and deliberately, "and nonsense, Brother Anselm."

"Did I do wrong, Abbot Gregory?"

"The finances ..." stormed the Abbot Gregory slowly, "... of this ..." he looked across his nose, up it and then down it again, "... Abbey are not such ..." the Abbot Gregory stood up at this point and turned away, "... that we can dole out ..." – Anselm the Monk hated the way the Abbot stretched out his sentences when he was scolding him. He was sure the Abbot did it deliberately just to lengthen the process of humiliation – "... dole out ..." he repeated, "... food and shelter to any beggar on the street!" The Abbot Gregory banged his ring-encrusted fist upon the back of his chair.

"But ... the Lady Emilia de Valois is not a beggar, my lord Abbot ... she might even donate money to ..."

"D'you know what that thing between your ears is called, Brother Anselm?" asked the Abbot Gregory.

"My head?" mumbled Brother Anselm miserably – he knew what was coming next.

"Then, if you know what it is, why don't you use it?" exclaimed the Abbot triumphantly. Brother Anselm knew from bitter experience that whenever the Abbot Gregory said anything like: "What do you keep in that head of yours – wool?" or "Why do you think God gave you something you keep your nose on?" that his humiliation was drawing to its climax in which the Abbot would mete out some punishment or other.

"Do you seriously imagine ..." the Abbot was now pacing about the room, "... the Lady Emilia de Valois would be tramping round the country on foot? Whoever this strumpet is, who has so impressed you, Brother Anselm, you may be quite certain she is not the Lady Emilia de Valois!" Brother Anselm winced – he was about to know his fate. "Your pocket money will be stopped for the next two weeks to pay for the food these ... charlatans ... will undoubtedly consume at our expense ... and another week to pay for the bed covers that we shall undoubtedly have to de-louse."

"Thank you, Abbot Gregory," said Anselm the Monk meekly. You always had to thank the Abbot for punishment – it was a rule of that particular house.

And so it was that Emily and Squire Alan sat down that evening at the long table of the hostelry of the Abbey of St Peter and St Paul to a supper of black bread and porridge, while Anselm the Monk served them personally as part of his punishment.

There were no other guests, and that made the whole occasion doubly irksome for the monk. He thought of the supper he would otherwise have been enjoying with the other brothers in the infirmary: plum pudding, braised small birds and a rabbit pie, a duck and three capons that he had personally selected. Not to mention the sweet custards and the six apple tarts that he had purchased.

Strictly according to the Order of St Benedict, the brethren should have restricted themselves to a diet of vegetables, but the Rule did allow meat to be served to the sick. And so, over the years, it had become the custom for the monks to eat in the infirmary, where they could help their sick brethren (whose appetites were weakened by sickness) deal with the abundance of venison, partridge, well-hung beef and good mutton that crowded their table, while the refectory itself stood empty and silent week after week.

Tonight, Anselm the Monk knew, the infirmary hall would be filled with the sweet voice of that young noviciate, Lucas, as he read the holy stories that all the brethren knew so well; the table would be gleaming with candle-light, and humming with the companionship of the monastery meal; the monks would remain silent, as their Rule commanded, but they would be signalling away to each other in the sign language they had developed for dining; their elbows would be working up and down as they quaffed their wine, and their hearts would be light as they munched the good food that Anselm the cellarer had provided.

Here in the guests' quarters, on the other hand, dinner was a rather gloomy affair. The food had little to recommend it and there were only two candles to light the entire hall – one per diner being the rule. The meal was, however, far from silent.

"Is this muck what you monks eat here?" The Lady

Emily de Valois hurled a loaf of stale bread across the table and would have hit Brother Anselm square on the nose had he not ducked. "That bread's six days old and this stodge …" she pushed her bowl of porridge across the table, "isn't fit for pigs! Call yourselves monks? I've known lepers who eat better!"

"We are but a poor order," mumbled Brother Anselm. To tell the truth, he was becoming more and more convinced that the Abbot Gregory was totally wrong. If this young woman was not the Lady Emilia de Valois, where on earth could she have learnt manners like this?

"You don't look as if you're starving!" Emily was continuing the attack. "You look fat enough for three monks! I bet you don't eat this hogswill! You and your fellows will be gorging yourselves in the refectory on pork and wine and white bread!"

Anselm the Monk felt bold enough to reply: "I swear to you that is not so." And it was true in a way: they were not eating in the refectory, and pork was not on the menu that evening.

"I know you monks!" Emily always got extremely cross around meal-times unless confronted by a meal that was exactly to her taste. "You live well enough for Earls! You don't go short of a fat capon or a goose! So … let me tell you this … if you continue to treat my squire and myself in this shameful and insulting way, I shall make sure that my uncle, Jean de Craon, the Archbishop of Reims, gets to hear about your behaviour. And when he does, he will pay a visit to this monastery that will make your Abbot … what's his name?"

"The Abbot Gregory, your Ladyship," Anselm the Monk had, by this time, very little remaining doubt about the Lady Emilia's credentials.

"That will have your Abbot Gregory soiling his silk shoes!" And with this, Emily picked up the bowl of porridge and hurled it at the monk. This time he hesitated and the bowl hit him full in the face. The thin porridge trickled down the inside of his habit and all over his fine linen undershirt – a misfortune made all the worse by the fact that he wasn't supposed to be wearing a fine linen undershirt in the first place.

Brother Anselm was convinced. He ran off to tell the Abbot.

· 38 ·

PRISONERS OF THE ABBOT

It was unprecedented for the Abbot Gregory to break off in the midst of a meal. It was unprecedented for the Abbot Gregory to rise up from the table and make his way to the hostelry to enquire about the well-being of the monastery's guests. The only thing that was not unprecedented was the abuse that he heaped upon Brother Anselm. "Why didn't you say? – if you were so certain she was the Lady Emilia?" his voice rasped across the chilly cloister, as they hurried, muffled up against the cold night air.

"But ..." said the wretched Anselm.

"You are nothing but a donkey's back-side, Brother Anselm!" the Abbot continued. "If the Archbishop starts poking his nose down here, goodness knows what he'll find! He might go through our accounts, for goodness' sake! He could insist on manual labour for every single brother! He could even force us to start eating in the refectory again!"

Brother Anselm groaned. He knew how serious that would be.

By the time they reached the hostelry, the cooks had already run ahead with platters of mutton in onion sauce, spiced pigeons, and flasks of wine with cheese and fresh-baked white bread. And all this had been laid in front of the Lady Emilia de Valois and her squire, before the Abbot and the Members of the Chapter (who advised him in all important matters) reached the hall. When they did, the churchmen bowed before their illustrious guest. Candles had been brought in by the score, and the whole place was beginning to look almost festive.

"Your Ladyship," said the Abbot in his most accommodating voice. "You are most welcome here. I apologize for the stupidity of Brother Anselm here, who failed to recognize you, and who therefore omitted to announce your arrival to me. I trust you have suffered no inconvenience as a consequence of his foolishness."

Ann looked at Emily in admiration: she certainly knew how to get things done!

"My Lord Abbot," said Emily. "We shall endeavour to forget your niggardly hospitality, since it was the fault of your subordinate ..."

"Your Ladyship is most gracious," said the Abbot, bowing low.

Brother Anselm never understood, to his dying day, why it was that everyone always blamed him for everything. But he knew enough to know what was coming next.

"I will see that Brother Anselm is punished." The Abbot glared at the unfortunate Anselm, and then flashed his most brilliant smile at Emily: "From now on, our hospitality is yours. May I offer you my own private rooms for your accommodation tonight?"

Emily nodded, and graciously accepted the Abbot's generous offer. Actually it wasn't quite such a generous offer as it sounded. The Abbot was not really offering to turn out of his own bed for the sake of his guests: he was simply offering them the suite of rooms that were reserved for his personal visitors. They were, of course, magnificent rooms.

"My squire Alan will stay with me," said Emily imperiously. "He guards my chamber."

"As your Ladyship commands," said the Abbot with a fleshy smile. "We are only too happy to accommodate your Ladyship's desires in any way we can. In the meantime, we shall send to the Golden Cross for your horses."

"That won't be necessary!" It was Ann, or rather Squire Alan, who was suddenly thinking fast. "Their stabling for the next three days has been already been paid for – it would be a waste of good money to change the arrangement."

The Abbot turned to Squire Alan, with the merest hint of a sneer. "They will be better stabled here and better fed. Allow me to have them brought here."

Squire Alan looked desperately at Emily.

"That won't be necessary!" said Emily – perhaps a bit too sharply. "I prefer to leave them where they are presently stabled."

The Abbot bowed. "Then I shall send my ostler in the morning to check that they are being treated with proper care and attention," he said. "One can never trust these public inns."

Ann sighed: "There is no need for you to trouble yourself, my Lord Abbot. My duties include the supervision of my her Ladyship's horses."

"Doubtless, Squire Alan," said the Abbot. "But I should feel I was a poor host were I to leave your lady's horses to the mercies of the Golden Cross. I must therefore insist." Ann and Emily exchanged glances. The Abbot's concern for their non-existent horses meant they would have to be up, out and away from the Abbey before day-break. But there seemed to be nothing else for it.

The Abbot's private chambers were indeed luxurious. To be sure they were not quite as luxurious as the Abbot's own "cell" in which he spent most of his days and nights, but they were handsome rooms for all that. From their lofty position in the high tower of the hostelry wing, the windows commanded a magnificent view all over the city of Troyes. You could see the city walls – famous for being shaped exactly like the cork from a bottle of wine.

Inside the chambers themselves was a large bed with a curtain, a smaller bed, a stool, an iron-bound chest and even – and this was what amazed Ann – even a table! To us that might not seem such a remarkable thing, but in Tom and Ann's day a table was something you set up on trestles for a meal. A table that stood there all day long was a novelty that had not yet reached beyond the rich and famous.

Emily chose the large bed, without any debate, and Ann thankfully threw herself down on the small bed. She blew her candle out, but Emily left hers burning.

"Alan," Emily's voice came out of the candle's glow.

"I'm sleeping," said Ann. "We've got to get up early if we're going to get away before the Abbot checks up on our mythical horses."

"I would never have thought of saying all that about having paid for the horses in advance," said Emily.

"It didn't do us much good," mumbled Ann.

"But at least we're going to get one good night," said Emily. Ann grunted without opening her eyes. She wanted to get as much sleep out of this night's lodging as possible ... and she was just finally drifting off when a butterfly brushed against her cheek. Ann shot bolt upright.

If you're trying to get a good night's rest, the last thing you want is butterflies interfering with you. Ann glanced around the room. Emily's candle was still burning, and she expected to see the giant shadow of an insect fluttering across the walls – but there was nothing like that. In the candle's soft glow all she could see was Emily's hand still where her own cheek had been a few moments before.

"Your skin is so soft," whispered Emily. Ann could now see Emily was kneeling beside the bed.

Ann took a deep breath. "Go back to bed NOW, Emily!" she ordered. "We've precious little left of the night as it is, we must sleep."

"But ... Alan ..." said Emily. "I can't sleep."

"You've got to sleep! We've got a long way to travel tomorrow if we're going to catch up with King Edward before he leaves Tonnerre," replied Ann.

"Alan ..." said Emily quietly. "I've never met anyone like you."

"Well," said Ann, "I've never met anyone like you, Emily."

Emily frowned for a moment and then suddenly smiled. "Kiss me goodnight, Alan," she said.

Ann leant forwards and kissed Emily lightly on the lips. "Now go to bed, for goodness' sake," she whispered. "You're getting cold!"

"Yes, Alan," she said. She was shivering slightly.

"Goodnight, Emily," said Ann.

"You are very strong, Alan," said Emily.

"Go to sleep, Emily!"

"Yes, Alan, I'll do whatever you say." And with that Emily crawled back to her bed and blew out the candle. But she didn't sleep a wink all that night. And when dawn showed its first rays in the sky, and Ann shook her, she was already awake.

"We'd better get out of here," whispered Ann.

"Right, Alan!" said Emily.

In a few minutes they were creeping to the door of the Abbot's private guest-room in the tall tower of the Abbey's hostelry wing. It was there that the first unpleasant surprise of the day awaited them. The door had been bolted and barred from the outside.

Clearly, they weren't going anywhere until the Abbot had checked the story about their horses.

· 39 ·

THE ABBOT GREGORY
HATCHES A PLOT

Abbot Gregory was in a surprisingly good mood that morning, as Anselm the Monk found himself yet again standing in front of his superior.

"But I don't understand," Brother Anselm was mumbling. "You say you are certain she is who she says she is – the Lady Emilia de Valois?"

"I have no doubt," said the Abbot. "Her clothes alone testify to it."

"Then why have you locked them in the guest-room tower?" Brother Anselm always felt he was several leagues behind the Abbot, when it came to politics – and he was sure politics were involved somewhere in this business.

"Brother Anselm." The Abbot had reverted to his slowest speech delivery. "Are you aware ..." Brother Anselm had a sinking feeling he knew where this was leading. "... that a head ..." Why couldn't the Abbot just spit it out like a normal human being? "... is usually capable ..." Brother Anselm gazed out of the window. "... of containing ..." Here it came! "... a brain?"

"Of course, Father Gregory," said Anselm.

"Then why ..." asked the Abbot with satisfaction, "... is it that yours ... of all human heads ... is an exception?"

"I have a brain, my lord ..."

190

"Then USE it!" thundered the Abbot. "Just THINK! If this is, indeed, as I am sure it is, the Lady Emilia de Valois, and if she has arrived here alone with no entourage other than a gallant young squire, and if they have, as I suspected all along, no horses, there can be only one explanation."

Brother Anselm's mouth worked up and down as if rehearsing an explanation, but no words came out.

"She has run away from her guardian, Brother Anselm!" said the Abbot, banging his fist upon his writing desk.

"Of course!" murmured Brother Anselm. He suddenly knew he would never rise to any rank higher than cellarer.

"If we return her to her uncle, the Archbishop, I have no doubt that he will reward us richly," smiled Abbot Gregory. "Things could go very well for the monastery …"

"Indeed," smiled Anselm, relieved that for once it seemed that he would escape punishment.

"Now," continued the Abbot, "you know that the Archbishop of Reims fled the city some days ago …"

"Did he?" Anselm the monk was never one for keeping up with the latest news.

"If you weren't so busy ministering to that fat belly of yours, you'd be more aware of what was going on in the world," snapped the Abbot. "The citizens of Reims besieged the Archbishop to stop him handing the city over to the English."

"My goodness me," said the cellarer rather feebly.

"Now, I understand the Archbishop is on his way to see His Holiness the Pope in Avignon. He was not intending to stop here at Troyes on this occasion, so you will send a messenger at once to intercept him and suggest that he pay us a visit after all."

"Immediately, Abbot Gregory!" exclaimed Anselm, happy to be of use.

"Wait a minute!" growled the Abbot. "Don't go prancing off before I've finished!"

"Sorry, Father!" said Anselm, turning back as the Abbot continued.

"You personally will make sure that our two little love-birds do not fly the nest before he arrives. I have no doubt that this … Squire Alan … will not enjoy meeting the Archbishop of Reims after absconding with his niece."

"You mean the Archbishop may show him into his Parlour?" smirked Anselm the Monk. The Archbishop's Parlour, you see, was well known to all and sundry – even though it was such a great secret.

But the Abbot Gregory was looking at Anselm the Monk with contempt. "You are a nincompoop, Anselm," he said.

BURGUNDY

• 40 •

TOM AND ANTON JOIN
THE HUNT FOR BANDITS

Anton hadn't slowed down the whole of the way, and Tom had been half-walking, half-running for days on end. Many a time he wanted to beg Anton to cut down his giant's stride, but there was something about the giant's determination that stopped him. Anton walked with his great ugly head up, staring ahead as if he were trying to get an early warning of distant dangers. He didn't speak much, but just maintained his steady pace as if his whole world depended on his getting to Avignon – which maybe it did.

"What place is that?" asked Tom one bright spring morning. They had just enjoyed a particularly luxurious night in a five-star barn. There had been good dry straw, several hens' eggs, which they had cooked in Anton's pan, and excellent water from a nearby spring. Accommodation couldn't get much better than that, thought Tom. But then he remembered the beautiful Emily's beautiful chamber in the Bishop's Palace at Reims, and he sighed. But whether he was sighing for the rich tapestries and the silk bed-coverings, or for the white slope of Emily's neck and the way her mouth turned up at the corners, I don't know.

"Dijon," said Anton. Tom was amazed at how much had gone through his mind in the time since he'd asked the question. "It's a great city. We might find a ride on a cart," said the giant. The idea of a ride put a spring into Tom's step, and he had no trouble keeping up with Anton all the way to the market square of Dijon.

There were several carts gathered in the main square, and a great bustle of people. Townsfolk were scurrying here and there, while others were staring at the great company of men-at-arms who were also assembled in the market square, sitting astride their nervy war-horses and high-bred chargers.

Anton approached the leading cart and asked the man where the convoy was bound for? The man looked rather shifty and refused to say, until he caught the eye of a sergeant-at-arms.

"We're bound for Lyons and then Avignon," said the sergeant-at-arms brusquely.

"But that's where we're heading for!" exclaimed Tom. "Can we get a ride?"

"No! Be off with you!" exclaimed the sergeant-at-arms. "This is too serious a business to give rides to beggars!" and he wheeled his great horse around and started barking out orders.

The carter, meanwhile, had been looking Anton up and down. As soon as the sergeant-at-arms was out of earshot, he leant over to Anton and murmured: "Mind you, you look as if you could make yourself useful!"

"I'll do whatever you want," said Anton, "if you'll give my young friend and me a ride."

"I need someone like you on a trip like this," said the carter. "Jump in the back when no one's looking." Then he started humming a tuneless tune and jiggling the reins.

Jumping in the back of the cart was comparatively simple, even though it was a high-sided wagon, with a canvas awning; but doing it when no one was looking was a bit more problematical. However, Tom and Anton hung around the wagon trying to look as if they were supposed to be there, and then, when a trumpet sounded from the other end of the market square, and everyone turned to look, Anton quickly bundled Tom into the back and then jumped in himself. He did it with such surprising speed that the trumpet had hardly finished the first bar when they were safely in the wagon. The next moment the horses strained, the wheels creaked, and the vehicle started to roll forwards. Shouts rang through the air, whips cracked overhead, horses neighed, and the townsfolk sort of half-cheered as the cavalcade got under way. There were about a dozen carts and wagons, and behind them came the troop of some sixty men-at-arms.

As the cart jolted and juddered its way out of town, Tom glanced across at Anton. The giant was frowning. "Well!" said Tom. "That was easy enough!"

"Hmm," murmured Anton. "There's something odd about the whole business."

"Odd? What's odd?" asked Tom.

"Look at this wagon," said Anton. "Doesn't something strike you as peculiar about it?" Tom looked around the inside of the vehicle. It was made of rough planking, and the canvas awning swayed as the cart moved; it would have been pretty odd as a plum pudding, but as a cart it was about as unremarkable as a cart could get – at least that's what Tom said.

"You don't see?" asked Anton.

"I don't see what you're seeing!" said Tom.

"I'm not seeing anything," replied Anton, who was by no means as simple as he appeared. "That's exactly what's so odd."

As the words left Anton's lips, Tom suddenly exclaimed: "It's empty! The cart's empty!"

"Exactly!" said the giant.

"Then why do we need a small army to guard us," Tom went on, "if all we're carrying is thin air?"

"It's as fishy as an old salmon cake," said Anton, and he peered out from under the canvas awning. Tom did the same on his side.

They had left Dijon well behind them, when the first odd thing happened. Just as they entered the small village of Fixin, they heard shouts from the head of the troop, and the whole convoy came to a halt.

The sergeants-at-arms clustered around in a conference with the leaders. Then about half the troop dismounted and – to Tom's surprise – started to climb into the carts. Four armed men, with swords and bucklers and spears, heaved themselves into the cart in which Tom and Anton were hiding. As luck would have it, one of them was the sergeant-at-arms who had refused them.

"So you came after all, eh?" he said, looking Anton up and down. "Well, you're big enough to be useful in a fight!" and even as he spoke these words there was a series of shouts that ran up and down the troop, and the carts started to roll forwards once again.

Tom peered from under the canvas awning: he could see the troop of men-at-arms peeling off from the convoy of carts, and heading up another road, with the spare horses following them in a pack.

"But you're no more than a child!" The sergeant-at-arms was looking accusingly at Tom. "This is no place for you!" And before Tom knew what was happening, he found himself being pushed out of the cart.

"Help!" yelled Tom.

"Jump!" yelled the sergeant-at-arms. "Ow!" he added, as he found himself pulled across the cart by Anton so that he was now staring into the giant's face, still crowned by his hat with the spoon stuck through it. Before you could say: "Leprechaun sandwich!", however, the other three men-at-arms had pounced on Anton and all four began threshing about – and the cart began rocking.

"Stop that!" yelled the carter – who already looked nervous enough for six kittens. "You'll turn the thing over!"

"Leave the boy alone!" yelled Anton, who by this time had all four men-at-arms sitting on him.

"Calm down!" said the sergeant-at-arms. "I'm only trying to save the boy's neck. This could be a bloody business."

"What could be a 'bloody business'? What's going on?" asked Tom.

The four men-at-arms looked at Tom as if he'd just walked bone dry out of the sea. "You mean you really don't know?" said the sergeant.

"We only just arrived in town," said Tom.

The men-at-arms allowed Anton to sit up. "Well! Welcome to the party!" said the one in the rough red tunic.

"We're going to have fun and games!" grinned the one with no front teeth and the staring eyes.

"The situation is this," said the sergeant-at-arms. "A band of English brigands have set themselves up in the hills above the village of Vergy. From there they are not only terrorizing all the farmers in the area, but they are stopping the traffic on the road to Lyons and Avignon and robbing tradesmen and citizens alike."

"So," said the one with no teeth, "we've prepared a little surprise for them!"

"We've put out word that this is a large convoy, carrying

treasure to the Pope in Avignon," the sergeant-at-arms went on. The brigands won't be able to resist attacking – especially when they see there are no guards …"

"But the only treasure these wagons are carrying is us!" grinned the toothless one.

"They'll wish they'd never come down to Burgundy!"

"Ouch!"

"Ow!"

"Oh!"

"Oof!"

This symphony of musical noises was achieved by the wagon stopping suddenly, and all its occupants being thrown forward into a heap – an unusual method of composition, it has to be admitted. "Sh!" hissed the sergeant-at-arms *troppo forte*. The players took a five-bar rest and waited, still in a heap, for the next cue. In the meantime each tightened his grip on his instrument (mostly swords) and tensed himself for the crescendo towards which the concert was clearly heading.

Tom felt a rush of excited alarm. The toothless man-at-arms, who happened to be nearest, moved very slowly and cautiously raised the canvas awning a quarter of an inch and peered out.

"There's more than a hundred of them!" he whispered. The others looked at each other in alarm.

"It's not possible!" hissed the sergeant-at-arms. "We were told they were no more than two dozen!"

"We're dead!" whispered the man in red, in a voice of awe.

"But there's one good thing," whispered the toothless one earnestly.

"What's that?"

"They're unarmed!"

"WHAT?" whispered the sergeant-at-arms as quietly as he could.

"And what's more – they're all female!" added the toothless one, grinning mysteriously.

The sergeant-at-arms pushed him aside and took a look for himself. "You idiot!" he growled. The wagons had been halted not by brigands but by a flock of sheep which the shepherd had suddenly decided to take across the road.

"Why couldn't you wait till we'd gone past?" the carter was yelling.

"I wouldn't be in no hurry to go down that road, no I wouldn't," sniffed the shepherd. "Them brigands don't let nary a wagon go through without taking what they want."

"Hurry up and get your sheep out of the way!" said the carter.

"There they are," said Tom quietly. He had just seen a movement and a flash of steel in the wooded hills above the road.

"Where?" said the sergeant-at-arms, wary of being made a fool of for the second time.

"Over in the copse beyond the bridge," said Tom. Yes! He could definitely see them, slipping between the trees.

"They'll probably attack when we get down to the river. No one's built up the causeway for years, and the going's slow and boggy," said the sergeant-at-arms. "Keep out of sight at all costs," and he pulled Tom away from the awning, as the last sheep crossed the road and the horses heaved the wagon forward again.

They rolled on down a gentle slope for what to Tom were the longest ten minutes he'd ever known. The tension in the wagon was like a rising tide, mounting higher and fuller inside each one of them. He could see white knuckles as the men gripped their swords. He saw sweat breaking out on the forehead of the toothless one with the staring eyes. He saw the chest of the man in the red tunic heaving with the excitement as the moments passed, and the wagons rolled forwards ... onwards towards the marshy path by the river, where bushes crowded up to the roadside.

They were almost there! The man in red tugged nervously on a strap of his heart guard. The toothless one grinned inanely, as if they were all somehow still in his joke about sheep. Anton – the giant Anton – looked almost as if he were asleep. Perhaps it was his way of conserving his great strength.

The first wagon rolled into the mud. A horse neighed in the bushes. And suddenly it happened! A dozen Englishmen, mounted on stallions and armed to the bristles, burst out of the bushes and blocked the road ahead.

The carter pulled his horses up short, and the creatures shied and tried to turn in their traces.

"So what's this then?" snapped the Captain of the Englishmen. "What d'you have in there, carter?"

The carter shrugged nervously, and replied in French that he could speak no English.

"Damn you lazy French cur!" yelled a round fat Englishman in a tattered blue tunic who happened to be on the Captain's right. "What's that you're gabbling?"

"I am just a poor carter – I have no quarrel with you!" the carter's voice was quavering. The sergeant-at-arms was squinting through a hole in the awning trying to see beyond the Englishmen to the higher ground. His instructions were not to attack until he saw Sir Gervais de Cotigny and the remainder of the troop arriving. What was keeping them?

Meanwhile the Captain of the English was smiling a broken-toothed smile. "We hear you've got the Pope's treasure chests in there – isn't that right?" he grinned. Once again the carter mumbled a reply in French.

"Speak so we can understand you, damn you!" bellowed the fat Englishman in blue.

"It seems we need to teach this French rabbit to speak

the King's English, boys!" yelled the Captain. He was dressed in a long mail coat, with a rough brown jerkin thrown over the top. At his words two of the others dismounted, and pulled the carter off his seat. He screamed, and glanced back towards the interior of the wagon. Why on earth weren't the men-at-arms coming to his rescue?

The sergeant-at-arms squinted through the hole in the awning. Why on earth weren't Sir Gervais and the rest of the troop here yet?

The Englishmen, it has to be said, were in a particularly good mood, the rumour was that the Pope's treasure amounted to over 20,000 gold francs – a fortune that would see their little band living in clover for the rest of the year – well, actually for the rest of their lives, but then brigands didn't tend to think too far ahead. Brigandage was an unpredictable line of business, and most brigands wisely considered it best to live only for the moment. And for this particular moment, these particular brigands were determined to have their fun with the carter of the Pope's treasure wagon.

Two of them threw him on to the muddy ground. They were not the most intelligent of men, and it was hard to imagine they had paid much attention at school – that is, if they'd ever been to school – but nevertheless they seemed very keen to pass on what learning they had. "First lesson in English!" said the large swarthy brigand with the broken nose, who was holding the carter by the hair. "You'd better learn to say: 'Help me!' So go on – say it! 'Help me!' " and, perhaps to clarify the meaning of the phrase, he hit the poor carter around the head with his mailed fist.

"*Aidez-moi!*" cried the carter in a loud voice.

"No!" bawled the swarthy Englishman. " 'Help me!' " And the rest of the brigands laughed as if there were no tomorrow – which, I may tell you, was to prove the case for many of them.

"AIDEZ-MOI!" screamed the carter.

"I heard you the first time!" grinned his unwelcome instructor. "Saying it louder don't turn it into English!"

"He don't seem to be paying much attention to his lessons, do he?" said his other English tutor. This brigand was short and bald, and carried a buckler strapped to his back. "Perhaps we should help him to concentrate?" And to the continued amusement of his fellow Englishmen, he pulled out a knife and proceeded to hold it under the carter's nose. "Now," he said, "it's quite simple. Every time you get a word wrong, I'll keep a score – on your left cheek ..."

"AU SECOURS!" cried the poor carter.

"No! 'Help me'!" said the swarthy brigand.

"That's one!" cried the bald one, and duly cut a line on the poor carter's cheek. The blood gushed out and the other brigands thought this was the wittiest piece of repartee they'd ever come across – they roared with laughter.

"Do something!" hissed Tom. From inside the cart they could all hear the conversation clearly, but Tom, who understood the English that was being spoken as well as the French, was the only one who could actually follow what was going on.

The sergeant-at-arms was still squinting through the hole in the canvas awning. "We have to wait for the rest of the company," he said in a low voice.

"But they'll kill him!" whispered Tom.

"Shut up!" whispered the sergeant-at-arms.

Suddenly Tom heard the carter scream again and the brigands laugh. "That's two!" said his tormentor.

"Teach him to say his prayers!" called the Captain of the brigands.

"*Pitié!*" cried the carter.

"That's three!" and the carter screamed again.

"Stop!" yelled Tom. He had leapt out of the back of the cart before the sergeant-at-arms could stop him, and was now standing in front of the Englishmen. "Leave my father alone!" The brigands looked up like a bunch of naughty schoolboys caught tormenting a dog. "He can't understand you," shouted Tom, "but I can!"

The Captain of the Englishmen broke into a broad, broken-toothed grin. "Well! Well! Somebody here does know how to talk proper!" The rest of the gang guffawed and looked to see what their leader would do. Rather surprisingly, however, the fat brigand in blue, to the Captain's right, gave a sort of squeak, and edged behind the leader, as if he were almost afraid of the newcomer. But Tom did not pay any attention to this – he was far too busy wondering what on earth he was going to say next. He had jumped out of the wagon with only the vaguest notion that he had somehow to delay matters until the rest of the troop arrived, if the carter were to stay alive.

"I'll teach my father English!" said Tom. He knew the brigands didn't have the slightest interest in teaching the carter anything, but he thought it might gain a little time.

"Oh, will you?" murmured the Captain. "Come here, little sprat."

Tom approached the man and tried to smile bravely. The truth was that he felt more nervous than if he were walking into a den of lions that hadn't eaten since Christmas.

"Now if you want your father here to keep his nose, you'd better tell us what's in this little convoy of yours!" The carter didn't know what was being said, but he must have got the gist, for he looked imploringly at Tom.

"It's on the Pope's business," said Tom – thinking with his mouth.

"Ow!" said the carter. The bald brigand had just gouged his cheek again – just for the hell of it.

"Hey! Stop that!" shouted Tom. "I'm telling you!" The brigands laughed.

"So tell us what you are carrying on the Pope's business, little minnow!" said the Captain.

"It's the tithes due to the Pope from all of Champagne and Burgundy," said Tom. Maybe he could buy time by entertaining the brigands with a little foretaste of what they were about to get their hands on. "They say there's more than 20,000 golden crowns, along with jewels and furs and some silver and gold from the Archbishop of Reims's coffers. Perhaps there's nearer 40,000 all told!"

He could see, by the way all the brigands suddenly caught their breath, that he was hitting the right notes. "And there's hams and wines and joints of beef all fit for the Pope's table!" he went on. He could see a sparkle kindle in the eye of each and every brigand, as they imagined the good times they were going to enjoy that very evening. "There's fat geese and ducks and even pheasants – ah! the Pope must eat well for the honour of God," said Tom.

The Captain was smiling dreamily. "Good ... good ... even better than we were expecting ..." he murmured, and then turned to the fat brigand in blue, pointed at Tom and said: "Cut his throat, Jack!" It was, Tom had to admit, a disappointingly sudden end to his little diversion, but Jack didn't seem to be about to cut anyone's throat. He was mumbling something to the Captain – Tom couldn't hear what – until the Captain suddenly turned to a big fellow in a steel jacket and snapped: "Baker! You do it!"

Tom wondered why on earth he hadn't taken the chance

to run away, as the big fellow grabbed him by the throat, but he hadn't. Perhaps he still thought he could play for time. "Wait!" he cried. "Don't you want to know?"

"Argh!" cried the carter. The bald brigand was still keeping score on the poor fellow's cheek.

"Know what?" asked the Captain.

"The truth!" exclaimed Tom. He was clutching at straws. The fellow in the steel jacket had pulled him backwards on to the ground, and now produced a pig-sticking knife about a foot long.

"The truth?" said the Captain. "What truth?" He motioned to Tom's assailant to stop.

"The truth about why they're sending this convoy to the Pope?" yelled Tom in desperation. "It's a trap!"

A shadow had suddenly passed across the otherwise

cheery Captain's face. "What?!" he said. Surprisingly the possibility of a trap had simply not occurred to him before.

But now Tom was yelling in French loud enough for the sergeant-at-arms in the cart to hear: "I'm telling them it's a trap! You'd better come on out and save us!"

"Search the wagons!" cried the Captain, but before a single person could move, there was a cry from behind them. The Englishmen turned to see a troop of forty mounted knights and men-at-arms sweeping down from the wooded slopes above the vineyards. Sir Gervais de Cotigny had finally made it!

"Bells of Damnation!" spat the Captain, and before the spittle was dry on his lips, all hell did indeed seem to be ringing in his ears, as the men-at-arms leapt from their hiding-places in the wagons and charged.

Tom's assailant, the brigand by the name of Baker, was a man of great strength. He used to boast that he was as strong as two oxen. Unfortunately he only had the brains of one ox – but he kept quiet about that, especially as it wasn't even a very bright ox. This factor had two effects on Tom's situation, one bad and one good. The bad effect was that it took Baker a few moments to register what was happening, and as a result he got as far as putting the blade of his pig-sticking knife to Tom's throat and actually cut the skin before he realized that they were being attacked. The good effect was that the moment he did perceive that all was not well he totally forgot about his mission to dispatch Tom (which would have been the sensible thing to do) and he also dropped his pig-sticking knife (which was a really stupid thing to do). While Baker was still gaping at the approaching army, Tom put a foot round his ankles and gave him a push so that the huge fellow toppled forwards into the mud. Tom then snatched up the pig-sticking knife and ran at the two men attacking the carter.

In retrospect, this was a pretty stupid thing to do, and even at the time Tom was surprised to find himself doing it – but, as luck would have it, the two brigands were equally surprised. They stopped trying to educate the carter, turned and fled ... straight into the arms of the sergeant-at-arms and the man in the red tunic, who had come round the other side of the cart.

Tom just had time to see two swords slice through the air and the two brigands stagger and sway in an unreal silence before he felt himself grabbed from behind. He span round, raising the pig-sticking knife above his head, and was just bringing it down into his assailant's heart, when he realized it was Anton. "Whoops!" he said (not a word often used in pitched battle) and neatly diverted the blade, so that his knife stabbed the side of the cart – giving it a nasty wound. "Sorry!" he said to Anton.

"They didn't hurt you?" asked the giant.

"I'm fine!" said Tom. "Did I cut your arm?"

"It's nothing." Anton shrugged – although his sleeve had been slashed and there was a trace of blood on the tear.

It was at this moment that the Captain of the brigands wisely decided it would be a waste of precious time to issue any more commands. The situation was pretty obvious, he thought: it was each man for himself, and may heaven help the hindmost! And since the help of heaven was not something that he himself placed much hope in nowadays, he wheeled his horse around and stuck his spurs into its flanks as far as they would go. Jack, the fat brigand in blue, was the next to follow, and then the others. The mud from the hooves of the horses flew high into the air, and the bandits fled down the road ahead.

Sir Gervais de Cotigny and his troop had no intention of allowing the English to escape, however. An encounter in which the forces of good so magnificently outnumbered the forces of evil was not an opportunity that arose very often, and they were going to make the best of it. Sir Gervais turned his horse's head towards the retreating malefactors, gave a rather over-dramatic signal to his followers, and the whole troop veered off across one of the most highly prized vineyards in the area. The wine of Gevry Chambertin would be in short supply this year.

In the meantime, the grooms had brought up the pack of loose horses, and there followed several minutes of utter confusion, as the men-at-arms who had been hidden in the wagons rushed about looking for their mounts. Anton grunted at Tom and nodded towards the two horses that had belonged to the dead brigands. Now normally such valuable animals would be regarded as the spoils of war, and as such they would be seized by the sergeant-at-arms in the name of the King, but in the current mêlée it was an easy matter for Anton and Tom to sidle over to them and grab the reins. The next moment Tom found himself astride a fiery war-horse, galloping in the midst of an armed troop of Frenchmen in hot pursuit of the English.

It was not at all what he was expecting, and Tom was not at all sure it was what he should have been doing. But he was.

· 41 ·

SQUIRE ALAN AND EMILY HAVE A CLOSE ENCOUNTER WITH A LAVATORY

Ann and Emily had spent the entire morning trapped in the guest room in the tower of the hostelry of the Abbey of St Peter and St Paul. The Abbot Gregory had very kindly paid them a visit shortly after matins. He had been in lively spirits and very sympathetic.

"Abbot Gregory, how kind!" murmured the Lady Emilia de Valois, pretending to stir from her sleep.

"Would you believe it!" the Abbot exclaimed as he swept through the door.

"What?" Ann was already well into her role as Squire Alan.

"It seems that your Ladyship's horses have vanished into thin air!" the Abbott confided to them. "Were they by any chance magical horses? Or perhaps they were simply invisible horses? I confess I am quite at a loss to know where to look for them. What does your Ladyship suggest?"

Emily gritted her teeth. The Abbot's good humour grated like pumice – smooth and diminishing.

"Those thieving rogues at the Golden Cross!" It was Squire Alan who responded. "They'd swear blue was white to get their hands on such a fine pair of thoroughbreds! I'll

211

go and give them a piece of my mind!" And she started making for the door, but the Abbot caught her by the arm.

"Squire Alan!" smiled the Abbot. "It is far too windy a day for either you or her Ladyship to venture outside. I advise you both to sit tight, while I enquire further into this matter."

"That's most kind of you," said Squire Alan. "But I'm not going to let those thieves at the Golden Cross get away with such a cheap trick. I must sort it out myself."

"My advice to you, young man, is to forget about those horses, and concentrate on what you are going to tell the Archbishop of Reims when he arrives later today." The Abbot's smile dropped for a fraction of a second – the merest blink of a snake's eye – and then he was gone.

Squire Alan looked at Emily, and Emily looked at Squire Alan.

"Well! That makes it easy then!" said Squire Alan cheerily.

"Easy?" said Emily.

"Yes," replied Squire Alan. "We've got no alternative. We have to escape!" And with that Ann started pacing around the chamber, examining every floorboard and every nook. She took particular interest in the window and the garde-robe.

Eventually she glanced at Emily and realized that she was sitting on the bed, smiling. "What have you got to smile about?" she asked.

"You," said Emily.

"Well, I'm glad you find me amusing," replied Squire Alan. "But I might point out that we are in what I would call 'a tight spot'. You'd be better employed helping me think of a way to escape."

"Oh! But you've already thought of one!" smiled Emily.

212

"How d'you know?" asked Ann.

"Well, Squire Alan," said Emily, "we women can tell these things."

"Like how?" Squire Alan was genuinely curious.

"For a start you'd been so preoccupied looking for an escape route that you didn't notice me one little bit. You didn't even notice when I was pulling faces at you. Then you suddenly nodded to yourself and looked round at me. So I knew you'd thought of something."

"But you're not going to like it," said Squire Alan.

"I'm going to like it even less when my uncle arrives," said Emily. "What's the plan, Alan?"

Ann moved to the window. "We can't get out of here," she said. "Too much of an overhang – and anyway they'd spot us before we were half-way down."

"Agreed," said Emily.

"The door's barred and bolted. Probably guarded too."

"Agreed."

"But there is one way out."

"Then let's go!" said Emily.

"Are you absolutely sure?"

"I'll do whatever you suggest, Alan," said Emily with a seriousness that took Ann by surprise.

"The only way down is here ..." Squire Alan had pulled back the curtain to the garde-robe. "There's a sort of chute going straight down to the cesspit, but there are foot-holds along the side there ... It's really hard and the chances of falling are not worth thinking about, but we should be able to make it ..."

Emily was looking at the hole in the board of the garde-robe with undisguised horror. There was, indeed, a chute – but it went down a long, long way. It was true that there appeared to be foot-holds down the side, but if you slipped or missed your footing it would mean a quick death. It was also true that the bottom of the chute opened to daylight and the chance of escape, but it also ended in the cesspit.

"It stinks!" said Emily. And it did. "It's disgusting!" she said. And it was. "It's dangerous!" she exclaimed. And she was right.

"But there's no other way," said Squire Alan.

"I'm too scared," said Emily.

"I'll go first," said Ann, "so if you slip at least I'll break your fall."

Emily stared at Squire Alan for some time. Then she walked about the room clenching and unclenching her fists. Eventually she turned and looked directly at her friend. "Alan," said Emily. "Do you think I can do it?"

"I know you can, Emily," said Squire Alan, more confidently than she felt. "We'll do it together." And she put her arm round Emily and gave her a hug. Emily leant against her, and took hold of one of Ann's hands. She was trembling.

"Let's do it, Alan," she whispered, and she raised Ann's hand to her mouth and kissed it.

"The best thing is not to think too hard!" said Squire Alan, disengaging her hand. She was already lifting off the wooden seat of the garde-robe, and a few seconds later she was lowering herself into the stinking shaft that dropped down to the cesspit. "And, whatever you do – don't look down!"

Ann was really saying this to encourage herself. As she braced herself over the sheer drop, the feeling of having nothing below her turned her stomach over like a pancake in a frying pan on Shrove Tuesday. But she pushed her back against one side of the chute and her feet against the other.

Then, cautiously, with one foot she searched for the first ledge, and began to edge her way down …

Ann tried desperately not to think about what lay below her … she tried not to faint from the stench that gripped her by the throat … and she tried to sound confident as she yelled up to Emily: "You can do it! It's not as hard as …" But at that moment, her foot slipped on a particularly slimy ledge and she jerked down several feet before she managed again to jam herself against the sides of the chute. Then she just shut her eyes and waited for the panic inside her to subside.

When she looked up again, Emily was on her way down.

"An inch at a time," Ann told herself.

"I can't get a grip!" Emily shouted from above.

"You're going too fast!" called Squire Alan.

"I can't help it!" cried Emily. She wasn't exactly falling, but then again she wasn't in what one might call a 'controlled descent' either. Ann braced herself across the empty gulf of the chute.

"Ohhh!" cried Emily, as her foot skidded on the slimy foot-hold, and she suddenly accelerated downwards, before finally coming up against Ann's braced body.

"Ow! You've got your feet on mine!" exclaimed Ann.

"Sorry!" said Emily. She shifted her foot on the ledge and Ann moved hers down to the ledge below.

"Just push with your legs and shove your back up against the side," said Squire Alan.

"Got it!" said Emily.

They were both breathing fast, their hearts were thumping in their chests, and – to tell the truth – they were both almost overwhelmed by the awfulness of what they were in the middle of doing. It was awful in the sense that at any moment they could fall backwards forty feet. It was also awful because the further down they got, the more disgusting the chute stank and the slimier the sides got and the more putrid.

Suddenly Emily was surprised to hear Squire Alan laughing to himself.

"W-w-what's the joke?" she asked.

"Well, I was just thinking," replied Squire Alan, "it's a funny place to keep your clothes."

"What?"

"Well – you know – 'garde-robe' – I wouldn't keep my clothes here, would you?"

"I wouldn't keep yesterday's dinner in it!" replied Emily, "and that's a euphemism too!" And suddenly the pair of them were laughing – stretched across the yawning void of the chute of the garde- robe – laughing as if they were hay-making in the sun.

And somehow or other, Ann managed to edge herself down and down, with Emily staying close, and she guided Emily's feet on to the right ledges and talked her down ... and down ... and down ... until they were just above the cesspit.

"Uh oh!" said Squire Alan. The trick would be to jump down and sideways far enough to miss the pit, which was directly under the opening of the chute.

Ann's feet were on a reasonable ledge, and if she could get her hands to it she might have a chance of swinging herself across and away from the cesspit. But try as she might, she simply could not reach the ledge with her hands. And she knew that as soon as she moved her feet away she would fall. So whatever she did she would have to do it very quickly.

"What are you waiting for?" asked Emily. The strain of keeping herself braced across the shaft was beginning to tell.

"I'm trying to work out how to fall," said Squire Alan.

"Falling out of a garde-robe is as easy as falling off a log," replied Emily – not very helpfully.

"It is if you want to land in the cesspit," agreed Squire Alan. And perhaps here I ought to make it clear that falling in a cesspit was even worse than you might imagine. In fact it had often proved a fatal experience for the chosen few who had tried it. Cesspits could be not only very, very smelly and very, very disgusting, they could also be very, very deep, and drowning in a cesspit is not the sort of exit from this world most sensible people would choose.

With thoughts like this uppermost in her mind, Ann felt behind her back, and discovered another ledge there. Again it was slippery and foul, but she thought if she could twist round as she fell she might just be able to swing herself out of harm's way.

"Well, here I go!" she called up. "Wish me luck, Emily!"

"Good luck, Alan!" called Emily.

And Ann jumped, twisting round as she did so. It was a jump that seemed to take for ever. Everything happened as if it were slow motion ... She just managed to get a hand to the ledge, but then her fingers slipped off, with the result that she hardly swung herself out at all and, instead of landing clear of the cesspit, she landed feet first in it. She would have gone right in too – right in over her head – but for the fact that she flung the top half of her body forwards across the edge of the pit, and, as luck would have it, was just able to grab hold of a hunk of weed. She lay there for a moment, half-stunned by the narrowness of her escape, with her legs dangling in the filth, before she was able to drag herself to safety.

"Mother of the Pongs!" exclaimed Squire Alan. Now

she had disturbed the top of the cesspit, the stench was truly unbearable.

"I can't take it!" cried Emily from inside the chute.

"It's quite tricky!" shouted Squire Alan.

"I'm coming!" screamed Emily.

"Wait!" yelled Squire Alan. But it was too late! Emily jumped, twisted around, caught the slippery ledge with the tips of her delicate fingers and swung herself elegantly across the cesspit and landed with her feet firmly on the ground.

"That was fantastic!" grinned Squire Alan.

"Let's get out of here!" said Emily.

They found themselves in a narrow space between the Abbey walls and the next building. It took them two steps to get out of the alley and into the street. It took them two glances to make sure the coast was clear. And it took them two minutes to run down the street, round the corner, down another side-street, and out on to the bank of the River Seine, which runs through the middle of the city of Troyes.

The riverbank was not the cleanest place in Troyes, because the good citizens were in the habit of dumping most of their waste into the river and on to its edges, and each house that backed on to the river had its stinking pile of refuse and ordure. The river, however, was still a river, and without another word the two fugitives jumped simultaneously into the water. It took a long time before they had rid themselves of the stench of the garde-robe – and to tell the truth, the smell stayed in their nostrils for some hours.

"I'm cold," said Emily. Squire Alan put a wet arm around her.

"Situation, Alternatives, Action," said Squire Alan,

trying to sound cheerful. "Situation: we've escaped, but the Abbot is bound to send someone after us as soon as he discovers. Alternatives: we either make a dash for it now and get as far away from the city as we can, or we lie low until the hunt dies down. Action ..."

"Let's go!" said Emily.

"Let's go!" said Ann, but Emily had caught her arm.

"Alan," she said.

"Yes?" said Squire Alan.

"Nothing," said Emily.

· 42 ·

BANDIT COUNTRY

The village of Gevry Chambertin is surrounded by well-drilled vineyards. The ranks of vines extend like troops on parade – disciplined and ordered. The countryside all around, on the other hand, is wild and unruly – perfect bandit country, in fact. And this was where Tom now found himself – against his better judgement.

To tell the truth he couldn't understand why Anton was so keen to join in the search for the rest of the English bandits who were hiding up in the hills. "It's none of our business," Tom had argued. "We've got horses now! We ought to press on to Avignon!" But Anton would not listen.

And now here they were riding up a narrow, wooded road, that corkscrewed between grey crags and outbreaks of rock. Every so often a ravine would open up beside the track, and Tom would glimpse a stream far below, rushing headlong in a frantic bid to escape from the rocks and crags. Even Tom, with his lack of experience, could see that it was the kind of countryside where a band of desperate villains could disappear as quick as weevils back into a biscuit. He could also see that it was the perfect terrain for an ambush ...

He glanced across at Anton, but the giant's broad face

was as placid as always – until he felt Tom looking at him, and it broke into a smile:

"These'll get us to the Pope in fine style!" he chuckled, patting his horse's neck.

"And what's your business with the Pope?" asked the man in front. He was a prelate of some sort – a high-ranking churchman. He was dressed entirely in red and wore his hood well over his head so that his face was scarcely visible. His voice carried authority and power.

"We seek the Pope's mercy," replied Anton simply.

"The Holy Father is full of mercy, my son. What have you done wrong?" asked the prelate. He was every inch a pontiff – a lord of the Church – and it struck Tom as odd that he should be on this expedition at all. Another odd thing about him was that his voice and his manner reminded Tom of somebody else – but he could not quite place who.

"We have done nothing wrong," said Anton. "We are going to ask the Holy Father's mercy upon our village and on all the poor farmers of the Champagne, who are robbed by the English and taxed by our own lords until we have nothing left to live on – let alone pay our tithes."

The burly prelate in red snorted. It may have been a laugh. "The Holy Father may be merciful," he said, "but even he cannot spare you what is due to God!"

As he said this, there was a rumbling from overhead, and the entire troop looked up to see … well, they couldn't see anything really because of an overhanging ledge. But they could tell something was coming down towards them – fast! By the time they could see it (it was a boulder about the size of a house) it was too late to do anything other than decide to get the hell out of the way! There was, however, no time to actually get out of the way. The

boulder seemed to hang in the air for a moment, and the men just seemed to sit there on their horses – frozen in time – before it fell.

From where he was at the rear of the column, Tom

couldn't see exactly what happened, but he could hear the screams of those who had survived. He glanced back up at the cliff and could see men looking over the top, but before his lips could even form the word "ambush", a frenzy of yelling and screaming announced that the boulder had now started to roll back down through the column towards the rear.

"Quick! Anton!" cried Tom, as he wheeled his horse around. But the boulder didn't want to be left behind! It began to pick up speed as it careered towards them – turning in the air like a vast quoit, knocking men and horses out of its way like skittles.

Tom dug his heels into his horse's flanks, but there seemed to be no escape. To the left, the hill dropped away into the steep ravine, and to the right the forest was impenetrable ... except ... what was that light through the trees? Tom kicked at his horse and urged the terrified animal into the undergrowth. The horse bucked and tried to turn back, but Tom kept its head forward and urged it through the saplings and brush, and finally broke through into a glade. Anton and a few others were hard on his heels, as the boulder blundered past, catching the last unfortunate horseman a glancing blow that sent rider and horse spinning through the air and down into the ravine.

The survivors hunched over their horses' shoulders. The thundering they could now hear was neither the pounding of the boulder, as it careered on its way, nor the echo of their horses' hooves against the rock-face: it was the thumping of their own hearts.

"Everyone all right?" asked a fresh-faced youth, who was wearing the livery of Sir Gervais de Cotigny. There were nods and grunts. "They may have more surprises in store for us," he went on, "so we'll go round by the other road – take them from behind!"

"Who will?" asked a heavy-set man in a mail coat with a bandage tied round his head.

"We will!" said the fresh-faced youth. He wore his hair in a cloud of curly locks.

"Maybe you will," said the man with the bandage. "I won't."

"Surely you're not going to let these English scum get away with a stunt like this?" said the youth.

"Exactly!" The prelate in the red robes had regained some of his authority. His hood had slipped back off his forehead, exposing his face for the first time. He was white-skinned and wore his fair hair in a tonsure. And the devil of it was that Tom felt certain he knew him, even though he had never seen him before. And before Tom could think more about the puzzle, the prelate had slipped the hood back over his head. Only his voice remained to nag Tom's memory.

But the man with the bandaged head was still complaining: "I agreed to fight alongside fifty men-at-arms," he was saying. "I never agreed to risk my neck with half-a-dozen novices – one of 'em a churchman! and one a child!"

"I'm not a child!" exclaimed Tom.

"And we're not just half a dozen!" shouted the youth, his fresh face blushing as crimson as the robes of the burly priest. "There's ten of us! And he's worth two!" Here he pointed at Anton.

"Well, good luck to you!" shouted the man with the bandage. And without more ado, he turned his horse about and galloped out of the glade and down the path in the wake of the boulder.

"Come back here, you rogue!" shouted the prelate, but the man had gone.

"Listen!" said the youth. "I am Jean – son of Sir Gervais de Cotigny! Heaven alone knows whether my father is still alive, but I swear this: I shall not leave this wood until I have avenged this cowardly attack! When we rode out, we pledged ourselves to rid these hills of the scourge of bandits, and shame on us if we turn back at the first blow!"

There was a murmur of slightly reluctant approval for these words. Then the churchman spoke: "God will reward us for our deeds today! Have no fear!" And somehow, whether they really thought it was a good idea or not, when Jean de Cotigny spurred his horse and cried: "Follow me!" – everybody did.

· 43 ·

BROTHER ANSELM GETS
THE BLAME

"What did you say, Brother Anselm?" The Abbot Gregory knew he was about to enjoy himself. He might be angry. He might be furious. He might be beside himself with rage. But these emotions were emotions he enjoyed – they made him feel alive and in charge of his life for a change.

"I said," repeated Anselm the Monk in a voice so small he obviously hoped nobody would hear it, "they don't seem to be there."

"Don't ... seem ... to ... be ... there?" the Abbott hit each word as he if he were hitting a nail into Anselm's coffin. "My dear Brother Anselm, either you haven't looked properly, or ..." – and here he drew a deep breath – "... or they have escaped. I trust the problem is the former: you haven't looked properly."

"Alas no! I searched the room high and low." Brother Anselm's voice appeared to be coming from under his sandals. He had deliberately put on his old sandals instead of his fine new shoes – in case the Abbot Gregory decided to confiscate whatever he was wearing on his feet. To have lost his new shoes would have been more than Anselm could have borne. "They have definitely ... gone ..."

"Anselm," said the Abbot Gregory after some moments

226

of silence, "if I find …" He got up and started to walk about the room. "If … I find …" Oh dear, thought Anselm, he's repeating himself – that's a bad, bad sign. "… That you … have lost this monastery the chance of winning the Archbishop of Reims's favour … I …" The Abbot was weighing his words very carefully now. "I … will personally see to it … that you …" How bad could a punishment get? wondered Anselm. The Abbot couldn't take his shoes away from him, because he didn't know about them. What could he possibly do that could make his life any more burdensome than it already was?

"… I will personally see to it that you are stripped of every single privilege; that you are stripped of your office as cellarer and that you are confined to your cell for the next six months!" That should do it, that would certainly make his life more miserable than it already was.

"But they were locked in, Father!" he pleaded. "I made sure they were secure – I did everything I could!"

"Clearly …" said the Abbot, "you did not …" He turned from looking out of the window and went up close to the penitent monk, so that his face was only a few inches away, and then he bellowed: "OTHERWISE THEY WOULDN'T HAVE ESCAPED! YOU BLUNDER-HEAD! YOU BRAINLESS LUMP OF LARD! YOU EMPTY-HEADED APOLOGY FOR A MAN OF GOD!"

"Tell me what more I could have done?" cried Anselm the Monk. Could that be a note of anger in his voice? "What more could I possibly have done?" he continued. "In the name of God! Why should I be held responsible for every single thing that goes wrong in this monastery? Perhaps they're magicians? Perhaps their horses *were* invisible? Perhaps they made themselves invisible too?! In the name of the Holy Saints! I AM NOT TO BLAME!" It

227

was the first time he had ever raised his voice to the Abbot. It was the first time he had ever stood his ground. The Abbot Gregory smiled a thin, unpleasant smile. He knew – without a shadow of doubt – that the next hour promised to rate among the most pleasurable in his life. To be presented with such a God-given opportunity of heaping abuse on Brother Anselm was something not to be rushed – it was something to be savoured. He would tease it out, enjoy every minute – and, finally, crush Brother Anselm like the cockroach he was.

· 44 ·

THE TOWN WHERE
EVERYONE IS DRUNK

Emily couldn't understand why Squire Alan was so cross with her. It seemed there was nothing she could do to please him. And she was trying very hard – which was not something that the Lady Emilia de Valois was in the habit of doing. She was much more used to *other* people trying hard to please *her*.

Take for example their escape from the Abbey of St Peter and St Paul: Emily had not once complained about the stench on her clothes from the chute of the garde-robe – nor had she complained about their exit from the city of Troyes in a cart of vegetables. It was certainly not a mode of transport she would normally choose, and yet Emily had breathed not a word about her discomfort as they lay together under the cabbages and carrots, with the smell of earth in their nostrils.

She had done her very best to remain bright and cheerful, even when Squire Alan had insisted that they jump from the moving cart into a muddy ditch. Emily's clothes had never been so soiled and crumpled and yet she never murmured a single complaint. She smiled at Alan and followed him for mile after mile across a vast plain, where the earth turned red and the road became a scar across the landscape – stretching on, as far as Emily could

see, for ever. Yet she kept smiling and even trying to
please him. She let him sit on one of her gowns when they
couldn't find anywhere dry. She gave him the largest piece
of sausage when they ate their lunch. Emily scarcely

understood herself. Perhaps most remarkable of all, she even managed to retain her temper when they reached Tonnerre.

Emily had been looking forward to getting to the charming little town of Tonnerre. Above the warren of little streets towered a new church, still under construction, a sure sign that the good townsfolk of Tonnerre still had money to jingle in their pockets despite the wars that were ravaging other parts of France. On the opposite side of town, the long roof of the Hospital showed they were also rich enough to look after their sick. The Hospital was one of the wonders of modern fourteenth-century France. It housed no less than forty beds, all neatly arranged in wooden alcoves against the walls, each with its own curtain, shelf and coffer. The townspeople of Tonnerre joked that it was worth getting ill just to enjoy such luxury!

But the real reason Emily had been looking forward to arriving at the town of Tonnerre was neither of these things. Emily had been looking forward to reaching the Hole of Dionne.

The Hole of Dionne was a pool of clear crystal water, that surged out of the hillside. Its waters were an extraordinary greeny blue and they were contained within a perfectly circular pool, surrounded with stone paving, where the women of Tonnerre could come and wash their clothes and themselves. There was a slate roof to keep the weather off and, in the winter, three roaring fires kept burning through the day to dry the clothes and to warm the womenfolk.

In her present state, the thought of this crystal pool had been keeping Emily going for many miles. She imagined removing her stained outer garments and

231

washing them in those limpid waters. She even imagined waiting until the menfolk had all been chased away, as they were once or twice a week, and then dipping herself into the clean, clear water of the pool.

So it was, indeed, a remarkable achievement that Emily did not completely and utterly lose her temper when she and Squire Alan finally arrived at Tonnerre, and found the town in a mess.

Back in the fourteenth century, litter was not usually considered a problem. In fact the word was not used to mean "a mess" until four hundred years later. In Tom's day a "litter" meant a bed or something rich people were carried around in. But it's a good word, and the streets of Tonnerre was certainly littered – but not with rubbish. The streets of Tonnerre were littered with bodies. Bodies lay sprawled in the narrow alleys, heaped in doorways and slumped against walls – some of them dead asleep, some of them dead drunk, and some of them just plain dead.

The Hospital was no longer full of sick townsfolk but was now chock-a-block with drunken men-at-arms snoring in their sleep. I'm not saying some of them weren't sick, but – if they were – it was self-induced sickness, and the place stank of wine and vomit.

Worst of all, even the Hole of Dionne was strewn with armed men, sprawling next to empty pots. A dozen large wine barrels lay abandoned around the edge of the pool, and in the clear waters of the pool itself a body was floating, bumping up against the drain.

Emily's dream of Tonnerre collapsed before her eyes, and yet she did her best to hide her disgust and vexation. She turned to Squire Alan. "I'm so sorry!" she said – as if the drunken soldiers were all her fault. "It's a beautiful place really."

"Well, good luck!" replied Squire Alan.

Emily grabbed his sleeve. "Where are you going?"

"Brittany," said Squire Alan.

"But you can't leave me now!" exclaimed Emily.

"I told you I'd have to leave you as soon as we found the English army," replied Alan. "And here they are!"

"The English army?" Emily looked around at the comatose soldiery. Of course! That's who they were!

"The King is probably quartered in the castle," Squire Alan was continuing. "Let's hope he's not drunk too," and he turned to go again. But Emily was clutching at him.

"Alan! You can't leave me here … among these scum …" Emily put her arms around the squire. "Please, Alan! Help me find the King!"

Squire Alan frowned. "Emily … I told you I'd help you find the English army but then you'd be on your own. You know I can't stay!"

"Ahhh! Who's this then?" a rough-looking fellow suddenly lurched out of a doorway and stood in front of Emily, peering drunkenly into her face.

"Get out of my way!" said Emily.

A few of the other bodies were, by this time, beginning to groan and turn over.

"What's a nice little lady like you doing here then?" grinned the man. His eyes were bloodshot, his breath smelt like the Fleet Ditch, and his hose were hanging half-way down his legs. He now had his hand on Emily's petite shoulder.

"Take your hand away!" said Squire Alan.

"Make me!" sneered the man. He was about half as tall again as Ann and about twice as wide. Ann squared up to him – willing herself back into her role as Squire

233

Alan as she did so. But before she could swing the punch that she undoubtedly intended to swing, the man crumpled to the floor with a silent scream.

"You've got to protect me, Alan!" said Emily. Ann looked from Emily to the man whom Emily had just kneed in the groin. He lay squirming and gasping on the floor. Emily gave him another kick for good measure, and the two turned and ran.

"I don't think you need much protection ..." said Squire Alan some time later.

"I do! I need *you*!" panted Emily, as they ran through the awakening revellers. "We're a team, you and I!"

They had run up the narrow path that led to the castle, and were now standing outside the main gate. A sentry was on duty, but even he appeared to be a little tipsy. Emily slipped her arm into Squire Alan's.

"Alan," she said. "I don't want you to go to Brittany. I want you to stay here!"

"But I told you!" said Squire Alan, disengaging himself from Emily's arm. "I injured the young Earl of Gisbourne in a practice tournament. The Duke of Lancaster wants me put in irons!"

"I thought you said the Earl of Grossmont?" said Emily.

"I mean the young Earl of Grossmont!" It wasn't like Squire Alan to forget his own stories.

"I'll speak to my uncle, the King!" replied Emily. "I'll sort it out ..." And Emily put her arms around Squire Alan. For the briefest of moments, Ann felt the urge to tell Emily everything – but again she stopped herself. It was almost as if she needed Emily's belief in her as Squire Alan in order to carry on.

"No! You can't!" said Squire Alan, trying to break

free. "It's more complex than that! I can't go back! The Duke mustn't catch me! I've got to …" But that was as far as he got, for the Lady Emilia de Valois had suddenly collapsed into Squire Alan's arms, and nothing Ann could do seemed to revive her.

"You'd better bring her inside," said the guard, who although he had drunk the best part of a flask of wine, was a man of great compassion. As a matter of fact he was, probably, the worst guard in the world. In almost every way he was unqualified for the position. He wasn't aggressive. He wasn't mean-minded. He wasn't vindictive or keen to see others suffer. What was worse, he was also interested in far too many things other than guarding. In fact, the only reason he was on guard-duty that morning was because everyone else was far too drunk.

"Here, give her a little of this remedy," he said, offering a small phial to Squire Alan. "It's a concoction of my own. Are you interested in herbs and medicine? I am. Very interested."

But right then, the only thing that Ann was interested in was how she was going to get away before the Duke of Lancaster caught her and sent her back to England.

· 45 ·

TWO BANDITS DOWN

The wooded hills above the town of Nuits St Georges, offer splendid facilities for the professional bandit. The woods provide plenty of hiding-places, and the hills give grand vistas, which the bandit can either enjoy for their own sake or for the sake of keeping watch on all the approaching paths. In fact, it was a mystery to Tom how he and his companions were able to get so far into this territory without being spotted.

"Stop!" hissed Tom suddenly. "Listen!" They could hear the distant strains of a popular English song, apparently being sung by a chorus of chickens.

"No wonder they're brigands," muttered Tom.

"What d'you mean?" asked Anton.

"Well, they'd never make any money as minstrels," replied Tom.

As Tom and his companions came over the crest of a hill, the singing got louder and then they caught sight of them: eight or nine brigands straggling back to their hide-out – clearly in high spirits.

At that moment, however, one of the brigands discovered that the wine-skin he'd been given was already empty. "Goats of God!" he grumbled – it was the fat brigand in the blue surcoat. "That's as much use as a piss-pot at sea!" and he flung the empty skin into the bushes, turned to grab another from the rogue behind, and, in doing so, caught sight of Tom and his party.

The brigand in the blue surcoat didn't shout: "Look out! They're after us!" or anything helpful like that. He simply turned and took to his horse's heels. The other brigands registered the expression on their comrade's face, but by the time they had turned to see what had caused it Tom and his party were upon them!

Without a moment's hesitation, every single brigand decided that cowardice was the better part of valour. The ground shook, the dirt flew up from under the hooves. Branches lashed riders and horses, as if whipping them on faster and faster, and Tom clung to the straining neck of his horse, hoping against hope that he could stay in the saddle, as they charged after the bandits.

A mile down the track, however, the way split – and so did the brigands. Tom and Anton, the prelate in red and one of the sergeants-at-arms followed to the right. The leading brigand twisted round in his saddle and yelled a curse at them. It was an elaborate curse – something about hoping they perished before their time in some sort of ... But they never found out what, because one of the other brigands interrupted:

"Look out!" he called. The brigand stopped, mid-curse, and turned to see a low branch overhanging the track. He began to duck, but too late! He rode straight into the branch, and the impact lifted him clean out of his saddle and threw him under the hooves of his companions' horses.

One of the horses reared. The next ran into it, stumbled and shot its rider straight over its ears, smashing him head first into a tree trunk. The man was knocked out cold. The remaining two brigands had just enough presence of mind to duck under the branch and gallop away.

The sergeant-at-arms leapt on to the brigand who had fallen under the horses' hooves. His dagger was already slicing through the air before the bandit had even begun to draw what was to prove his last breath. In the meantime, the red-robed prelate, with surprising agility and aggressiveness for so high-ranking a churchman, ran to where the second brigand was slumped against the tree trunk, with blood streaming from his head. Tom didn't see what happened, because he was already charging under the low branch, in hot pursuit of the two remaining brigands. All he heard were the muffled cries for mercy of the brigand, the curses of the prelate – that voice! Tom was certain he knew it! – and the shouts of Anton riding heaven-and-hell-for-leather beside him as they rode deeper and deeper into bandit country.

• 46 •

EMILY HAS NO LUCK
WITH THE KING OF ENGLAND

King Edward III had a hangover. Nobody mentioned it, but everybody knew he had, because he was even more irritable than usual. There had been a time, when he was younger, when the King had been a pleasant companion. He had even been quite fun at times. But he was now increasingly morose. The siege of Reims had not helped one little bit.

The whole idea had been that since he was styled King of England and of France, he should actually take over France. It had seemed a pretty good wheeze. The current King of France, King Jean, had been captured at the Battle of Poitiers, and was now safely in prison in England. France itself was in most satisfactory chaos, with warring factions and uprisings adding to the havoc and devastation caused by the English raids. Under such circumstances, Edward had been advised, the people of France would be only too thankful to welcome a strong leader who could pull the country together. And who better than himself – King Edward III?

So he had brought this vast army of ten thousand men to sit outside the gates of Reims, where the French traditionally crowned their kings. There he had waited for the grateful people to throw open their city and welcome

239

him in as their saviour. No less a person than his cousin, Jean de Craon, the Archbishop of Reims, had assured him that this is what would inevitably happen. It hadn't.

Edward had sat outside Reims, like a stuffed goose (as he put it), waiting and waiting, and nothing had happened. They couldn't fight anyone because nobody would come out and fight them. And all the time, the great army of ten thousand men needed feeding and paying, and tempers got shorter as supplies got scarcer, until it became quite clear to the King that he was going to look like a complete idiot. It made him furious!

Then, however, by a wonderful bit of good luck, the Duke of Burgundy did a very foolish thing. He sent ambassadors to the English King offering to pay him a large sum of money in return for being left in peace. Edward didn't think twice. He ordered his army to pack their bags and straightaway march down into Burgundy. This, you see, improved his bargaining position no end.

Nevertheless, abandoning hope of being crowned King of France was a bitter pill for Edward to swallow. The whole enterprise had cost more than he could ever hope to pay off, and he had been counting on all those extra revenues he'd get as King of France. Now all he could do was try to wring as much money out of people like the Duke of Burgundy as he could and then go home. The whole thing was a shambles. No wonder he was mammothly pissed off.

And on top of all that he now had a dreadful hangover.

"I don't think this is a good moment to talk to the King," whispered Squire Alan. Ann had been trying to get away ever since they first arrived, but something had kept preventing her. Emily herself had become so clinging that – short of physical violence – there was no way Ann could break free.

"No! You mustn't leave me, Alan!" Emily pleaded. "Not yet! Just wait until I've spoken to my uncle, the King. You can keep out of sight ... The Duke of Lancaster need never see you ..." And she had buried her face in Squire Alan's arms and sobbed her heart out there.

What could Ann do? She sighed. She swore this was the last time she'd ever help a spoilt rich brat like Emily, but she went with her. By good fortune, it seemed that the Duke of Lancaster was away raiding somewhere, and would not return for a day or two – so now, here they were, in the King's audience chamber, waiting for the herald to announce Emily's presence.

"You won't go away?" asked Emily.

"No. I'll stay here until you've spoken to the King," replied Squire Alan, "but then I'm off. No six ways about it."

"Shth Lady Milia De Valwarr, y' Mashipsty!" the herald suddenly declaimed. I forgot to say that while King Edward III had a hangover, he was in a considerably better state than most of his courtiers. They were still drunk. The problem was that when the English army had taken over the pretty town of Tonnerre, they had discovered no less than 30,000 tonnes of wine all neatly stored in the cellars of the town. It was more wine than the English soldiery ever thought could possibly exist. And it was good wine. They tasted it. Within an hour of taking over the city, the entire army was drunk.

King Edward had bowed to the inevitable. There was no way he could stop his hungry, exhausted and demoralized army from drinking their way through this glorious treasure trove. So he decided to let them do it. They could have four or five days of solid drinking. There would be plenty of time to sober up and then get on with the serious business of blackmailing the Duke of Burgundy.

As the drunken herald finished his announcement, fifty red-rimmed eyes turned to look at Emily. Squire Alan shrank back into the shadows.

Emily had cleaned herself, and had found a skivvy to press her gown and dress her hair. She looked, once again, every inch the lady that she was. Watching from the corner of the chamber, Ann marvelled at Emily's charisma as she stepped forward to greet the King of England.

"Ah ... the Lady Emily, niece ..." muttered the King, closing his eyes and passing his hand across his forehead, as if to wipe away the pain throbbing between his temples.

"Your Majesty!" said Emily bowing low. "It has been many years since I have had the pleasure of gazing upon your ..."

"Just get to the point," said the King, "I feel like a rat's codpiece!"

"If you please, Majesty," continued the Lady Emilia de Valois, "I have a request that I should be ..."

"Just say it!" groaned the King.

"My brother, Guillaume de Valois, is at present a prisoner in London, awaiting payment of his ransom ..."

"A useful sum, as I remember." The King's eyes rolled up into his lids as he recalled the amount he had demanded for the release of Guillaume de Valois. He remembered it well – it would be enough to rebuild a whole castle.

"I have reason to believe his life is in danger!" said Emily. "Since my father's death the family estate has had no one to guard it. There are many who would like to get their hands on it ..." Edward III nodded sagely. He was one of them. "My brother is unable to assert his rights from his prison in England, and I fear there are those who wish to take advantage and steal his lands and property!" Edward III nodded again. He knew exactly what she meant. "But

242

worst of all, uncle, there is one who, I believe, is plotting against my brother's life – seeking to kill him while he languishes in an English prison and then assume his birthright ..."

"Enough!" snapped the King. Then he leant forward and whispered something into Emily's ear. The rest of the court could not hear what was said, but I can reveal to you that what the King of England muttered into his niece's ear was this: "Before you say something you might regret, Emilia, I must warn you to put these foolish thoughts aside. No one intends to kill your brother while he lies in prison. It would be most dishonourable. Besides, he is here ..."

It was the first time that Ann had ever seen Emily taken aback. She gasped, turned pale and started to tremble like a leaf.

"What!" exclaimed Emily. "My brother is here!"

But she did not get any further, nor did she hear the King mutter: "No! Not your brother ... I meant the person you are talking about ..." because at that very moment someone she knew only too well entered the audience chamber and smiled at Emily. Emily's heart hit the floor with a clunk – actually she'd just knocked over a stool – and her eyeballs leapt out of their sockets as if they were trying to get a better view at the man who stood there before the King of England – the man whom she least wanted to see in all the world: Jean de Craon, the Archbishop of Reims.

"Uncle!" she murmured.

"Emilia!" said the Archbishop. "How good of you to seek me out like this."

HOW TOM LEARNT
ANTON'S TERRIBLE SECRET
AND MET SOMEONE HE DIDN'T
WANT TO

"We've lost them!" muttered Anton. And it was true. He and Tom had chased the two brigands up on to a high hill, crowned by a deserted castle. One tower had fallen into ruins and the other was roofless and stuck up like a single broken tooth in a skeleton's mouth. Dense woods stretched right up to the crumbling walls, and as they gazed forlornly at this desolate ruin Tom suddenly realized their predicament. They had both been so intent on the chase that neither had realized the sun was getting dangerously low on the horizon, and the shadows beneath the trees were growing thicker by the minute.

"We'd better find somewhere to spend the night," said Anton.

"I'm glad you're here, Anton," said Tom.

Above the trees, they could just make out the weather vane of a small chapel that stood alone, under the lee of the deserted castle. "We'll head for the church," said Anton.

There was a chill in the air as they rode into the untended graveyard that was overgrown with bindweed and bramble. Tom couldn't help feeling that the silent tombstones were guards on sentry duty, but Anton was already at the chapel door, rattling the lock.

"I've had enough of sleeping in graveyards," said Tom.

"Then in we go!" said Anton, and he heaved against the heavy door. It creaked a couple of times but stood firm. Tom joined in. Again the door creaked: once, twice and then – quite suddenly – there was a splitting sound and the wood gave way around the latch.

"Anton!" exclaimed Tom, as he peered into the dark interior. "There's someone in there!"

"It's just the rats," laughed Anton.

"Hedgehogs from Hell!" exclaimed one of the rats.

"That's no rat!" muttered Anton.

"I'm not so sure!" said Tom. "I know that voice!"

They edged their way into the darkness. There was a frantic scuffling and then a crash as something fell over. "Boiling bed-bugs!" exclaimed the voice. Tom was just about to call out, when he realized that a figure was rushing towards them. He felt a blow across his temple and the next minute found himself reeling to the floor, but at the same moment he heard a cry and a crunch as Anton brought the man down. "I've got money! And wine! Barrels of it! You can have it all! Don't hurt me! Aaagh!" whimpered the man in English.

"What's he say?" asked Anton. Tom translated into French.

"You scoundrel!" It was as if all Anton's gentleness had suddenly evaporated in the heat of the moment, cooled in the chill air and was now pouring back down as distilled hatred. "You offer me the things you've stolen!? You leave our women and children to starve, and then try to buy your own miserable life with their goods! You are not worth the air you breathe!"

"Mercy!" cried the man, who needed no translation to understand that Anton was not wishing him Good Luck

245

Accompanied by a Long and Healthy Life. An impression which Anton reinforced by drawing his knife.

"Wait!" cried Tom.

Now it so happened that – at that very moment – a sort of miracle occurred. The setting sun had dropped so low that one ray suddenly struck through the little window of the chapel. It hit a white tombstone on the wall and shone down on to the altar steps to reveal Anton – half kneeling on a corpulent figure. It was the fat brigand in the blue surcoat, and the sun's ray lit up the man's face sufficiently for Tom to be able to see who it was.

"I knew I knew that voice!" Tom exclaimed. The brigand's eyes flicked momentarily away from the knife in Anton's hand to Tom.

"Tom!" he gasped.

"Sir John Hawkley!" cried Tom.

"Die like a pig!" yelled Anton. The words jerked Tom out of his astonishment – he leapt forward and grabbed Anton's arm.

"What are you doing, Tom?" cried the giant.

"I know him!" said Tom.

"You know this piece of vermin?!" exclaimed Anton.

"His name is Sir John Hawkley!"

"He's a brigand and a thief and a murderer!" said Anton.

"But ..." said Tom.

"But what?" said Anton.

Sir John, who had understood not a word of all this, turned on his most remorseful look for Tom's benefit. "Tom! By all the Balls in Bethlehem! As I love you more than my life! Ask this oaf to let me go!" And he emitted such a pitiable whine that I believe the Devil himself would have had second thoughts about casting him into hell.

Anton twisted Sir John's face back so he was looking him straight in the eyes. "Before I kill you, I want you to understand what you and your fellow scum have done to my country!" Anton growled. "Tell him what I just said, Tom!" Tom duly translated.

"Satan's Sunday Stew!" cried the knight. "I swear I'll never steal another chicken, Tom! Tell him to leave me alone!"

"You and your miserable companions found our country rich and peaceable – our barns were full of grain and our cellars overflowed with wine. You came and stole everything from us! Tell him, Tom!"

Tom translated.

"Tell him I'll change! Tell him I'm your friend!" yelled Sir John. If Sir John had been well into his cups before, he was stone cold sober now.

"The farmers don't dare to till their land for fear of you!" continued Anton. "And the fields, where wheat and barley once ripened in the sun, are now overgrown with weeds! Villages are deserted! Fine farmhouses abandoned!" All Anton's pent-up rage, that had built up over the last several years, was suddenly roaring out. "You have turned my country into a place of fear and emptiness! Tell him. Tom!" And Tom translated.

"It's not just me!" exclaimed Sir John. "It's the others!"

But Anton had not finished. "And where you could not scare the farmers off the land, you have simply burnt it – so that all one can see for miles around is scorched earth and blackened homes! You have brought misery and death to my people!" Anton had Sir John by the throat and the great man's eyes were bulging.

"Devil's Dumplings!" croaked Sir John. "He's choking me, Tom! Do something! Save me!"

"You have killed our menfolk, and shamed our women! You have slaughtered our wives and murdered our daughters!" Anton was now banging Sir John's head against the ground in rhythm to his words.

"Help me! Tom! For the Pity of Christ's Wounds! Help me!"

"You killed my wife!" bellowed Anton. "You killed her before my own eyes! And ..." His voice suddenly went razor-quiet as he said: "And you murdered my daughter! In front of me! You fiend from hell!"

"It wasn't me, Tom!" Sir John's voice could hardly leave his throat. "Honest as St Peter at the Gate!" His colour had gone bright red and his thoughts were clearly straying towards the after-life. "Tell him it was someone else! I didn't kill his wife and daughter!"

"To slit your throat would be too good for you!" roared Anton.

"Please stop him!" whimpered the knight.

"Anton!" cried Tom. "Don't!"

Anton turned to look at Tom. The hatred in his eyes was so extraordinary, so intense – so unlike the Anton that Tom had come to know – that Tom felt his insides turn to ice.

"Give me one good reason why we shouldn't slit this dog from belly to snout and pull out his insides so he can watch while the rats gnaw his entrails?" Anton's face had gone white, and his voice had turned cold and eerily controlled. "Give me one good reason why we shouldn't torture him and then kill him so slowly that he feels every inch of death? Give me one good reason why we should not inflict the pain and suffering on him that he has inflicted on others?"

"Because ..." Tom really felt there was no answer. "Because surely God'll punish him for any evil he's done on

248

this earth. We shouldn't put ourselves in the place of God – to be judges of good and evil!"

"You're wrong, Tom!" exclaimed Anton. "If we don't judge good and evil ourselves, then there is no hope in the world! If we deny ourselves the right to say what is right and what is wrong, then this hell's spawn …" and here he banged Sir John's head on the stone step a couple of times for emphasis, "and his kind will rule our world and make Hell on Earth!"

"But Sir John isn't evil …" said Tom. "He's a rogue … he's a coward … he's an ungrateful fat-head … but he's not evil!"

"What's that you're saying?" gasped Sir John. It was lucky he couldn't understand French, thought Tom.

"I'll tell you how I saw my child die with my own eyes," whispered Anton. "The English devils had overrun our village, they dug a pit and in it they put a great fire. They told us that they called this pit 'Hell'. Then they ordered us villagers to stand in front of them – one by one – and demanded from each of us a ransom of two marks or the equivalent in chickens, pigs, cheese and eggs. If any villager could not pay, the English would whoop and laugh and shout out: 'To Hell with him!' and they would throw the poor wretch into the fiery pit!

"When I was summoned and asked to pay the ransom, I paid up, although it left me and my family with exactly nothing. I had no idea, you see, that they would demand the same ransom of my wife and daughter … I stood there and watched as they called up first my wife and then my daughter. 'No!' I cried out. 'You have already taken for them! I gave you all I had!' But I might as well have been shouting at the Devil himself.

" 'To Hell with her!' they cried and threw my wife into

the pit. And then my daughter stood before them ... my sweet daughter ..." Anton's voice faltered. He shut his eyes, and Sir John struggled but was held down by a huge hand.

"But it wasn't Sir John ..." Tom ventured. "He didn't actually throw your daughter into the pit. It was someone else."

"Do you think there is any difference between them?" asked Anton. Sir John had given up struggling and was lying as still as a mouse in a cat's claw. Sweat was glistening on his temples. "No! They are all one and the same! Don't you remember? They have ceased to be human. Oh! They may look like humans! They may laugh and cry and swear like human beings, but they are really tigers! And we must cease to be human too. We must choose to be tigers like them or be the dumb oxen that the tigers will tear to pieces!"

"We can't kill him," said Tom quietly.

Anton looked at his young friend for some moments and then asked: "Give me one reason why not?"

"Because he is Sir John Hawkley," replied Tom quietly, "and I am his squire."

AVIGNON

· 48 ·

TOM AND ANTON COME UP AGAINST A BIG PROBLEM

Tom was not at all sure that he liked Avignon. He had been to busy cities before, but never one quite as busy as this. It was as if the number of people and the number of houses didn't quite add up – which was exactly the case. Even though the place was a permanent construction site, with new buildings and works down every street and at every corner, there were still not nearly enough buildings to house all the people who had to live there.

The truth was that Avignon was not really designed to be the home of such a great and magnificent personage as the Pope – complete with all his chaplains and secretaries and lawyers and doctors and stewards and attendants and cooks and pantrymen and porters and cellarers and blacksmiths and soldiers and sergeants-at-arms and guards and all the other hangers-on – not to mention the cardinals with all their chaplains and secretaries and lawyers and doctors and stewards and attendants and cooks and pantrymen and porters and cellarers and blacksmiths and soldiers and sergeants-at-arms and guards and all their hangers-on.

Now back in Rome it would have been fine. There was plenty of room for the Pope and all his minions in Rome.

In Rome there was a magnificent Palace with endless kitchens and stores and bedrooms and offices and audience chambers and so on and so on. But in Rome there was also a snag. A big snag. A very big snag.

You see, over the years, a lot of people in Rome decided they preferred the Emperor (who lived in Constantinople) to the Pope. In fact, a lot of Romans were heartily sick of the Popes. One Pope had become so unpopular that he only just escaped from the city with his life, and since then not a single Pope had dared to go back.

That was why the present Pope was now living in the French provincial town of Avignon – and why the place was bursting at the seams. The good people of Avignon had already discovered that being host to the most powerful potentate on Earth had its down side.

A lot of the citizens of Avignon had been moved out into the countryside, and their homes were now occupied by the cardinals, who had turned the houses into palaces, fenced them off from the *hoi polloi* and put armed guards on duty. In some cases they had even closed off whole streets, so that the population now had to get past by climbing up on to catwalks! It was all most inconvenient, and many a citizen cursed the day the Pope had arrived in town.

For their part, Tom, Anton and Sir John Hawkley had arrived at Avignon on board one of the many barges that plied up and down the great River Rhône, carrying all manner of goods and people in between the great cities of Lyon, Valence, Pont St-Esprit, Orange and Avignon.

For Tom's sake, Anton had spared Sir John's life, but had insisted on taking him prisoner. For Sir John this was a torment worse than any death, or so the knight claimed.

252

"Tom! Tom!" Sir John had woken Tom up in the middle of the first night. "Take my knife and slit me throat for me, would you?"

"Sir John!" Tom really didn't think Sir John Hawkley actually meant him to do any such thing, but he was still shocked.

"I tell you I'd rather be boiled in the Devil's arse than have this! To be captured by a serf! A stinking peasant! Christ's armpits! Slit me throat for me, Tom – or untie me and let me escape!" (Ah! That's what he really wanted!) But Tom had done neither. And the great man lay there cursing and moaning until thankfully he fell asleep.

The next day, Sir John Hawkley had whined and wheedled and cursed and threatened, but nothing would persuade the giant to release him, and the noble knight was forced to walk in front of Anton and Tom with his head hung low and his hands tied behind him.

As their journey had progressed, however, and they'd made their way down through Beaune and Macon towards the great metropolis of Lyon, the giant had relented sufficiently to release Sir John's wrists. He had made sure that Sir John was treated properly and had everything he needed to eat and to drink (which in Sir John's case was considerable), and he always allowed Sir John the best bed for the night.

It was as if Anton's anger was evaporating as the river took them further and further south.

Sir John's indignation at being the prisoner of a peasant also seemed to evaporate as he discovered the advantages of Anton's hospitality and protection. In fact when Anton finally relented and said to the knight: "Sir John, I quit you – you are free to go", the knight looked a little ruffled.

"Well, let's not be too hasty," he said. "Perhaps I should

just go on being your prisoner until we reach Avignon."
And nothing they said could dissuade him.

Now here they were in Avignon, and if Tom had expected Sir John to take his leave of them, he was mistaken. "I'll just make sure you get in to see the Pope," said Sir John, pausing to swig a little of the strong wine that Anton had thoughtfully provided for him that morning. "You never know, you might need me," said the knight, wiping his lips.

From the riverbank, the trio were looking up at the great Palace of the Pope that dominated the city. It seemed somehow far away, even as they looked at it. And when they tried to approach it, they soon found that if it was difficult to get near the great houses of the cardinals, getting near the Palace of the Pope himself was impossible. Well, almost.

The Pope had plenty of enemies even among the good people of Avignon. You didn't get to be head of the Holy Church just by being nice to people … It should come as no surprise that the present Pope, whose name was Innocent, was a bag of nerves. He hardly slept a wink all night, and during the day he was constantly on the alert for spies and assassins and poisoners. His Palace was the safest, most security-conscious building that modern architecture could devise. It had only one entrance – and that was heavily guarded. It had few windows – and those were high up and small. It was really a fort built in the middle of a town. It was, to put it simply, the Palace of Paranoia.

Tom and Anton and Sir John Hawkley climbed the rocky path from the river up to the Rock of Doms. They had passed under four windmills and a gibbet, on which a couple of rotting bodies swung in the slight breeze.

"Good to know that's ready there for you, Sir John!" muttered Anton.

"What did he say?" exclaimed Sir John, who by this time had a pretty shrewd grasp of the giant's sense of humour.

"He said you ought to try and avoid ending up there, Sir John," replied Tom. Then he stopped and gazed up at the ramparts that now loomed above them. "Look at those walls! We'll never get in from here!" They were standing on the public bleaching-ground directly under the northern walls of the Pope's Palace. Here the women of Avignon were in the habit of spreading out their sheets and linen to whiten in the hot sun. The walls on this side had been built without any entrance, and so high that there was no possibility whatsoever of the washerwomen of Avignon storming the Pope's Palace!

"We'd better go to the main entrance," said Anton. But that was easier said than done. They quickly found that they couldn't get within spitting distance of the Palace gates – not that they wanted to spit at them, you understand. Their motives were most respectful, but the streets that led to the Pope's Palace were blocked by armed guards.

"Where d'you think you're going?" the Papal Guard was even now shouting at Anton.

This was the moment Tom had been waiting for. "*Epistulam habeo … debeo Papa de manu dare*," he said in his best Latin, and waited for the words to have the magic effect that Father Michael had promised.

"Oh really?" replied the soldier. He was wearing a very bright, multi-coloured livery that had cost the exact amount that Anton's village had spent on food during that past year. But (perhaps fortunately) neither Tom nor

Anton was aware of this. "And I suggest you kiss my backside!" said the guard.

It wasn't a particularly witty thing to say, but it made the guard laugh and it made his companion laugh too. He was another guard.

Anton looked a little puzzled. "You don't understand," he began. "My friend has a letter – he must give it to the Pope! We've travelled all the way from Champagne!"

"And I suggested ..." said the humorous guard, his eyes twinkling like billy-o, "that you ..." – he indicated the three of them – "might just as well kiss ..." – here he turned round and pointed to his posterior – "my backside."

Oddly enough, the guard's backside was actually rather attractive. It was party-coloured in the bright yellow and crimson of the Pope's livery, but it was still not the sort of thing you'd want to kiss. Even Sir John Hawkley, whose French was limited to not understanding anything at all, got his drift and growled.

"Listen," said Tom. "I am a translator for the Pope, and I have been commissioned to give him this letter ..." and here he took the letter from Anton, "into the Pope's hands personally."

"And I could stand here all day listening to your life story," said the guard with a grin, "I really could. It's fascinating. But before you say another word I must point out that without a pass neither you – nor your friends – get a foot beyond this spot." And suddenly the guard wasn't smiling any more. He was levelling his pike at Tom's throat.

· 49 ·

A LUCKY ENCOUNTER

"It's so exasperating!" exclaimed Tom. He and Anton were lying in the straw up in the loft of one of the old boathouses that in those days stood beside the River Rhône. Sir John Hawkley was propped up against the wall in the corner. The great man had purchased a skin of wine and was contentedly sipping from it. "We've come all this way," said Tom, "and now we can't even get near the Palace gate!"

Sir John burped in the corner. Since Anton and Tom were speaking French, that was all he could contribute to the conversation. Anton shrugged. "Perhaps it was all a foolish idea anyway," he murmured to the roof of the boathouse. "Why would the Pope bother himself with the likes of us? He takes his money from us until we have no more to give. What more can he want from us? I suppose if I were the Pope I wouldn't want to speak to us."

"But you would," said Tom. "I bet you would!"

Sir John suddenly had something to say after all. It wasn't much, but it brought the conversation to a halt. "Sh!" he said. Someone was opening the boathouse doors. Anton squirmed himself into a position where he could look down into the boathouse below. The water slapped and gurgled against the walls of the shed, and threw up sparkling

258

reflections of the moon. Tom peered through another crack in the floorboards, and saw a barge nose its way into the mooring. Two men with lanterns stood on board, while a third pulled the barge into its place. Then one of them started examining the cargo, while the other two watched and conferred with each other in subdued undertones.

"Do you see who it is?" hissed Tom to Anton.

"It's that prelate! The one who chased the brigands with us ..." whispered Anton.

Tom peered down and nodded. He could see the mysterious hooded figure in red inserting a key into a heavy iron-bound coffer. "They're opening up the chest!" murmured Tom. And that was clearly the idea. But it was proving a bit more difficult that it should.

"This lock's rusty!" snapped the red-robed churchman. "Make sure you have it replaced!"

"Yes, Your Worship," said one of the others as the prelate raised the lid of the coffer.

"What is it?" whispered Tom, peering down from his hiding-place. "Can you see what's in it?"

Anton shook his head. "Uh uh! But whatever it is belongs to the Pope," he said. "That's the Pope's insignia on the side!"

"I think the Pope may be going to get a real surprise!" exclaimed Tom.

"Whatever do you mean?" Anton was looking at Tom – half-amused.

"Are you any good at diversions?" asked Tom.

———

The Pope's Chamberlain heaved a deep sigh. Little beads of sweat broke out under his red hood. This was one of the moments he liked best. Lifting the lid of the strong-box always sent a thrill up his spine. There was something quite other-worldly about revealing those vulnerable little money-bags just sitting there, waiting to be counted. To tell the truth, it was the nearest the Chamberlain ever came to a spiritual revelation.

Of course, it was very unusual for him to arrive with the barge. Normally he would be in the boathouse waiting for it. But there had been problems with the supply recently. The collectors had blamed bandits on the road – particularly in the region of Burgundy.

Now the Chamberlain was one of the most important people in the Papal Palace, and as a matter of course he would delegate the investigation of such things to some subordinate. But this was the matter closest to his heart – the matter of Papal finances. He decided that there was only one person he could trust to find out what was happening to the money.

"It's all very easy to blame bandits," he had told His Holiness the Pope, "when in fact it's simply a case of someone keeping a little bit on the side for themselves." After all, he thought privately, that's what he'd do.

In fact, that's exactly what he was doing at this very moment! And now he had to give everyone their cut. He opened a bag and handed some coins to the bargeman – a big fellow in a red cap and a rough fur jacket. That was his cut. Then he handed three bags to his manservant. That was his own cut. Best to get that business out of the way. Now he would be able to …

But he wasn't! There was a piercing shriek from outside the boathouse. All three of them span round as if the Pope himself had caught them at it.

"Perhaps it was somebody sneezing!" said the bargeman.

"Nobody should be sneezing out there at this time of night!" snapped the Chamberlain.

"I'll go and see who it is," said the bargeman.

"No!" snapped the Pope's Chamberlain. "I'll see for myself!" He shut the coffer and locked it. "Keep an eye on this fellow. I don't want to find we're a bag short," he muttered to his servant. Then he hurried out through the door of the boathouse. For a few moments they saw the light of his lantern shining on the water under the door – then it disappeared.

Then there was silence. Not a suspicious silence, but a silence all the same. A silence which told nothing. And it went on ... and on ...

The Chamberlain's servant looked at the bargeman, and the bargeman looked at the Chamberlain's servant. The time ticked away, and still the lantern did not return.

"Do you think he's all right?" whispered the bargeman.

"He's been gone a while," admitted the Chamberlain's servant.

"Perhaps the Pope's sent his spies?" suggested the bargeman. "Go and have a look."

"What? And leave you alone with the money chest? You must think I'm soft in the head or something. You go and have a look."

"I'm not going out there on my own! It might be dangerous out there!" The bargeman pulled his red cap further down over his head, as if for protection.

"Well, we can't sit here like mugs of milk," said the Chamberlain's manservant.

"Then you go!" said the bargeman.

"We'll both go," said the manservant, glancing round the empty boathouse. The treasure chest could look after itself for a few moments.

Outside the boathouse it had started to rain. And when I say "rain" that's a euphemism. This wasn't just "rain", this was ... well there isn't really a word in English for it: "an inundation", "a deluge", "a downpour" – you go and look it up in the Thesaurus. But not one of these words really gives any idea of this particular rain. A roll of thunder grumbled from up the river. The heavens opened and the water came down like spears, with the solid shafts sticking up out of the ground. The light from the manservant's lantern reflected against the vertical lines of rain and turned them into bars – imprisoning the two men in their immediate world. They could hardly see three feet around them.

"Quick!" said the Chamberlain's manservant, and he ducked into the shelter of a small lean-to. The bargeman followed. "Damn!" yelled the Chamberlain's manservant as he tripped over something and went sprawling into the dark.

"What's that?" asked the bargeman.

"How do I know?" said the Chamberlain's manservant. The lantern had gone out when it crashed to the floor.

"Mmnckmmunngh!" said the thing that he'd tripped over.

Re-lighting a lantern, six hundred years ago, was a bit of a palaver. And doing it when you were soaking wet was even more of a palaver. There were no such things as cigarette lighters or safety matches. You had to use a tinderbox and strike sparks from a flint on to a bit of cord or cloth. So it was some moments before what happens in the next paragraph actually happened.

"Mmmmckkkkmmmgggggg!" continued the thing, as the lantern finally sputtered into life, to reveal a large carcass of red, bundled up in a corner.

"It's him!" exclaimed the bargeman.

"I can see that!" the Chamberlain's manservant said, already removing the gag from his master's mouth. "I'm not a ..."

"A monster!" cried the Chamberlain. "Ten feet tall! Huge teeth and eyes!"

The Chamberlain was normally the most imperturbable of men. He was normally as cool as a cucumber in a bucket of ice, and he disliked fantasy and exaggeration almost as much as he disliked people who were poor. So you can imagine the effect of his words on the servant. The poor fellow turned white and began to shake.

"It leapt out on me!" continued the Chamberlain. "I didn't have time to scream! Wait! Where d'you think you're going?"

"I'm getting out of here!" cried his manservant, but he stopped at his master's command.

"This is the Devil's business!" cried the bargeman, and – not taking any notice of anybody's commands, whoever they were – he disappeared.

"Untie me!" ordered the Chamberlain. And – as scared as his servant was of the Chamberlain's monster – he was even more scared of the Chamberlain himself. So he untied him. "We're not leaving here until we've got the tithes on the cart," said the Chamberlain.

I should have explained that the treasure chest was not a treasure chest in the sense of a pirate treasure chest – full of stolen booty – wrested from its owners at the point of a sword. No! This was the Pope's treasure chest, full of tithes – that tenth of their worldly possessions that Christians in those days gladly gave the Church to further God's work on Earth. Of course, if they didn't give it, they were threatened with excommunication and the prospect of spending Eternity burning in the fires of Hell, but nonetheless it was God's money, and monster or no monster, rain or no rain, said the Chamberlain, they were going to get it back to the Pope's Palace.

As soon as his servant had released him, the two of them rushed back into the boathouse, picked up the chest and manhandled it out to the horse and cart that was waiting in the rapidly drowning street. And all the time the Pope's Chamberlain was cursing and panting and complaining that the chest felt heavier. Which it was.

· 50 ·

HOW TOM GOT INTO THE POPE'S PALACE

Tom hardly dared to breathe. He knew it was a daft scheme. Anton had said it was a daft scheme as soon as Tom had proposed it. "But can you think of any other way of getting into the Pope's Palace?" Tom had asked, and because Anton couldn't, he'd done it.

"But how will you get out?" asked Anton.

"I don't know. But I'll tell you what! You know the bleaching-ground?"

"Under the north wall?"

"Watch for me there. If I can't get out I'll send a signal," Tom said, although he had no idea how he was going to do it. He must have sounded convincing, however, because Anton had gone off to cause a diversion.

Anton's diversion consisted of his doing his impression of a night-hawk in distress (not somebody sneezing). Then, when all three of the Pope's men had left the boathouse, Tom had persuaded Sir John to give his wineskin a rest for a few moments. They had both then jumped down from the loft and opened up the coffer. It was almost half full of money-bags.

"I'll have some of those!" exclaimed Sir John Hawkley, helping himself. Tom ignored him. He was too busy trying to decide if there was room for him to hide in the chest and still be able to breathe. It was going to be a tight fit, Tom could see that, even though Sir John was doing his very best to make more room for him. And of course there was always the possibility that the Chamberlain might open up the chest again when he came back, but Tom decided that was a risk he'd just have to take. He took a deep breath, just as Sir John was fishing out his fifth bag of money, and, with his heart beating, he climbed into the coffer and lowered the lid. Sir John obligingly locked it, and fled back upstairs to the safety of the loft – six money-bags richer. (He'd snuck another one just as he was closing the lid.)

As it was, the Chamberlain and his manservant were in such a hurry to get out of the boathouse, they simply carried the chest off, without bothering to check it.

That had been the best bit of the journey.

Unfortunately Tom discovered the reason that more people don't travel as small change or even gold bullion is that it has a pretty rough ride. For something that human beings love more than anything else, money is treated surprisingly badly. It's heaped together in piles, it's slung into bags and thrown about and dumped on the ground and chucked into carts and heaved off them and chucked to the stone floor ...

"If money bruised easily, it wouldn't be gold and silver, it would be black and blue!" thought Tom.

That was certainly the condition Tom was in by the time he reached the Pope's Counting House. The chest finally came to rest, and for a few peaceful moments Tom lay back and was able to enjoy the luxury of groaning silently to himself in peace and quiet.

Now I'm not quite sure exactly what Tom had expected to happen, but I do know it wasn't what did happen. Perhaps he imagined that the coffer would be taken into the

266

Pope's Palace, and set down in front of the Pope himself, and then opened – whereupon Tom would leap out and make his plea on behalf of Anton's village. The Pope would be so surprised that he would listen to what Tom had to say, and would quickly see the justice of the villagers' request. He would immediately dictate a letter giving the village full permission to pay no tithes until they were in a position to do so, then he would pat Tom on the head and give him some venison pie.

If that was indeed what Tom was hoping for, I'm afraid he got ten out of ten for optimism and nought for accuracy.

He lay there for some time and nothing happened. No one opened up the chest. No one tapped on it. No one did anything to it. Tom could hear the busy comings and goings of the Counting House. He could hear the chink of coins on tables. He could hear the scratch of quills on vellum. He could hear guards snapping to attention as distant doors creaked open and shut. He could hear the busy murmur of the notaries of the Apostolic Chamber doing their calculations. The coffer was ignored.

For a moment, a feeling of panic seized Tom. What if the coffer were simply dumped in a storehouse and forgotten about? He might be locked in it for hours or days or even weeks before anyone discovered him! Tom suddenly had the urge to bang on the chest and scream out: "Help! Let me out!" But – quite suddenly – he heard a key turn in the lock of the chest. And before he could decide what to do, the lid was opened.

A clerk peered in, screamed and banged the lid down again.

But Tom wasn't prepared to be trapped in there for a second time. He leapt up, pushing back the lid.

"Guards!" shouted the Chamberlain.

"Please!" shouted Tom. "I mean no harm! I have a message for the ..." But before he could say "Pope", four guards had burst across the Counting House and seized him in a stranglehold around his neck so tight he could hardly breathe, let alone speak.

"Take him out and dispose of him!" said a tall, thin-faced cadaver with hollow, sunken eyes. He was the Chief Notary of the Apostolic Chamber, and his instructions were to liquidate any intruders into this – the Pope's Holy of Holies.

If Tom had thought he'd been treated roughly as a bit of bullion, he soon discovered that an intruder into the Papal fiscal boudoir was treated even more summarily. The guards didn't seem to regard him as a living creature – which isn't perhaps surprising when you think about what they were about to do to him.

"Wait!" It was the Chamberlain's voice that cut across the uproar of the Counting House, where the normal quiet concentration of the place had erupted into cacophony. Nothing like this had ever happened before. Everybody was suddenly talking at once.

The clerks in the Counting House were not normally allowed to talk, and the humdrum routine of the place, as each applied himself to his task in silence, was unbroken from year's end to year's end. For something out of the usual to happen was unprecedented. And Tom's truly amazing appearance from inside one of the strong-boxes seemed no less amazing than a conjuring trick! Indeed, there were many notaries and clerks there who swore, in later years, that Tom had leapt out of the coffer in a puff of smoke and that the smell of brimstone hung in the air of the Counting House for days afterwards.

The Chamberlain, however, was not a party to all this

astonishment. He was astonished, but he was damned if he was going to show it.

"Silence!" he roared, and glared round at the staff. "How dare you raise your voices in His Holiness's Counting House! Have you no sense of piety?" He really meant it. As I said, the fiscal side of religion was the Chamberlain's only contact with divinity.

"You!" He turned on Tom. "What the devil are you doing here?"

"- _ _ - - _ -******!!!!!!!" said Tom.

"Let him go!" ordered the Chamberlain.

"But ..." began the Chief Notary of the Apostolic Chamber.

"I said let him go!" commanded the Chamberlain.

The guards released Tom from their strangulating grip. Tom fell to the floor, gasping for breath. "I'm sorry," he croaked. "Couldn't get into the Palace! Important message for Pope!"

The Chamberlain smiled the ghost of a smile. "So, my little sprat," he barely spoke – the words seemed to ooze from under his top lip. "What was your name again?"

"Tom."

"Tom. Ah yes. And where is your friend the giant?"

"He's waiting for me. I'm delivering a message from his village..."

"Yes ... I remember ... a village that wants to be excused its tithes ..."

"They can't pay! They have nothing! You should see the way they live! Underground! Like animals! If only the Pope knew ..."

"And you have a letter?" said the Chamberlain kindly.

"Yes," said Tom. "From Father Michael – the village priest."

"Show me," commanded the Chamberlain. Without thinking, Tom pulled the letter out from his jerkin, and the next moment the Chamberlain snatched it from his grasp and held it up for the whole Counting House to see.

"Here it is!" said the Chamberlain. "A letter from a village that thinks it can't afford to pay its tithes!"

The whole Counting House gasped and laughed in surprise, and yet what the Chamberlain did next was, in many ways, the most surprising thing of all. He strode across to the coffer and lifted the lid, which had fallen shut during all the confusion. Then he turned to the guards and said: "Put him back!"

Before Tom could think what was happening, the guards had seized him and shut him up – back up in the coffer.

"Take this to the Lower Hall!" was all Tom heard, before he felt himself lifted up again and manhandled out of the Counting House.

· 51 ·

THE MOST
EXTRAORDINARY ROOM
IN THE WORLD

Tom felt himself being carried down a long flight of steps. The sounds of the Counting House faded in the distance. He heard a guard jump to attention. The Chamberlain muttered something, and the guard moved again. Then the sound of a door – a heavy door – being unlocked and opened ... Then another ...

The noises from outside now seemed to be pressing up against the coffer. The footsteps of the guards echoed against close walls. "It must be some sort of passage," he thought. "It's certainly a deserted bit of the Palace."

Then the sounds of keys, another lock, another heavy door opening. Then the coffer was banged down on a stone floor.

"Get out!" said the Chamberlain.

Tom heard the guards' feet retreating quickly. Then the heavy door closed. Silence. Tom heard the Chamberlain walking backwards and forwards.

"Perhaps he's trying to decide what to do with me?" thought Tom. And he was just about to shout out a few suggestions when the lid of the coffer opened.

"Get out!" said the Chamberlain for the second time.

Tom obediently climbed out and looked around. He didn't know it yet, but he was standing in the most extraordinary room in the world.

271

It was not the biggest room he had ever been in, but it had an elaborate vaulted ceiling. There were no windows – save one tiny slit high up – and the walls were plain. And yet, as Tom looked around him by the light of the flaming torch that the Chamberlain now held in his hands, he somehow knew this was a special place ... a very special place indeed ... but how special he simply had no idea ...

"So ... little Tom," said the Chamberlain, "little Tom who wants to change the world ..."

"No! I don't want to change the world!" said Tom. "I just want to tell the Pope what's going on. If he only knew ..."

"Do you know where you are?" asked the Chamberlain.

"No," replied Tom.

"You are very privileged to be here," said the Chamberlain. "Only three people have the keys for this room: the Treasurer, myself and His Holiness the Pope," said the great man.

Tom looked around the room. "Then why are you showing it to me?" he wanted to ask. Alarm bells were ringing all over his body, but what he said was:

"Is this ... the Pope's Treasure House?" Now he was getting used to the light, Tom could see a lot of sacks against one wall. In the centre were stacks of big iron chests like the one he'd arrived in. In fact the more Tom looked, the more big iron chests he could count.

"Not the Pope's!" said the Chamberlain. "This is God's Treasure House. From all over Christendom, people send their contributions to enable the Church to carry out God's work on Earth. This room is where all that wealth is stored until God needs it. This is God's storehouse of earthly riches."

"Do I detect a euphemism!" wondered Tom, but he carried on looking round the room with a reverential

expression on his face. In those rusty chests and dirty sacks
lay all the wealth of the world. More money than anyone
would ever see in their lifetime. More money than the King
of England had in his coffers. More money than most

people could possibly imagine even if they sat there imagining until Doomsday.

"Is that why there are no windows?" asked Tom. "To stop people stealing God's wealth?"

"You're sharp enough to cut the meat!" replied the Chamberlain. "Hard to believe though it is, there are villains in this sinful town who would rob God himself, if he were to spend the night here. The Pope cannot be too careful in guarding what belongs to God."

Tom nodded. He could see the argument. But he couldn't see what all this had to do with him.

"And now I am going to show you a secret. A very big secret indeed," said the Chamberlain. "Pass me that iron bar."

Tom passed an iron bar, that was lying nearby, in as nonchalant a way as he could, even though every instinct inside him was screaming: "Don't trust this man!"

The Chamberlain put the bar into one of the cracks in the great flagstone floor and leant on it. To Tom's surprise, the seemingly solid floor broke away and the flagstone came up, like a trapdoor, revealing a void beneath.

The Chamberlain gestured to the iron chests and sacks that surrounded them. "This," he said, "is just the small change! The real wealth is underneath ..." and he grinned like a werewolf. "And nobody knows – just us!"

And suddenly, as Tom stared at those jagged wolf's teeth, he realized this man was not just the Pope's Chamberlain and not just the red-robed prelate who had chased bandits – Tom also knew him of old. He was the creature of his nightmares. He was the Devil at his door. He was the Archfiend. He was Nemesis. He was the Man in Black.

· 52 ·

WHAT HAPPENED UNDER
THE POPE'S FLOORBOARDS

"Are you the Devil?" cried Tom. "You've been chasing me long enough!"

The Chamberlain's face broke into a smile that could very well have been the Devil's, for all I know, but he shook his head.

"It amuses me to tell you the story, little Tom," he said. "After all, you should learn something before you die."

Tom made a mental note that he was not going to die if he could possibly help it, but he nodded gratefully – as was evidently expected.

"His Holiness the Pope has been much concerned, in recent years, by two unfortunate matters," said the Chamberlain. "First, moneys due to God were not arriving in Avignon. Some people said there were bandits in the hills of Burgundy, robbing the holy tax collectors. Some said it was the holy tax collectors themselves lining their own pockets.

"Secondly, His Holiness was aware that someone was intercepting his mail and thus other parties were learning the secret business of the Holy Church.

"Now, you understand that these were both matters I did not wish to entrust to anybody else. Indeed there is no one else in the Papal curia whom I would trust to carry a loaf of bread without stealing the crumbs. So, I decided to play the spy. I first disguised myself. I coloured my hair black, and I darkened my skin ..."

"And you dressed in black," added Tom.

"That was a little over the top, I grant you," said the Chamberlain, "but it was a great outfit. Then I volunteered to deliver His Holiness's letters myself. This brought me to the Archbishop of Reims's court and, of course, to the court of the English King Edward, where my investigations led me to the scriptorium of the Duke of Lancaster. There I found, to my astonishment, that the Papal correspondence was being translated not by a churchman but by a boy. I decided to take the young sparrow with me, to see if I could make him sing. However, the good people of Reims took it into their heads to storm the Archbishop's Palace and I was lucky to escape with my life. Indeed I was all but strangled by a half-crazed prisoner in the cells."

"I thought the Cannibal had done for you!" exclaimed Tom.

"Good luck favours the wicked, my son. That is something you would have found out, had you lived longer ... The fellow was too impatient to get his teeth into my flesh. He'd only half-strangled me when he tried to start his meal ...!"

"Always make sure your food's dead," Tom nodded.

"I gave him a taste of his own medicine!"

"You ate him!?"

"No, idiot! I strangled him!"

"Lucky him."

"After that," continued the Chamberlain. "I decided to dispense with disguise. I thought I might need all the authority of the Holy Church while I was chasing bandits in the hills of Burgundy. Imagine my surprise, then, when I discover myself riding side by side with this same young sparrow. He does not recognize me, and I, of course, say nothing – meaning to snare him later – but he eludes me in the heat of the chase. I expected never to see him again.

"Some time later, however, I open one of His Holiness's treasure chests – and what happens? Believe it or not, this same sparrow leaps out and starts chirruping some nonsense about a village that refuses to pay its tithes! I start to think he must be spying on me!

"Then I tell myself it's ridiculous. The boy is hardly more than a child ... I decide that the best thing to do is to forget about it ... to forget about him ..."

Tom had never liked the way the Chamberlain looked at him – not when he was the Man in Black – not when he was the red-robed prelate – and especially not now.

"But why have you brought me here?" asked Tom. "Why are you showing me all these great secrets ..." But even as these words were leaving his lips, Tom realized he already had a pretty shrewd idea ...

The Chamberlain was advancing towards him. "You got into the Palace as part of the Pope's treasure, little sparrow. And you are going to stay part of the Pope's treasure. I am going to keep you in the safest place in the whole wide world ... somewhere where no one will find you ... ever ...

Tom backed away from the black hole in the flagstones ... The Chamberlain had a dangerous smile on his lips and a light in his eyes that was almost zealous. Tom backed away. He knew he couldn't escape. He knew the Treasury was locked and guarded. But he couldn't think what else to do except to back away ... and back away he did ... again and again ... as the Chamberlain kept on advancing towards him.

And suddenly everything seemed so hopeless: his life, his

dreams of becoming a squire, of becoming a knight, of fighting in good causes and winning Emily's hand, of seeing all the places he'd dreamed of – the shores of Africa, the dusty lands of Arabia, the Tartar Khan, the cities of China, the forests of Russia ... it all seemed hopeless ... His mission to save Anton's village, to make the Pope understand the misery and destruction and the suffering that people were enduring day after wretched day throughout the land because of war and because of oppression ... hopeless ...

Tom glanced quickly round the Pope's Lower Treasury ... It was astounding to think that this whole, solid stone floor was false ... as false as Judas's kiss ... as false as a brigand's truce ... All those tithes that hard-pressed peasants and honest working folk gave to their parish priests ... all that wealth that was raised in the name of Christ and the Holy Spirit, wealth to give to the poor, wealth to promote the Holy War, wealth to build churches to the greater glory of God – it all ended up being hoarded away in here ... under the Pope's floorboards!

This was the grubby secret at the heart of Christendom.

"Got you!" The Chamberlain had leapt across the room and grabbed Tom by the collar. But Tom dived to one side – behind a stack of treasure chests – and the Chamberlain lost his grip. And still Tom kept backing away – by this time, they'd almost done a complete circuit of the Lower Treasury.

"You'll not stick me under the Pope's floorboards!" exclaimed Tom.

"You can't escape!" snarled the Chamberlain, and once again he ran at Tom, and Tom dived over a pile of money sacks, rolled across the floor and fell straight into the hole in the flagstones!

"Oh no!" cried Tom, as he fell the six or seven feet into the secret space beneath the floor and cracked his head against the stone sides.

"That was easy!" cried the Chamberlain, and he started pushing the huge flagstone back into place.

It took Tom a moment to recover his senses. When he did, all he saw was the paving sliding closed above him. "Stop!" cried Tom. "You can't!" But even as he said the words, the Chamberlain's face appeared in the remaining gap, and one glance at those cold, mocking eyes told Tom he could.

Tom tried to push against the flagstone, but the weight of it and the strength of the Chamberlain were too much. He was as helpless as a lobster in a pot. The huge paving slid remorselessly across the hole. Once it reached the exact slot where it fitted, its weight would carry it down into place, and Tom would never be able to move it. He would be sealed into the cramped space beneath and left there to die – buried alive under the Pope's floor.

"You should have kept your nose out of other people's business!" The Chamberlain grinned down at him. "You should have learnt that worms must avoid the boot that will crush them ..." And he shoved the giant flagstone another inch towards its resting-place. And Tom pushed with all his might against its weight, but he could get no purchase on it, and he watched helplessly as the gap closed to a couple of inches.

The Chamberlain put his eye to the slot. "Oh! Here's your letter, little sparrow. It'll be safer with you!" he said, as he dropped the letter through the crack. "Goodbye, little sparrow ..." And with that he gave a last heave, and Tom gave a last hopeless push against it. The flagstone slid across the final remaining inch of light ...

But there is usually a moment, in all stories, where the luck turns, and this, I am very pleased to be able to inform you, is that precise moment in this story. For as the flagstone slid across into its final resting-place (entombing Tom and making all his struggles and adventures up to this moment pointless), it suddenly stuck.

The reason it stuck was that it came up against an obstacle. This obstacle was an object that belonged to Tom. It was something he had been given a long time ago when he had first set out from his village back home in England. He had been given it by Odo, the ditch-digger.

"You may have need of it," Odo had said. And, at the

time, the words had struck home to Tom the enormity of what he was doing – running away from home into a dangerous and often hostile world. But curiously enough, although he had been carrying the object ever since, this was the first time he had actually used it. And he was certainly not using it in a way that either he or Odo could ever have imagined.

It was the knife that Odo had given him, all that time ago, that Tom now pulled out and stuck up in between the flagstone and the edge of the hole.

"Get that out of there!" snapped the Chamberlain and he stamped his foot on it, intending to knock it down into the hole. But, as luck would have it, the handle of the knife had caught on the edge of the paving, so instead of being kicked down, it stuck where it was and went clean through the Chamberlain's foot!

The Chamberlain gave a roar of pain that all the Palace would have heard, had the Chamberlain been anywhere but the Lower Hall of the Treasury. He let go of the paving stone and reeled back, clutching at his foot. The knife was yanked out of Tom's hand and stayed skewered right through the tenderest part of the Chamberlain's foot. It must have been excruciating.

Tom didn't waste a second. He jammed his fingers up through the last quarter of an inch of gap and, with a great heave, pushed the flagstone aside. Then he grabbed the letter, leapt up out of the hole and ran to the Treasury door.

"Quick! Quick!" he yelled to the guards outside. "The Chamberlain's hurt himself!" The Chamberlain was rolling around, desperately clawing at his foot, trying to remove the dagger, but with no success.

The two guards rushed across to the unfortunate man. Tom did not hesitate. He bolted out of the door and was just about to race off down the narrow passage that led to the Counting House when he stopped. I think I would have carried on running, but Tom stopped. He turned and ran back to the Lower Treasury. He stuck his head back in and shouted:

"I'll tell them you're all in here … tomorrow. Bye!"

Even with the din of the Chamberlain's yelling, the two guards heard what Tom had said and turned just in time to see the heavy door of the Lower Treasury close upon them. They dropped the Chamberlain and sprinted for the door in time to hear the great key turn in the great lock.

It was very satisfactory, thought Tom, that no matter how much those three yell in there – no one will be able to hear them. He had until tomorrow to do what he had come to do. He pocketed the key and strolled off to find the Pope.

· 53 ·

DINNER WITH THE POPE

It so happened it was dinner-time in the Pope's Palace. The great bell was tolling, and now, as he made his way towards the Cloister Courtyard, Tom could hear the noise of hundreds of people heading for the Grand Tinel, as the great dining-hall was called. The notaries and clerks, the servants and stewards were all jostling for a place at the great event of the day. Visiting dignitaries were being shown the way to the Grand Tinel, past the queue that was already forming at the door, where guards were searching everyone. There were more guards standing in strategic places, keeping their sharp eyes on the crowd as it passed to and fro.

Tom kept himself well out of sight. He had found a small alcove in the cloister from which he could watch the comings and goings, but he knew that the moment he stepped out there into the throng he might become an object of suspicion.

As he stood there, he thought about the Chamberlain and the two guards locked in the Lower Treasury. How long would it be before they were missed? He felt the key heavy in his pocket. How long would it be before that was missed? He probably had less time than he hoped.

The bell continued to toll, summoning everyone to the Pope's dining tables. Everyone, that is, apart from Tom. And suddenly, despite the gathering crowds and the cheerful

283

bustle around him, Tom felt desperately alone. He wished he had Anton there beside him. He could just see Anton's gentle face wrinkling into a frown as he considered what they should do next.

Tom looked across at a party of important people marching with noses in the air across the Cloister Courtyard towards the Grand Tinel, while others fawned and bowed and scraped alongside them. What proud, important people they looked. How could he – a country boy from a dirt-bound village lost in a remote England of field and furrow and hedgerow – possibly communicate with these silk-clad prelates, in their fur and gold brocade?

And then a memory slunk into his mind – almost half-ashamed of presenting itself. He was back in a dark alley staring through a window at a blind old woman ... a blind old woman who may not even have existed ... and yet (the memory insisted) it might be important: he must remember what the old woman had told him.

And now he acknowledged the memory, it stepped out into the light and stood up straight, and he saw in his mind the old woman as she murmured:

"You have enemies in high places. Important men who would like you out of the way ... Remember that you possess something they do not have ..." Those were her words. She'd been right about the enemies in high places. You couldn't get much higher than the Pope's Chamberlain! But what on earth could he possess that these urbane men of state did not?

"It is something they cannot make and something they cannot take ... and something they will never understand ..." The words drifted through his mind as the party of important people approached the steps opposite the cloister where he was concealing himself. And suddenly his heart leapt into his head and dropped through his feet simultaneously! His eyes opened twice as wide again and his head ... well ... if it could have twizzled round and round like a quintain*, it would have done.

The party of important people, with all their hangers-on and fawners, started up the steps that led up to the Grand Tinel, and as they ascended, Tom could see who they were. And he didn't know whether he should laugh or cry, whether he should shout "Hallelujah!" or whether he should scream with rage. Actually, he knew he shouldn't do any of those things. For there, coming up the steps, dressed up like the Queen of Sheba, in purple and gold and satin and jewels and with rings on his fingers was none other than the tortoise with stomach ache ... otherwise known as Jean de Craon, the Archbishop of Reims.

It was like a nightmare – one of those dreams in which no matter how hard you run away, you always end up back where you started from. And – like all nightmares – it threw together totally unbelievable combinations of people. Tom blinked. The Archbishop was escorting on his arm a beautiful, dark-haired, smiling woman.

"Emily!" breathed Tom to himself, and his world fell apart.

Emily looked radiant. She smiled and she bowed her head to the fawners and flatterers of the Papal Court. She was dressed magnificently and looked like ... well ... she looked like a princess.

Before he knew what he was doing, Tom had stepped out

---

* A quintain was a target used for practice jousting. It was mounted on a post and swivelled right round. On one end was the target and on the other a bag full of sand. If you didn't hit the target square on, the target would swing right round and the bag of sand would hit you over the head and, as likely as not, knock you off your horse.

of the shadow of the cloister and was giving an exaggerated bow to the passing entourage. The Archbishop was marching on, nose in air, but Emily caught sight of Tom out of the corner of her eye, and she turned and looked straight at him. Tom performed an elaborate charade of licking the Pope's boots (he just couldn't help himself) but Emily showed not a glimmer of recognition. She swung her head back to the front and took a grip of the Archbishop's arm as the entire party was ushered through into the Grand Tinel.

Tom stood there for a moment in a state of utter confusion. He was sure she'd seen him. She'd turned and looked straight at him. Why hadn't she at least waved?

And then his mind cleared. Suddenly he realized what the blind old woman had been talking about. He realized what he had that all these great and important people were lacking. He suddenly realized what it was that they couldn't make and that they couldn't take and that they would never understand. And yet, as the old woman had said, he had it. He wasn't quite sure how he could use it – but just the knowledge that he had it gave him a curious unfounded confidence.

But he also suddenly realized something else. He had to get a job. That was the only way he was going to appear inconspicuous.

———

Tom decided to follow the smell of the food. He slipped through the cloisters of the Pope's Palace, down a passageway that lead to the rear of the building, and up a flight of stone stairs. There he found himself in Hell's Kitchen. Well, that's what it looked like to Tom.

The room seemed to be one huge fire, over which two

whole sheep and an ox were roasting, along with pots and cauldrons hanging from chains held up over the fire on blackened iron brackets. The fire took up the centre of the room, and clouds of smoke were rising up from the cooking meat – up and up. Tom followed the smoke up and discovered a very surprising thing. The room had no ceiling. It just went on up – and there, far, far above, right in the middle of the room, impossibly high up, he could – for a moment – see the sky. Then it was concealed again in the clouds of fat-filled smoke.

What Tom was looking at was a state-of-the-art chimney. In fact the whole room was a chimney. The Pope had, naturally, insisted on the very best and most advanced cooking facilities in Christendom!

Around the perimeter of the kitchen, skivvies and cooks bustled with the duties of the meal. A line of servers – some of them young squires like Tom – came and took up pans and pots as ordered and carried them out. The only light in the Pope's kitchen was the roaring firelight, and Tom was able to slip himself into the line of servers as easily as a fish slips into the sea. A chef indicated a large cauldron and moments later Tom was staggering towards the door with it.

He stepped out into the Grand Tinel – the Pope's dining-room – and almost dropped the cauldron.

He had been in some extraordinary rooms recently, but this took the dog's biscuit. It was vast. You could have fitted Tom's entire village into it. Down one side, windows as tall as most churches allowed the sun's light to flood across the room and illuminate the huge expanse of the wall opposite – every inch of which was painted. There were hunting scenes and fishing scenes and scenes of courtly dances and …

"Hurry up there, boy! The Sauce-Chef needs that quickly! Quickly!" cried the Steward, and Tom hurried across to the Sauce-Chef. But as he handed the cauldron over, he couldn't stop himself looking up at the ceiling of the Grand Tinel, and he nearly dropped it again.

"Mind what you're doing!" said the Sauce-Chef, pointing his baton at Tom.

"Sorry!" said Tom. He bowed to the Sauce-Chef and stepped to one side, against the wall, so he could take in the scene for a few moments.

The ceiling was vaulted and high – very high – higher than any other ceiling Tom had ever seen – and it was painted midnight blue and covered from end to end and from side to side with stars.

"The Pope may eat under the stars like a poor shepherd," thought Tom to himself, "but he certainly doesn't eat a poor shepherd's diet!" And as he glanced around at the piles of meat and fish and vegetables, the memory surfaced of whey-faced villagers crowding in underground dens, gnawing on roots and scraps, and living in fear of death by hunger, death by the sword and death by disease.

And suddenly Tom realized, with a dreadful certainty, that his mission here was pointless. Even if he could gain the Supreme Pontiff's ear, it suddenly seemed obvious that a Pope who lived in splendour like this would never agree to cancel a village's tithes just because they were poor.

"Hey you!" another steward was pointing at Tom. "Don't just loll there! Can't you see the Carver's all piled-up?"

The place was so vast Tom hadn't noticed that he had only got as far as the serving area, which was separated from the main part of the hall by a series of screens. Centre-stage, in front of the great fireplace, stood a huge, fat man, dripping with sweat and working away with a huge carving knife. The Carver was slicing chunks off a side of beef as if he were a devil tormenting a lost soul in hell. He was surrounded by huge platters on to which he was piling the meat. Tom took two of the full ones.

"To the table! To the table!" cried the steward. "His Holiness is coming! His Holiness is coming!" And the next minute Tom had stepped through the screens into the dining-room itself.

Pandemonium had broken out, as people hurried to take their seats before the imminent arrival of the Supreme Pontiff. A herald was calling out names, and stewards were rushing here and there showing guests to their appointed places – the most important ones nearest to the Pope's dais, and the least important furthest away. The long trestle tables stretched down each side of the Grand Tinel, and in the centre was another long table on which all the food was being laid out.

The Grand Tinel was called the Grand Tinel because it was where they stored the wine barrels – what they called in Latin the *tinellum*. And all down one wall, high on top of each other, was piled barrel after barrel, containing the wines from the vineyards of Burgundy and Champagne and the Languedoc.

Tom could see the tortoise with stomach ache – the Archbishop of Reims – sitting at a table close to the Pope's dais. Emily was beside him. So without more ado, Tom marched straight up the long hall towards them. He knew Emily had seen him, but he couldn't be certain if she'd nodded back? Was that hint of a smile for him or not? He thought on balance not.

Emily seemed so remote. Tom felt the same as he had felt when he had first seen her lying asleep in her bed: the physical distance was nothing, but there was a gulf between them so deep and so wide that it might just as well have been from here to the moon.

The Archbishop, meanwhile, was too absorbed in watching the Pope's dais to notice anyone else in the room. Tom laid the great platters of meat down on the centre table as near to Emily as possible.

But before he'd even turned around, there was a commotion and three sharp raps on the wooden dais. Everyone who was sitting scrambled to their feet, as the side door opened and into the hall walked the Greatest Man on Earth – the Supreme Pontiff, the Holy Father, the Vicar of Christ, the Bishop of Rome, His Holiness Pope Innocent VI.

There was an absolute hush as he stepped up on to the dais. Surprisingly, for a clergyman, Pope Innocent VI sported a beard. He had a long nose and a pinched face. His eyes kept darting around the Grand Tinel as if he were expecting a hired assassin to leap out on him at any moment.

And, as a matter of fact, that is exactly what was going through the Pope's mind at that precise moment. It always did when he stepped up on to that wretched dais in that ghastly big hall.

Pope Innocent VI peered out across the sea of faces. Look at them! Any one of those prelates and notaries and clerks and guests could be plotting his death even as they bowed so low and so ingratiatingly towards him. Most of them he wouldn't trust further than he could throw a dagger. And the rest he wouldn't trust to see his pet chicken across the road! The cardinals were the worst – sitting there in their red robes looking as if butter wouldn't melt in their mouths. Every last one of them was plotting his downfall. He knew it! And the bishops and the archbishops were just as bad – there was not a single one that didn't envy him and that wasn't scheming to steal his hard-won seat as Pope – God's anointed one – the Most Powerful Man on Earth!

The Pope slumped down on the Cathedra – the enormous Papal throne under its sumptuous canopy. He fluttered an irritated finger at the Chief Steward, who banged his staff upon the dais and the diners all resumed their seats. Then the whole ghastly charade began to unwind as it did each and every dinner-time.

First the interminable grace. It was that sneaky cardinal Lamarque saying it today, as if he meant a single word of it. Then, grace over, a dish of food was placed in front of the Supreme Pontiff. He eyed it with distaste. Food had long since lost all its savour for him. Then his Official Taster stepped forward and bowed. The Pope nodded back and then pointed arbitrarily at a section of the plate. The Taster hesitated for no more than a ghost's breath and then dipped his spoon into the portion of the food indicated and put it in his mouth.

The Pope's eyes were now fixed upon the Taster. They never left him even for a fraction of a second as they watched the man chew the morsel thoroughly, thoughtfully, testingly. After several chews, the Taster nodded, seemingly satisfied that the food had not been poisoned with anything obvious like arsenic or belladonna (both of which imparted a bitter tang to the experienced palate), and then he swallowed. This was the key moment.

The Pope watched with riveted attention. It wasn't that he was particularly interested, it was just that he didn't dare take his eyes away for fear the Taster (given half a chance) would spit the poisoned food out of his mouth and trick him. So the Taster always made an elaborate gesture of swallowing, to reassure the Pope that it was well and truly in his gut.

The Pope still kept his beady eyes on the Taster. The whole room kept their eyes on the Taster. Would he suddenly collapse screaming in a writhing heap of toxic agony? It had happened within living memory, but not that often. Still, it gave a frisson of excitement to every meal. Some diners, I am afraid, laid bets on the result.

Sometimes the Pope would wait a couple of minutes, and if the Taster didn't fall down dead, His Holiness would begin his meal and everyone would sigh with relief. But sometimes – if His Supreme Holiness was feeling particularly nervous – he would wait for twenty minutes or more, while his fellow diners had to sit in silence, and watch the plates on the centre table get cold.

Today, however, the Pope was in a fatalistic mood: whatever will be will be. After a couple of minutes the Taster was still not displaying any adverse symptoms, so Innocent VI shrugged and started to pick at his food with his knife.

Now I don't want to go on too long about the Pope's eating habits, but there was something you ought to know about the Pope using a knife: nobody else was. Well, they didn't need to because their food had already been thoughtfully cut up for them by a gentleman known as the Pope's Carver. The Pope was anxious to save his dining companions all the effort and trouble of cutting up their own food. It was really most considerate of the Supreme Pontiff – especially since no one was allowed to enter the same room as himself carrying a knife.

So, since forks hadn't been invented in those days, it was spoons and fingers only at the Pope's dinner parties.

After some moments of toying with his food, Pope Innocent VI finally stuck a crumb into his mouth, and that was the signal for the servers to rush to the centre table and start serving the meal. A buzz of conversation rose up at once.

Tom grabbed a bowl of … well, he wasn't quite sure what they were … but he grabbed the bowl anyway and went straight over to offer whatever it was to Emily. He could feel his heart beating as approached her table.

Emily was talking to a fat jolly-looking prelate who sat on her left. He was gazing into her eyes as if he were looking for a lost sovereign. Tom coughed and bowed, holding out the bowl of thingamajigs. Slowly, and with infinite disdain, Emily turned those beautiful grey eyes towards him. Emily's eyes had lost nothing of their sparkle, but they were cold.

Tom smiled. The eyes told him nothing. Emily was now looking past him. Now she was whispering to the Archbishop, who sat upon her right, and pointing at the Pope. Tom's mind went into a turmoil. What had happened? This was Emily, wasn't it? And yet he didn't seem to exist for her.

He wanted to whisper: "It's me! Tom! Emily! I'm here!" But he managed to stop himself. And, as the Archbishop

squinted at the Pope, Emily suddenly turned and gazed straight at Tom and very quickly reached out and took a whatever-it-was from the bowl.

Tom's mouth opened a fraction to speak, but something in Emily's manner made him stop.

"You may take those pomegranates elsewhere," she commanded.

"But ..." Tom bit his lip as the Archbishop turned back to look at the bowl of fruit.

"Pomegranates," grunted the Archbishop and reached his hand towards the bowl. Tom saw Emily go pale. She glared and nodded at the bowl. Tom looked down. There was a small fold of paper tucked among the fruit. The Archbishop's hand was hovering over it!

"Look out!" cried Tom, and he snatched the bowl of fruit away from the Archbishop.

"What the devil!" cried Jean de Craon, Archbishop of Reims.

"There's a hornet in the fruit, Your Holiness!" said Tom. "I saw it just as you were about to put your fingers on it. Here!" And he picked out a pomegranate with his own hand and handed it to the Archbishop. "Better my hand be stung than a hand that belongs to a servant of Christ." And he gave a low ingratiating bow. Tom, you see, was already learning the manners of the Papal Court.

The Archbishop narrowed his eyes and glared at Tom. "I've seen you somewhere before, haven't I?" he growled.

"Of course! He looks like the boy who rescued me from the mob at Reims," exclaimed Emily. "But look! He has different colour eyes. Perhaps it was his brother?"

"Hmm," grunted the Archbishop suspiciously, and turned away to stare at the Pope again. Whereupon Emily waved her hand imperiously to dismiss Tom.

Tom took the hint. He bowed and hurried back to the centre table with the bowl. In the hustle and bustle of squires and servants it was a simple matter to pluck out the fold of paper and slip it into his sleeve. He then picked up an empty platter and marched deliberately back to the serving area behind the screens to read the message that Emily had left.

By the time he found a corner where he could tuck himself away in order to read it, he found he was trembling with excitement. He unfolded the message and read: "Tom Disaster Help".

"Oh great! That's really useful information!" thought Tom. "Thanks a lot, Emily!" But at least he now knew she was pretending not to know him. He also knew that she must want him to do something ... but what? And in any case what was the "disaster"?

Now at this moment I have to tell you something that might seem a bit beside the point, but, as you will see, it isn't. I have to tell you about the cost of paper in the mid-fourteenth century.

The usual thing that scribes wrote on was vellum or parchment – that is, an animal skin scraped and prepared as a writing surface. By Tom's days these skins were very fine and excellent for the purpose. Many a scribe pooh-poohed the introduction of new-fangled paper and said it would "never catch on". Vellum was permanent and beautiful. Paper was not as strong or as long lasting. Paper, however, had one distinct advantage. It was cheaper. You could get 25 sheets of paper for the price of one piece of vellum.

Even so, as you can imagine, paper was a pretty expensive item. You didn't have scribble-pads or paper bags or scraps of magazine to write messages on in the fourteenth century. Nor did you have fountain pens or ballpoints. Emily's message was scribbled on a scrap that she must have torn from an official letter of some sort. And she had written with the only thing that had come to hand, in between seeing Tom outside and his serving her the pomegranates. She had dipped her finger into the wine and then scrawled her message over the top of the original writing.

Tom could still read the original document clearly. It was written in the official hand of one of the Papal notaries. It was in Latin and it appeared to be part of a special indulgence and dispensation from the Pope allowing Jean de Craon, Archbishop of Reims, to marry the Lady Emilia de Valois, daughter of the late Duke de Valois, Lord of the lands of Picardy etc.

Emily was to marry her uncle the Archbishop of Reims! But that was impossible! In those days marrying your cousin was regarded as incest! And, in any case, Archbishops shouldn't get married at all! Ah! But then this was Avignon. This was the Court of God's Own Representative on Earth ... and where there were vast amounts of money involved and where His Holiness's eye alighted with favour, there was really nothing you couldn't do.

Tom found a blackened stick from the fire, and scrawled on the other side of the paper: "Your room – tonight". For a plan of action he had to admit it was a bit vague, but it would have to do. Anyway there wasn't any more room on the piece of paper to elaborate. Tom folded the scrap up and stuffed it inside one of the very small roasted birds on the platter he was now carrying back into the Grand Tinel. He just hoped he could make sure she picked the right one.

· 54 ·

HOW THE POPE'S DINNER
WAS INTERRUPTED

There was one thing that Tom had not taken into account, as he bowed before the Lady Emilia de Valois, soon-to-be-bride of the renowned and feared Jean de Craon, Archbishop of Reims, and that was the Archbishop's greed. No sooner had Tom offered up the platter of small roasted birds to the Lady Emilia than the Archbishop leant across with a sniff, reverently muttered: "Quails!" and stuffed one at his mouth.

As good luck would have it, he missed the one with Tom's note and picked up the one next to it. But Tom's relief was short-lived.

"No, thank you," said the Lady Emilia, declining the proffered delicacy. "I don't eat small birds." If Tom could have kicked her, he would have. As it was, he rolled his eyes upwards and then nodded urgently at the birds.

"The chef tells me, these small birds are particularly good," he said, nodding to the one with the message. "They have a special stuffing inside them, which I think your ladyship would really appreciate."

"Mine's got no stuffing!" exclaimed the Archbishop indignantly and he grabbed the very quail that Tom was trying to get Emily to take.

"Ah! Neither has that!" exclaimed Tom, and he grabbed the quail back from the Archbishop.

"What the devil!" exclaimed the Archbishop, trying to grab it back again. But Tom stepped back. The Archbishop lunged across the table, trailing his sleeve through a plate of sauce. "Damnation!" he exclaimed.

"I just noticed this one's got a bad leg ..." Tom hoped he'd say something sensible in a minute. "I mean it's been burnt ... Look! This one's fatter!" And he handed the Archbishop another. As it happened, the one he now handed the Archbishop was indeed considerably fatter and bigger than the previous one. So in this case the Archbishop's greed saved the day for Tom. The great man looked at the fat quail with some satisfaction, snatched it from Tom and started searching for the stuffing.

"I like them a little burnt," smiled Emily and promptly took the quail containing the message. "Oh yes! That's for me!" she declared, and before the Archbishop's tongue had probed into his small bird's abdomen, she had slipped the message out of hers and concealed it in her sleeve, as easily as a conjurer in a thick fog.

"Hey! This one's got no stuffing either!" exclaimed the Archbishop, withdrawing his tongue from its intimate investigation, but it was too late. Tom was already half-way down the Grand Tinel. He had to find Emily's room, lie low until nightfall, and then try to get them both out of the Palace before daybreak. But as he strode down the tables, he couldn't help glancing back at the Pope.

Pope Innocent VI had no appetite these days. He sometimes wondered if, perhaps, even this was a sign of God's even-handedness. The Almighty gave all this power and wealth with one hand, but with the other He took away a man's capacity to enjoy it.

And why oh why did the Creator subject his humble-servant-on-Earth to the torture of these remorseless, nerve-wracking dinners? Why should he – the Supreme Pontiff – be forced to sit all alone on this wretched dais, eyeing all those fat prelates stuffing their faces with his food, while he tried to guess which one was eventually going to poison him? Day after day, dinner-times were always the same terrible combination of nerve-wracking boredom and indigestion ... But wait a minute!

A thrill went through the Pope's body. He went hot and then cold. His blood raced. Something different was happening! Danger! Alarm bells rang all over his nerve-endings! And yet it didn't look dangerous! The Pope simply froze. He didn't know what to do. He just hoped somebody else would do something soon.

In front of him stood a young man – no more than a boy really. He was standing up as straight as a whipping-post, and he was saying something. Of course, the Pope couldn't be expected to listen to what anybody said to him at a time like this! It was unheard of! For someone to address him unbidden – in the middle of a meal like this – was forbidden! It was wrong! It must be Satan rearing his ugly head and making fun of him – of the Supreme Pontiff! Stop him, somebody! Stop him!

Tom couldn't believe he was doing this. He had told himself not to. He had told himself it was a waste of time and that he risked destroying his chances of rescuing Emily, and yet here he was – marching back up the length of the Grand Tinel towards the Pope on his dais!

No matter how many times he told himself that rescuing Emily should now be his only objective, he couldn't help remembering those thin, pale faces in the underground village. He couldn't forget that the reason he had come to

Avignon was to speak with the Pope – to tell the Pope about the sufferings of Anton's people.

He told himself the Pope would not listen. But then how did he know that for sure? Until he actually asked the Pope to relieve those poor villagers, he was only guessing. And here he was, not twenty feet away from the great man.

Nobody else was speaking to the Pope. He was sitting there looking bored out of his head. Tom could simply walk up to him, say what he had to say, and see what happened. "Don't do it!" screamed Tom to himself.

"I have to," said his other self. "I can't let them down. I can't let Anton down. Besides, the Pope might take pity on them."

"No chance!" he told himself.

"I have to try!" said his other self, and – sure enough – here he was, at this very moment, addressing the Pope.

In the general hubbub, no one had noticed this is what he was doing – so far. Even the guards (who were supposed to be keeping such a watchful eye on the Supreme Pontiff) were too busy licking their lips and wondering if any of that wonderful food would find its way to the guardhouse. And so it was that Tom was able to stand up straight in front of the Pope's dais and say the following in his best Latin:

"Your Holiness, forgive me for intruding on your meal. But I have been asked to bring a petition from your loyal and faithful children in the village of Comertrix in the region of Champagne. They have suffered at the hands of the English, who have killed their kith and kin and robbed and stolen everything they possessed. They have suffered at the hands of their own lords, who demand taxes they cannot pay. And they ask the Holy Father if he will excuse them from paying their tithes until such time as they are recovered enough to pay ..."

And at this point, Tom pulled the letter he had been carrying out of his tunic and offered it to the Pope.

The Pope saw the young man pull something from his jerkin. That was the last straw! It could have been a knife!

"GUARDS!" screamed the Pope. Tom didn't wait for the response. He simply threw the letter at the great man and ran. The Pope, convinced that the letter was a poisonous snake, ducked under the table yelling: "Vipers!" which, of course helped to confuse things even more. Ladies screamed and leapt up on to the tables, and even gentlemen started stamping the floor as if to kill any creepy crawlies that might have slunk into the Pope's dining-hall in addition to themselves.

Tom dived through the first guard's legs and sprang up on to one of the wine barrels that were stacked along the wall and from which the Grand Tinel derived its name. As the next guard lunged at him, he leapt up on to a higher barrel. The guard missed but his pike went straight through the side of the lower barrel and a fountain of red wine gushed half-way across the Grand Tinel, soaking diners and servers alike.

Tom was now on the top level of casks, running down the length of the wall towards the serving-area. Half a dozen guards charged at him and half a dozen pikes either hit the wall as Tom ducked or sliced through more wine barrels. More and more jets of red wine fountained into the air.

"That's the Tonnerre!" cried one of the cardinals. "Save some for me!" And as the wine rained down upon him, soaking his crimson robes with crimson liquid, he grabbed a jug, emptied out the water and rushed to the fountainhead.

"The Sablet!" cried the Cellarer, as his most reasonably priced local wine shot all over a wall painting of Carnival versus Lent.

"The Côtes du Rhône!"

"The Burgundy!"

"The Bordeaux!"

The cries went up from cardinals and bishops as they saw their favourite wine casks spouting forth arcs of the precious juice through the air, across the tables, across the guests and over the plates and prelates of the Pope's Court.

"Snakes!" yelled the Pope. "Poisonous toads! Spiders! Wriggling things!" But now no one was listening to him, and as the guards charged after Tom, they fell over the cardinals scrambling to save the wines, with jugs and jars and silver goblets. And as they tripped, their pikes sliced into yet more barrels (you might have thought they were doing it deliberately!) and the wine rain descended on the dining-room of the Pope as if expense were no object.

By this time, almost everyone had forgotten the object of the guards' attentions, and as the cardinals fought the guards and the guards fought the bishops, Tom stood on the last wine cask and stared at the chaos that had broken out around him. And as he stared, the corners of his mouth creased up and suddenly, unexpectedly, he found himself laughing. The Pope's dinner guests all looked so ludicrous and yet so serious. That's what the old woman had meant! That's what Tom still had that all these great prelates and politicians had lost! They couldn't see the joke any more.

For Tom the last laugh was being able to leap from the cask, over the screen, and disappear through the throng of servants who had rushed to see what all the commotion was about.

• 55 •

HOW TOM AND EMILY
RESCUED SQUIRE ALAN

After the events in the Pope's dining-room, Tom had enough presence of mind not to run. No point in advertising that you're wanted by the Papal Guard, he thought. So he strolled out through the main door of the kitchen as if he were the most innocent soul in the Palace (which, for all I know, he may very well have been) and on to the terrace above the cloisters.

"Now," he told himself, trying to calm his nerves. "All I have to do is find out where Emily is sleeping and then somehow … though goodness knows how … we'll get out of this place." It was at that moment that his plans fell apart – though in the best possible way. For there, at the far end of the terrace, was a figure waiting for him – a slight, slender figure.

"Emily! Thank goodn …?"

Emily didn't let Tom finish. "Tom!" she cried and threw her arms around him, kissing him and hugging him. Tom was instantly breathless and happy, but suddenly aware that Emily was crying.

"Emily!" he whispered. "It's all right! You don't have to marry the Archbishop! We're going to escape! I'm going to save you!"

"We can't!" said Emily, tears streaming down her face.

"Yes, we can!" said Tom. "I've got a plan! I'll get us out of here – you'll see!" Tom was suddenly head over heels in love with Emily all over again. He was now her knight in shining armour. He would carry her off somehow, and they would travel the world together and then live for ever in a grand house with a chimney and ... But something in the way Emily was looking at him told him to hold his dream in check. "Why can't we escape?" he asked.

"It's Alan!" she said. "They've arrested Alan!"

"Alan?" Tom felt suddenly pulled in the opposite direction. He felt guilty that he had not been thinking about Ann – his best friend.

"Yesterday. They dragged him away." Emily wept.

"Why did they arrest him?"

"I don't know!" cried Emily. "But we've got to find him! I can't leave here without him! Oh Tom!" she cried throwing her arms again around Tom's neck. "I love him!"

"But ..." said Tom, and then realized he had nothing else to say. But what? But you can't love him because I love you. Because I am going to be your knight in shining armour. Because I have built up a foolish dream out of hope and nonsense? Because Alan is Ann?

Tom held Emily against him as her body was convulsed in sobs. How could he tell her any of this now? His own feelings seemed suddenly irrelevant, and the other ... Well, Tom searched and searched his mind but he couldn't find a good way of saying it: "Alan is Ann". The more he thought about it the more it seemed that it was something between Ann and Emily and – strangely – nothing to do with him at all.

"Come on," said Tom. "We'd better find Alan and then get out of here while we still can."

The keeper of the dungeon was sitting in a stone recess drinking from a wineskin. He was a heavily built unshaven man, with broken teeth and the hairiest ears Tom had ever seen. The key to the dungeon hung from a hook on the wall directly in front of him – no more than a yard from his nose (which was the hairiest nose Tom had ever seen).

"Keep him talking," whispered Tom as they peered down into the dungeon. Although the Palace itself was new, it must have been built on the foundations of an older building, and Tom and Emily were now standing in what had once been a doorway at the top of a long flight of ancient steps.

"What shall I say?" asked Emily.

"Anything," said Tom. "Just keep him talking and – whatever you do – make sure you stand directly in front of him."

"What are we going to ..." Emily began, but Tom was already half-way down the steps.

The dungeon keeper didn't look up. He was alternately throwing dice on to the stone ledge in front of him and taking swigs of wine.

"We've come to visit the Squire Alan," said Tom. "Where is he?"

The dungeon keeper spat on to the stone floor, and tossed his head towards an iron grille, at the end of the passage. Behind the grille shadowy figures could be seen.

"Open up for us then, my good man," said Emily imperiously, as she came and took up a position square in front of the dungeon keeper. Tom shrank out of sight behind her. The keeper looked slowly up at Emily and deliberately took another swig from his wineskin

"And what makes you think I'd want to go and do a thing like that, milady?" he grinned in a way that made Emily's stomach turn over.

"Because I am telling you to," said Emily. "I need to

speak to him." Meanwhile, behind her back, Tom was busy examining the dungeon key that was hanging on the wall. Very carefully he reached into his jerkin and pulled out the key he had stolen from the Lower Treasury.

"On whose authority?" asked the keeper, throwing the five dice on to the stone and spitting again.

"On the authority of the King of France!" declared Emily, and here she slipped a gold sovereign in front of the dungeon keeper. Nothing could have riveted his attention more successfully. Tom heard his intake of breath and, before the jailer had breathed out again, Tom had the key off its hook and had hung the Treasury key in its place.

The dungeon keeper looked at the king's head engraved on the coin and scratched his crutch in the kind of way that men don't do in front of ladies. "This is the Court of His Holiness the Pope," said the keeper grinning slyly. "King John don't have much say around here."

Emily threw another coin on to the stone ledge where the dungeon keeper was sitting. "Perhaps two kings have more power?" she said.

"Oh aye! I dare say they do, but this here is Church business, and the scriptures say there were three kings," smiled the dungeon keeper. He was normally a slow-witted oaf, but not where money was involved.

"Here! Go and buy yourself the Pope's pardon," snapped Emily, throwing yet another gold coin on to the stone ledge, "and may you still rot in Hell."

The dungeon keeper snatched the sovereign up and looked around shiftily. "I'll not open up for the likes of you," he snarled quietly, "but you can speak to him – a couple of words, mind you – no more!"

As Tom and Emily hurried over to the grille, the keeper automatically glanced over at the key to the dungeon.

There it was – swinging slightly on its hook. He turned his attention back to the golden coins and threw the dice once more.

"Alan!" whispered Emily through the bars. "Where are you? Alan!" Several of the shadowy figures stirred in the gloom of the unlit dungeon, but Ann did not appear. "Alan!" she called again.

"Alan!" called Tom. "Where are you? We don't have long!"

There was a silence, and then a weak voice came out of the darkness. "Tom? Is that you, Tom?"

"Yes! We've got to talk to you!" called Tom. "It's urgent!"

A shadow slipped out of the darkness, and in the sputtering light from the dungeon keeper's candle they could see it was Ann – Squire Alan ... and yet it was neither. The face was scarred and bruised and there was dried blood beneath her nose. The squire's clothes were torn and – even in that gloom – Tom could see in those eyes a look he'd never seen before. There was a vagueness ... a sense of unreality ... perhaps the look of someone who had been through something very terrible ... and who knew there was more to come.

"Alan!" exclaimed Emily. "What have they done to you!" And she clutched at him through the bars and pulled him towards her.

"Listen, Alan!" whispered Tom urgently. I'm going to give you something, understand? Hide it as soon as I give it to you. And then join us by the door to the Grand Tinel!"

"Alan! Alan!" Emily was sobbing and kissing him through the bars. "What's happened? Why have they done this?"

"That's enough!" the dungeon keeper had risen to his

feet and was making his rather unsteady way towards them.

"Distract him!" whispered Tom out of the corner of his mouth.

But Emily was too preoccupied. "Your poor face!" she cried. "Your nose, Alan!"

Tom suddenly pulled Emily forcibly away from the bars and hissed in her ears, "The keeper! Get him away or we're done for!"

"Keep the noise down!" the keeper was saying. "D'you want to have the whole Papal Guard down here?"

Emily, pulled herself together and caught the dungeon keeper's sleeve. "You're a dull-eyed oaf and no mistake!" she said, pointing him back towards the coins that still lay on the stone slab. The dungeon keeper narrowed his eyes and looked back from Emily to Tom and back again.

"What on earth's she on about?" thought Tom.

"What you talking about?" grunted the jailer.

"You mean to say you didn't notice that one of those sovereigns was counterfeit?"

The dungeon keeper dashed back to the coins. At the same time, Tom quickly poked the key through the bars.

"Alan!" he hissed. "It's the key to this place. We'll take care of the jailer. Meet us upstairs!"

"Run for it!" whispered Emily.

The dungeon keeper looked up from examining the gold coins, "Hey! Stop!" he cried. "Cheats! Fraudsters!" and he gave chase, up the long flight of steps that led to the courtyard. He was surprisingly fast for someone so fat and someone who had drunk so much.

"Was one of them counterfeit?" gasped Tom as they leapt up the steps two at a time.

"Not as far as I know!" replied Emily.

"Great distraction!" muttered Tom.

By the time they reached the head of the steps, the dungeon keeper had almost caught up with them. "You owe me a sovereign!" he was shouting.

"No we don't!" shouted Tom, turning round on the very top step. "Go and have another look at it!" And with that he grabbed the iron bar that was all that was left of the old doorway at the head of the stairs, and swung out with his feet, kicking the dungeon keeper in the chest. The man gasped, flailed his arms and fell backwards – head first – down the long flight of stone steps. His head cracked again and again against the stones and he started to fall like a rag doll. Down and down he banged, turning over and over like a huge toy thrown down by a giant child.

But Tom didn't have a chance to say sorry or even to feel

horrified at what he'd done, because, as the jailer's limp body came to rest in a heap at the bottom of the stairs, several shadowy figures emerged from the gloom behind him.

"Wait for me, Tom!" It was Ann – Squire Alan – who was the first to race up the stairs towards the light. Once on ground level, she looked less worn, less terrified, but she still had a strange air of unreality about her.

"Let's get out of here!" exclaimed Tom.

"But HOW?" exclaimed Emily.

And that was the problem.

THE AMAZING ESCAPE
FROM THE POPE'S PALACE

How to escape? The problem was particularly acute because at that very moment they heard cries and shouts coming from the courtyard outside. Drunken and disorderly diners were reeling out of the Grand Tinel and the Papal Guard was being mustered in the courtyard.

"Uh oh!" muttered Tom. "No good making for the main gate!"

"Isn't that the only way in and out of the Palace?" asked Emily.

"I think so," said Tom.

"Then we're pooped!" said Emily.

"Look out!" exclaimed Squire Alan. A dozen Papal Guards had suddenly appeared at the further end of the cloister.

"This way!" shouted Emily, and she took off under the arches and across the courtyard and disappeared into a small door in the corner. Tom and Ann followed. They found themselves climbing up a twisting stone stairway, and all the while they could hear the guards clattering after them.

"I'm done for!" cried Ann. The torment had returned to her eyes.

"In here!" cried Emily. They ducked through a door and Emily slammed the latch and slid a bolt across. "That'll hold 'em for a minute!" she said.

"But where do we go?" whispered Ann. Tom could see panic beginning to seize her. She was starting to tremble and he knew her mind was flying in all directions – unable to focus. It was all so unlike Ann … the resourceful Squire Alan who always had an answer for everything. But there was no time to wonder what had happened to her. The guards were already hammering on the door.

Tom looked around. They were in Emily's chamber, and Emily, of course, was busy piling clothes into a bag.

"Not now, Emily!" shouted Tom. "We're not taking your wardrobe with us now!" In all his life, in all his adventures, he'd never felt so utterly trapped as he did now. Getting into the Papal Palace had been hard enough, but the place was also built to stop people getting out. As Emily had said: there was only one way in and out. That's how the Pope liked it. But they were not about to give themselves up – so they had to clutch at straws.

"There's a window on the east side that's not too high!" Emily was panting. "It's our only chance!" And she threw her bag of clothes at Tom and raced off out of the further door of the chamber. Tom glanced across at Ann. She was staring at the door as it shuddered under the impact of the guards' shoulders. It was as if the will to escape had been sucked out of her.

"Come on!" shouted Tom, and he had to drag Ann forward. Somewhere behind them they heard a crack that might have been the chamber door giving way.

"There!" cried Emily, pointing towards a small window at the far end of the next chamber. It hardly looked big enough to squeeze through, but even as Tom's heart sank, a dozen guards burst into the chamber and blotted out the light from the window.

"Up!" yelled Tom, and he hurled himself through a door in the corner where another spiral staircase led them higher. Without knowing where they were going, almost without hoping for anything, they locked the door and ran up and up and up. And when they came to a higher chamber, decorated with murals of hunting and fishing, they didn't stop to admire it – even though it was one of the most expensively decorated rooms in Christendom. It was, in fact, the Pope's bedchamber, although admittedly the elderly fat man who was sitting on the Pope's bed, trying on one of the Supreme Pontiff's robes, wasn't the Pope. It was his butler, who was in the habit of trying on his master's things, when the great man was occupied in other business. But neither Tom nor Ann nor Emily stopped to inquire about this, and as the elderly fat man gave a scream Tom again yelled: "Up!" and up they went again, with hope seeming to leak out from their boots with every step they took.

The spiral staircase continued to corkscrew up and it grew darker until they were in total blackness and couldn't see where they were going. It was a moment of complete despair that was compounded when Tom, suddenly found the stairs ended in something solid.

"It's locked!" cried Tom.

"What is?" hissed Emily.

"This door!"

"Let me try!" Emily pushed Tom away and in the darkness he heard a click and suddenly an explosion of light filled their vision.

"It wasn't locked," said Emily. "You panicked!"

"Clever dick!" muttered Tom, and they stepped out on

to the roof of the Chapel of Benedict XII. A parapet ran the length of the chapel's pitched tiles. The three had emerged from the Trouillas Tower, and now found themselves leaning over the crenellations, gazing down into the courtyard far below. For some reason they all started whispering.

"What do we do now?" whispered Tom.

"We've had it!" whispered Emily.

"I can't go on!" whispered Squire Alan.

"Wait a minute!" shouted Tom. "This is the north side of the Palace, isn't it! Of course!" And with that he started scrambling up the pitched roof of the chapel. He'd reached the top of the ridge before he realized the others weren't following.

"Something's wrong with Alan!" Emily shouted. She was holding a weeping Ann in her arms.

"I'd forgotten Anton!" cried Tom.

"Who's Anton?" shouted Emily.

"Just follow!" shouted Tom. He slid down the other side of the gable roof, and stopped himself with his feet against the stone parapet. Then he leaned over and looked down over the bleaching-ground, and the Rock of Doms where he and Anton had first approached the Pope's Palace. To the west the River Rhône was hurrying under the long bridge of Avignon to the sea. Ahead on the summit of the Rock of Doms, the windmills still turned and the gibbet hung up its grisly cargo for all to see. In the foreground, underneath the vast high northern wall of the Palace, the washerwomen were bustling about the bleaching-ground as if life were perfectly normal, and as if the Papal Guard were not hot on anyone's heels, nor the Pope's darkest dungeon waiting ready to swallow them up for ever.

"Anton!" screamed Tom at the top of his voice. "Anton!

Are you there?" Suddenly he saw the giant, standing with Sir John Hawkley and a small band of armed men far down below on the rocks. "Anton!" shouted Tom with all the urgency of complete despair. "Up here!"

It took Anton a few moments to locate where the voice was coming from. Then he waved and shouted back.

"Are you all right?"

"No! The guards are after us!" returned Tom. "We're trapped!"

It was at this moment that Tom turned and saw Emily's head appear above the ridge of the roof. "Alan won't come!" she yelled.

"I'll get him in a minute!" screamed Tom, and then shouted over the parapet, "Anton! What'll we do?"

"Only one thing you can do!" Anton yelled back – his voice faint from such a long way down.

"What's that?"

"Jump!" shouted Anton.

For a moment Tom thought his friend had gone over to the other side. He thought: "Anton's been told to try and get us to kill ourselves so there'll be no blood on the Pope's hands!" Then he thought he must have misheard.

"What did you say?" Tom shouted down.

"I said you'll have to jump!" Anton's voice came up from far below. "It'll be all right!"

"Did he just say what I think he said?" asked Emily nervously. She had just slid down the roof and had landed with a bump against the parapet. Now she peered nervously over the edge at the rocky ground so far below.

"He did!" exclaimed Tom. "We've got no choice!"

"But jumping off high roofs usually involves somebody killing themselves," murmured Emily.

"It's all right!" said Tom. "Anton's got it figured out!"

He could see Anton and the other men grouped around a white square down below. "He's got one of the sheets!" exclaimed Tom. One of the washerwomen was running around, beating the men with her fists and pleading with them to put it back on the bleaching-ground.

"He wants us to jump into it." Tom tried to say this with all the confidence he didn't feel. "The sheet'll break our fall!"

To tell the truth, it was such a long way down – such a very long way down – and from this height the sheet looked so very small – so very, very small – that the idea of jumping into it was about as welcome as the idea of sticking your head into a shark's mouth.

"You must be joking!" cried Emily. "I'm not jumping down there!"

"Then you'll have to marry the Archbishop!" said Tom. Somehow he had gone steely calm. He knew they had no choice. Anton's voice came up from below.

"Jump!" he was shouting. "Before they spot us! Jump!"

"Jump!" cried Tom. "Or d'you want me to go first?"

"I can't!" cried Emily.

"Watch!" cried Tom and he picked up the bag of Emily's clothes and threw them over the parapet. The bundle fell ... slowly, slowly ... it seemed to be falling for ever ... down and down and then suddenly there it was in the sheet!

"Bull's eye!" shouted Anton.

"Oh, Tom!" cried Emily.

"It's the only way out!" whispered Tom.

"But what about Alan?"

"I'll get Alan," he said. "Please jump."

And Emily jumped.

It was even further down than it looked. She fell and fell, and as she fell the wall of the Palace whizzed past her on one

317

side and on the other the River Rhône stretched imperturbable, and she was just thinking the river will always be there like that when she landed in the sheet. The men gave a whoop and tossed her up again and broke her fall.

Tom watched her falling with his heart in his mouth. It would work. Of course! It had to work! The beautiful Emily was not going to die on a beautiful day like this! But he didn't take his eyes off her until he saw her land fair and square in the middle of the outspread sheet.

Then he waved at Anton. "Wait a minute!" and he scrambled back up the roof tiles. Ann was standing on the other side of the gable as if she had lost all her will-power. Her head was down and she was gazing at her shoes.

"Ann!" called Tom. "We're going to escape!"

At that moment a guard appeared on the top of the Campane Tower at the opposite end of the Chapel. "There they are!" he yelled at the top of his voice. Everyone in the courtyard looked up and the guards started to run here and there.

"Quickly, Ann!" hissed Tom. But Ann didn't move a muscle.

Tom scrambled down the slope of the roof and took Ann in his arms. "You've got to come with me, do you understand? Whatever happened to you – whatever they did to you – you're going to be all right – we're going to escape!"

"They found out I'm a girl," said Ann. "They say I'm a witch. They're going to burn me!"

"No, they're not!" cried Tom. "Come on!"

"Stop there!" shouted the Sergeant of the Guard, who had just appeared out of the Trouillas Tower door.

"Why?" shouted Tom.

"You can't escape!" yelled the Guard.

"Want to bet?" yelled Tom. "Come on, Ann! You remember you got me up that wall when we first met? Well now I'm going to get you down one! It's you and me, Ann!"
Ann turned and looked into Tom's eyes and suddenly the

spark returned in her own. She leant over and she kissed him on the cheek.

"Tom! It's still you and me!" she smiled.

"Stop!" cried the guard, as he raced along the parapet. But Ann and Tom were scrambling up the tiles and over the roof-ridge before he'd taken a dozen steps.

"You mustn't think!" cried Tom. "Just do it! Emily did it!" He looked down at the white sheet that seemed so impossibly small below them, and even as he turned to urge Ann on, he realized she was already leaping from the edge of the parapet and falling, falling, falling down towards the bleaching-ground.

Tom watched in horror as he realized she was slightly to one side. He heard Anton shout. He saw the men move, become confused, the sheet went slack and folded for a moment and then, just as Ann reached them they pulled it taut and she landed, awkwardly, on one side of the sheet. The thing tore, but they tossed her up all the same and her fall was broken. She fell on to the rocky ground but only from a few feet. A moment later Ann stood up and waved back at Tom.

"There he is!" The Sergeant of the Guard's head appeared over the ridge of the roof, and then another guard appeared and another.

Tom looked down at the small white square below. He'd seen the sheet tear. Surely he couldn't jump now?

"Get him!" cried the Sergeant of the Guard, and swinging his leg over the ridge tiles he started to clatter down towards Tom.

Tom looked back down at Anton and the others down below on the bleaching-ground. They were looking up for him. Were they waiting for him to jump or just wondering what to do?

"Got you!" yelled the Sergeant of the Guard reaching his hand out as he landed with a thump on the parapet.

"Oh no you haven't!" exclaimed Tom, and – to the utter astonishment of the Sergeant of the Guard – jumped into the abyss. The Sergeant of the Guard's bark of authority suddenly turned into a cry of horror.

"Oh no! Wait!" he yelled. "Stop!"

"Oh my God!" cried another guard.

"Eurrrrch!" went the others. But there was nothing they could do.

Tom fell and fell and fell and watched the top of the Pope's Palace recede and become part of the sky until he was suddenly engulfed in white and rising up again as Anton and his men tossed him up and then – next moment – he was tumbling on to the solid ground and everyone was grinning and shouting and Anton was saying, "Let's get out of here!"

And in less time than it takes for the Pope to make sixpence they had all vanished into the twisting alley-ways of Avignon.

· 57 ·

THE TERRIBLE THINGS
THAT HAPPENED ON THE BRIDGE
OF AVIGNON

But, of course, it wasn't as easy as that! The guards, who had been gaping from the parapet, got their act together before Tom had time to realize he was actually still alive. They scrambled back to the ridge of the chapel roof and began shouting down to the courtyard below.

"Follow me!" yelled Anton, and he ran off across the bleaching-ground towards the river. Tom and Ann and Emily followed, and Sir John Hawkley huffed and puffed behind them, with the small gaggle of men-at-arms behind him.

"By all the pimples on the Pope!" yelled Sir John as he ran. "We'll never make it!"

They scrambled down the Rock of Doms like a small avalanche of arms and legs, and landed in a heap on the riverbank. The Papal Guard had already appeared down the road at the city gate.

"The bridge!" yelled Tom, and they ran towards the famous bridge of Saint Bénézet, which lies almost midway between the rock and the city gate.

The gatehouse to the bridge was, like everything else in the Pope's city, closely guarded, but, as luck would have it, the guard on duty was in the habit (on Thursdays) of entertaining a certain Mathilde, for whom he had a great affection of a not altogether fatherly nature. On this particular Thursday, he had decided to make a clean breast of his passion to Mathilde herself. He had persuaded her to sit out of the general line of vision, in his little office, and had just steered the conversation round to the need for her to divest herself of her heavy cloak and perhaps a few other garments, when a breathless group of people rushed past. The guard knew he should have challenged them – and so he would have done on any other day or at any other time that Thursday. It was the one and only time in his life that he allowed his personal inclinations to interfere with his duties as a guard. As a matter of fact he never got the chance to make a similar mistake, because he was dismissed from his post the very next day. He did not marry Mathilde, as it turned out that she had her sights set on an elderly merchant in the town who had not many years to live, and instead he married a rather plain but cheerful girl named Martha. He then became a pie-maker of some renown. But I digress.

The keeper of the bridge realized he had made a grave error the moment that the Papal Guard arrived, demanding to know why he had let eight dangerous criminals through. The interrogation, however, was mercifully brief, as the guards hurried through the gatehouse on to the bridge in pursuit of their quarry.

As far as Tom was concerned, crossing the famous bridge of Avignon was one of the scariest things he'd ever done in his life. It was a peculiar feature of the bridge that it had been constructed without sides or barricades or fences – indeed, without anything to stop pedestrians, horses or even wagons from plunging off the bridge into the storm-filled waters below. The Bridge of Avignon was simply a cambered road set high across the River Rhône. Every year, especially when it was icy, people skidded, slipped, stumbled, staggered, jumped, and generally fell to their deaths from the bridge of Avignon with appalling regularity.

It was particularly dangerous for the average pedestrian when he found himself half-way across the bridge with a wagon or ox-cart bearing down towards him. Stepping aside meant teetering on the unprotected edge of the bridge while the cart blundered past, its wheels slipping on the cobbles and its cargo swaying in front of the terrified pedestrian's nose.

But even that was nothing, Tom decided, compared with crossing the bridge with the Papal Guard chasing you and arrows flying over your head.

"Break my bones!" screamed Sir John Hawkley. "They'll turn us into pin cushions!" Another bolt from a hastily aimed crossbow slammed past Tom's ear with a "whumph!" and then clattered against the stone of the bridge.

"Tom and Squire Alan!" It was Anton yelling above the general confusion. "Save the Lady Emily! Tell Sir John to get his men behind the wagon!" They had at this point caught up with a slow-moving ox-cart laden with wood that was going in the same direction. Tom yelled Anton's instructions to Sir John.

"Not for all the beef in Burgundy!" Sir John shouted back. "Hey! What're you doing?" The giant Anton had just grabbed hold of the knight and unceremoniously thrown him bodily on to the wood cart. Sir John screamed and ducked down into the piles of logs as another arrow whizzed over his head.

"You three!" Anton turned to the men-at-arms and mimed for them to get behind the wagon, which had now come to a stop. The men-at-arms tucked themselves in behind it and started to fire their crossbows back at the Papal

Guard. The first volley of arrows checked the guards and they flattened themselves on the cobbles.

"Run, Tom!" yelled Anton. "Run! I order you to run! You've got to save Emily!"

"Come on!" said Squire Alan, and they grabbed Emily's hand and ran as hard as they could towards the further end of the bridge.

"Fight, Sir John!" Anton was yelling. But whether it was that Sir John didn't understand Anton's French, or whether he was suddenly more interested in forestry, Sir John merely burrowed himself down into the pile of wood.

"Aaaargh!" One of the men-at-arms was hit by an arrow. It went straight through his head as he was looking round the side of the wagon. He staggered forward and then pitched off the side of the bridge into the turbulent water below. Anton leapt forward – not to save the man, but to save the man's crossbow. He just managed to grab it from him, but the quiver of bolts was still strapped round the man's back as he disappeared into the raging muddy waters of the Rhône.

A crossbow without arrows is about as much use as a roll of drums without a performer. Anton tried to take a bolt from one of the other men-at-arms, but the man resisted and Anton suddenly realized with a sinking feeling that the man was already down to his last two bolts. The other man-at-arms was in a similar condition. The Papal Guard must have sensed this, for they suddenly leapt to their feet again and came charging at the wagon.

"NOW!" yelled Sir John, standing up and heaving several long logs from the pile off the end of the wagon. For now it must be revealed that Sir John, unusually for him, was not simply keeping himself out of harm's way among the wood. He had done something extremely odd for him. He had

formulated a plan. And – what was even odder – here he was now putting the plan into action. He stood up and heaved more and more logs on to the bridge in the path of the charging guards.

The logs bounced on to the bridge, rolled towards the astonished soldiers and then knocked the legs from under them. Two guards stumbled backwards and screamed as they fell from the unprotected edge of the bridge. The other two looked panic-stricken and turned to run as Sir John heaved out more logs and sent them rolling across the bridge. One of these swung round to the side and swept yet another guard overboard.

Three more guards, who were bringing up the rear, stopped for a moment, confused. One of them, however, raised his crossbow and let fly a bolt. Sir John saw him taking aim and ducked down again. The bolt fled true and straight from the bow, skimmed the pile of logs on the wagon, dipped and then buried its shaft up to the feather in the flank of one of the oxen. The beast roared and reared and sprang forward, but the other ox shied to the side, and before anyone realized what was happening, it was plunging over the edge of the bridge, pulling the cart with Sir John Hawkley and the two men-at-arms with it. Anton, who was standing on the near side as the cart swung round, tried to push it away from the edge, but even his giant's strength was not enough. The heavy wagon had gained its own fearful momentum. The first ox swung in space for a moment – its legs scrabbling for solid ground. The second ox struggled to avoid the same fate, but the weight of its companion dragged it on and then both were hanging in space, bellowing and roaring, as the cart rolled slowly and then suddenly quickly after them.

Tom, Ann and Emily had almost reached the other bank, but when they heard the fearful din, they turned in time to see Anton swept in front of the wagon wheel and flung off the bridge. Then the cart plunged off the edge with the great logs falling among the humans like bits of luggage. The next moment they all disappeared into the angry, mud-filled waters that rushed them off under the bridge of Saint Bénézet and out of the sight of men towards the immense obscurity of the sea.

· 58 ·

AND SO ON

"It's not my fault that I'm a girl," said Squire Alan. But Emily kicked the stool and then kicked the table.

"You've been making a fool of me all this time! Both of you!" and she turned and glared at Tom. And Tom sat there silent. He didn't know what to say. He didn't know what he felt. He wanted to say: "I'm not a girl", but he knew that wouldn't help.

"How could you let me go on thinking ... Oh!" And here Emily kicked Tom and then kicked Squire Alan – Ann – for good measure.

"Look," said Ann. "Nobody was trying to fool anybody. I have to be accepted as a squire to survive. I'm not doing it simply to trick people."

"But who is this Peter de Bury anyway?" It was Tom's turn to sound indignant. "You've never mentioned him before."

"I told you, Tom. He's the squire to Sir Richard Markham who is fighting with Sir Robert Knolles ..."

"And are you in love with him?" complained Tom.

"We met two years ago. When he left for the French wars, I swore I'd come and find him," said Ann. "That's the only reason I joined up with Sir John Hawkley in the first place."

Emily kicked a table, a wooden chair, the wall, the newel post of the staircase and the cat. Tom wished he could do the same.

"Meow!" complained the cat.

"So I'm off to Brittany. If either of you want to come with me, you're welcome."

"Well, you can stuff that!" said the Lady Emilia de Valois, in a most unladylike tone. "I'm going to England to rescue my brother. Are you coming with me, Tom?"

Tom sat on the staircase and swung his legs from side to side. He shrugged. "Let's sleep on it," he suggested.

The next day before the sun had risen Tom was already sitting on the milestone outside the little inn where they had taken lodgings.

He gazed into the distance, towards the gorges of the Ardèche, the mountains of the Cévennes and the old volcanoes of the Auvergne. Beyond, he knew, lay England and his sister Katie and Old Molly and a way of life that now seemed so long ago and far off that it belonged to another person. As his eyes searched the horizon in the first rays of light, his mind ran back over all the things that had happened since the day the Man in Black had abducted him from the Duke of Lancaster's scriptorium. He remembered seeing Emily for the first time, the revolt of the townspeople of Reims, the escape from Chalons, the underground village, and Anton. And there his thoughts came to a dead stop. He couldn't accept that the giant, who originally had been meant to kill him, the giant whom he had come to love, was dead. And Sir John Hawkley? Could he be dead too? No ... Tom shook his head. How could death be so casual? Did it all mean nothing? Their lives? Their deaths? Nothing?

Tom shut his eyes, and when he opened them again, the

sun had just poked its head above the horizon. The new day had begun. New adventures lay in store. But which way Tom would go was anybody's guess.

THE END OF THE SECOND ADVENTURE